Love Match

Roberta Leigh

D0188555

FAWCETT GOLD MEDAL • NEW YORK

LOVE MATCH

© 1979 Roberta Leigh

Published by Fawcett Gold Medal Books, a unit of CBS Publications, the Consumer Publishing Division of CBS Inc.

A selection of the Doubleday Romance Library Book Club.

ISBN: 0-449-14331-7

Printed in the United States of America

First Fawcett Gold Medal printing April 1980

10 9 8 7 6 5 4 3 2 1

Love Match

I

When Suzy Bedford's editor asked her to write the biography of Millie Queen, three-time winner of Wimbledon, she thought he was joking. Not only was her knowledge of tennis minimal, her liking for it was even less. But this, far from being a deterrent in Bill Walters' eyes, was a positive asset.

"If I send a tennis buff along to interview her," he explained, "all I'll get back will be the usual sycophantic mishmash. And not to put too fine a point on it, I'm up to here"—he gestured to his throat—"with stories of Millie Queen the tennis tiger. What I want to know about is Millie the woman, Millie the girl, Millie the—"

"Kid?" Suzy cut in sweetly. "I'll write you a better Western than I will a tennis story!"

"I don't want a tennis *story*," Bill Walters said edgily, "I want a piece written from the heart. Something with punch and feeling. An in-depth look at a phenomenon. That's what she is, Suzy. A phenomenon. And you're the girl who can get to her. I want you to find out what she's like off court; why she's still so ambitious when she's already worth a fortune; how she sees her future as a woman." Beady eyes surveyed the girl in front of them. "I know you can't even see to tap a tennis ball over the net," he grunted, "but in my book that makes you the best person to get me what I want."

"You're the boss," Suzy said. "I just hope you know what you're doing."

"If I don't, I won't be the boss for long! Now go and see Charlie and collect some expense money to tide you over for the next six weeks."

"That long?" Suzy said, astonished.

"I don't want a two-thousand-word article with a three-inch headline. The Millie Queen story is good for a four-parter, and I want you to work full time on it."

"It won't take me six weeks."

"Not the actual writing, maybe, but getting all the information you need might take longer."

Suzy swallowed a sarcastic retort. Bill Walters was evidently serious about this project and she must be the same if she wanted to keep her job.

"I'm sure Millie Queen won't be staying in London for as long as that. She's playing in Rome two weeks from now."

"So what's wrong with you going to Rome? Afraid of getting your bottom pinched!"

"You mean I'm to follow her around?" For the first time Suzy began to be interested in the project. "I suppose you know the peripatetic life these tennis pros live?"

"I happen to be a fan," Bill Walters replied. "And like I said, I want a written-from-the-heart life story about our wonder girl."

"Has she agreed to it?"

"Lord Robson signed the contract with her yesterday. We'll be promoting the Millie Queen story with full-page ads and a television promotion."

Suzy was impressed by the news and flattered that she had been asked to help create it. When a newspaper tycoon like Lord Robson allowed himself to become involved in one of his newspapers' stories, then it was indeed going to

8

be an important circulation booster. The Millie Queen Story. Suddenly she saw her byline fading.

I'm not supposed to be ghosting the story for her, am I?"

"No, you're not. It's a biography. So climb down off your ego and go see Charlie." She was by the door when he called to her again. "Make a good job of this and you might get yourself the column you've been angling for!"

With a smile as meaningless as she knew her editor's promise to be, Suzy went to see the accountant. She was delighted to be given the chance of writing something more serious than the frivolous pieces she had been doing since coming here, but could not help wishing that the subject was more deserving of her literary ability than a tennis star. Still, millions of people loved the game, and as a journalist she must remember she was catering to the mass media; at least so long as she continued to write for a newspaper that considered the mass media all-important. She smiled wryly at her pretensions. A year ago she had thought herself the luckiest girl in the world to be offered a job on the *Sunday Digest;* yet here she was turning down her nose at an assignment that, had it come at the beginning of her career, she would have given her eye-teeth to do. Of such ingratitude was ambition fashioned!

Lightheartedly she raced down to the second floor and Charlie Brand's office.

"Looks as though Bill Walters has taken his hand out of his pocket," the accountant remarked as he gave her an air travel card and then made out a check for five hundred pounds. "What did you do to him?"

Suzy grinned. "I'm being paid all these expenses not to tell you!"

"And the rest! You've still got the bloom of innocence on you." The check was handed over. "Don't forget to keep a clear reckoning how you spend it all. Those tax bastards watch every penny."

Promising to do as he said, she headed for the reference library where cuttings of the famous and infamous were kept.

A quick glance at the Millie Queen files told her she was in for a long read before embarking on her first interview with the tennis champion. It would be pointless to meet her until one had learned all the salient facts about her career and character.

Two hours later, salient facts absorbed, the meeting seemed even more pointless. What could one write about someone when everything worthwhile seemed to have been said already? No wonder Bill Walters had not wanted to put a sports writer on the story. Whatever she herself produced, it would have the doubtful virtue of total disinterest in the game.

Pushing the files back into the drawer and clutching the thick bundle of photostats she had made of some of the more interesting articles, she went to collect her car from the underground garage. Was her dislike of sports the reason for her ineptitude at it, she wondered, or had her ineptitude caused the dislike? It was the chicken-and-egg syndrome and she would never know the answer.

She reached her car and dumped the files on the back seat before sliding behind the wheel, a taller than average girl with slender body, corn-gold hair and violet-blue eyes. Those eyes were now thoughtful as she headed for home in her dusty little two-seater. Much as she disliked the assignment, if she did it well it could be exactly the chance she was looking for. Bill Walters might not keep his promise to give her a column of her own, but she should be able to persuade him to let her tackle more serious features. Equally important, if the biography was successful it might give her the impetus to write a novel, which she had been wanting to do for the last two years. The only trouble was that she could not find a plot. No sooner had she done research into one subject, than her interest switched to something else. One month she was determined to unveil the scandal of the beauty business; the next month she was intent on exploding the myths of the publishing field. All of which proved to her that she was not ready to do either. Somewhere, somehow, she would find a subject that would

10

fire her imagination long enough for her to put pen to paper and begin her magnum opus.

Parking her car in the mews where she lived, she let herself into the little house that had been her home since she had come to London. If she had to travel around with Millie Queen for the next few months, she would only be able to use this as a base. Suzy looked around the sitting room with a pang of regret. It had been left to her by her grandmother and she had lovingly refurbished and redecorated it when she had taken it over, careful to retain its Old World charm and to replenish the window boxes with the same aromatic herbs that her grandmother had first planted in them twenty years ago. Apart from being excellent for flavoring soups and casseroles, the herbs gave the rooms a delicate fragrance that delighted all visitors.

Dropping her outdoor things on a chair, she went into the bedroom to change into slacks and sweater before making herself some supper. Cooking was the one activity she enjoyed, and she wished she had been asked to write about one of the great chefs instead of a girl whose lifestyle was at such variance with her own. However, she was not expected to explain the intricacies of hitting a ball from one side of the net to the other, nor make her readers appreciate the thrill of winning tournament after tournament. Show Millie Queen the woman, had been her order, and show her she would.

But was Millie a woman or an automaton? The tennis star might look pretty and feminine but, in order to withstand the terrific strains of her life, she obviously had the stamina of an ox. Suzy devoutly hoped she did not also have the same intelligence!

With a sigh she sat down to eat. The hard-hitting life of a tennis professional looked like being her own for the next six weeks, and she thought of it with growing trepidation. By tomorrow she would know the worst. At ten o'clock she was meeting the champion in her suite at the Savoy, where she was staying while competing in this week's indoor tournament.

11

Suzy's first sight of Millie Queen did little to allay her fears. She was like and yet unlike her photographs. Chunky, with a snub nose and alert brown eyes, she was younger in looks yet older in manner than Suzy had anticipated.

"I can't think why my manager got me into this," was her abrupt greeting as she gave Suzy a bone-shattering handshake. "I don't need the money or the publicity, and if you want to do my biography, I'm sure you could have got everything you needed from your reference library."

"I'm not interested in doing a rehash," Suzy said firmly, deciding in the face of this attack that the only way to establish any *rapport* with the girl, was to be honest. "My intention is to try to see you in a different way. If I don't, there'll be no point writing about you."

Millie shrugged, as if she had heard such statements many times. "I suppose you're one of my fans?"

"I'm afraid not." Suzy hesitated. "Actually, I don't like the game."

"You don't like. . . ." Astonishment made it impossible for Millie Queen to finish her sentence. Then the brown eyes narrowed. "That's a good gimmick, if I ever heard one."

"It isn't a gimmick, Miss Queen. I know very little about tennis, and what I do know, I don't care for. I sometimes watch a big match on television, but that's because of the excitement it arouses. I'm not interested in the game as such."

"You don't believe in flattery, do you?"

"I don't see the point of it where you and I are concerned. I could start off by flattering you, but if I'm going to follow you around for the next six weeks I wouldn't be able to keep it up. And then where would we be? That's why I think it's best for me to be honest."

"Honesty's a word I've never associated with the press," Millie Queen said abruptly. "They say nice things to my face, then go away and write a pack of lies."

"I only intend to write the truth," Suzy assured her. "Though it will be the truth as *I* see it and not as *you* would like it to be."

12

"That could be as distorted as the rubbish your fellow journalists write about me!"

"I hope not. I've already told you, Miss Queen, if I can't find something new to say, I won't say anything."

"Can there be anything new to say about me?"

Suzy smiled. "If everything that's been said so far are lies—and according to you they are—then there must be lots of new things for me to say! But don't take my word for it. Wait and let my first article convince you."

The champion shrugged and flung herself down in the corner of one of the settees in the opulently furnished sitting room.

"I suppose we might as well start then."

"Start what?"

"The first interview."

Suzy bit her lip, wondering how to say what she wanted without antagonizing this tetchy young woman.

"I hadn't planned to interview you in the normal sense. What I'd like is to be with you as much as possible and try to get an idea of the way you live and think."

"At least you give me credit for being *able* to think! Some of your fellow journalists make me out to be an idiot!"

Suzy laughed. "I can see I'd better get used to the 'fellow journalists' tag!"

Millie Queen looked faintly apologetic. "I know I sound rude, but I'm so cheesed off with the press that . . . okay Miss Bedford, you win—for the moment. I promise not to compare you with your colleagues, if you promise not to act like them!"

"I'll do my best." Suzy felt more at ease as she sat down. "If there are any particular things I'd like to know about you, I'll ask you, but for the most part I'm just going to be your shadow."

"You mean you want to see me at my worst!"

"Or your best."

A flash of humor softened the hard features of the sun-tanned face.

"Very well," Millie Queen said. "You can help Bessie."

"Who's Bessie?"

"My secretary. She's inundated with work and she's always complaining that she needs another pair of hands."

"I'm not here to get to know your secretary," Suzy protested.

"Well I'm not going to have you follow me around twenty-four hours out of twenty-four."

Suzy did not reply, deciding to let her silence indicate her acceptance of the tennis star's suggestion. Gradually she hoped to change the girl's opinion of her, but she knew it was not something that could be hurried. Trust was as slow growing as a plant in winter.

Yet from this inauspicious beginning there swiftly developed a warm friendship between the two of them. It was probably because they were so dissimilar in character and ambition that one did not pose a threat to the other. Only in their determination to succeed, were they in any way similar.

"I suppose you must think I'm as lazy as a sloth," Suzy commented one afternoon when they were sitting chatting, Millie on the settee, her feet up and resting to conserve her strength for playing that evening in London's largest indoor stadium, Suzy curled up in an armchair.

"You're not lazy," Millie replied. "But you use brains and I use brawn."

"Don't give me that! It requires as much brain as brawn to win a tennis match."

"I'm glad you appreciate the cerebral effort."

"I find tennis a bore," Suzy protested, "but I'm not such a fool as to think you just go on court and play pat-a-cake! You put a great deal of thought into it. You have to know your opponent's weakest points and find the best way of overcoming their strongest."

"Sometimes I think that's the only thing I do know," Millie said, unexpectedly serious. "Tennis has been my life for so long that I don't have any other. It's all I've been trained to do since I was a kid. Play tennis."

"Were your parents keen players, too?"

"I didn't have any parents."

"I'm so sorry." Suzy was discomfited not to have re-

14

membered such a fact from the press cuttings she had read.

"I didn't mean it literally," Millie said quickly. "My folks are alive and well and living in South Dakota! But you asked me if I had parents, and what I meant to imply was that I only had a male and female coach! They were never like an ordinary mother and father. They absolutely lived for the game. They weren't in the championship class themselves and when they realized I was—well, you can imagine how they reacted. They made up their minds I was going to achieve all their ambitions—plus any that I had of my own."

Suzy sought for but failed to detect any bitterness in Millie's voice. But she had to be sure, for here could be the linchpin on which to base her first article.

"Ambitious parents can be the very devil," she said casually.

"Without them I'd still be playing Sunday tennis."

"You might have been happier. No pressure, no practice sessions, no diet—"

"No money, no fame, no traveling," Millie continued with a rueful smile. "I guess one can't have everything in this life. It's the swings and the roundabouts, isn't it? If I'd had the sort of childhood I wanted, I wouldn't be where I am today."

A low sigh followed, making it seem as if being where she was was not what Millie wanted. Suzy was not sure how to continue on the same subject, or even if she should.

"My childhood was very dull by comparison," she said at last.

"And mine wasn't dull enough. For as long as I can remember I've had people pushing me to get to the top; first in my home town, then in the States and finally in the country."

"Finally in the *world*," Suzy corrected. "You should be very proud of yourself. You're probably as well known as your President and you can run for more than two terms!"

"That's the problem," came the prompt reply. "There's no letup till your stamina gives out."

"I don't see any gun behind you. You can always retire."

15

"And do what? Take me off the tennis court and I'm useless."

Suzy was shocked. "Useless at what?"

"At everything. Do you know I'm not even sure how to boil an egg?"

"You'd soon learn."

"Maybe. But if I got married and had children, I'd make sure they learned things like that from the moment they could walk and talk."

"What happens if they'd prefer to play tennis?"

"I'd strangle them!"

Suzy laughed, feeling she had been given her first glimpse of the girl behind the tennis champion's façade. Yet Millie was not a girl. She was twenty-seven and a woman, with a woman's need to feel wanted, to give tenderness, to mother. I must be careful not to read too much into a couple of wistful statements, Suzy thought. Millie's got an attack of nerves and is saying anything that comes into her head. Tomorrow, with another victory behind her, she might say the exact opposite. Yet it was too much of a temptation not to pry further.

"How is it that you've never got married?" she asked.

"Are you asking me as a friend or a journalist?"

The atmosphere of intimacy trembled like a glass about to shatter, and Suzy knew how hard it was going to be to gain Millie's trust.

"Can't one be both?" she replied. "I can't divide myself into compartments. If I did, I wouldn't feel an integrated person. Everything I do—think—feel—goes into my writing at some time or another, in some way or another. Just as everything *you* are goes into your tennis. But that doesn't mean I'd break a confidence. If you don't believe that, then I'm not the right one to do your biography."

The gamine features sharpened as Millie pondered the answer to her question.

"Fair enough," she said at last. "For a journalist, you're remarkably honest!"

"Compliments yet!" Suzy smiled. "Watch out, Millie, or you might find yourself trusting me."

16

Millie smiled appreciation of the comment and lay back upon the settee. The room was quiet. Double glazing muted the noise from the street far below and there were no homely sounds to be heard in the suite. Inexplicably, Suzy was aware of the emptiness of living in a hotel.

"I would hate it if I never had a settled place to stay," she commented. "Until now I didn't realize what a home-body I was. I love my little house. I wish you could see it."

"No!" It was a sharp refusal. "Hotel suites are good enough for me. I don't want to get attached to bricks and mortar. I have to be free."

Thinking of Millie's five hours' daily practice at the nets and her continual traveling, Suzy wondered if the girl knew the real meaning of freedom. But she hesitated to verbalize her thoughts. If they were to indicate Millie's true feelings, she must say them for herself, without any prompting.

"I *was* engaged, you know," Millie said abruptly. "But it didn't last. I'd just won my first major title and was all set to play Wimbledon. But Don couldn't see why tennis was so important to me. He wanted me to marry him and give up the game."

Knowing Millie's competitive spirit and earlier ambitions, Suzy marveled at the unknown Don's stupidity.

"He was right, of course," Millie continued, confounding Suzy's thoughts. "At least right for *him*. The only way we could have been happy together was for me to have given up playing."

"But you were just starting to be a success."

"Maybe that's the time to quit! Once you're at the top, it's a terrible temptation to try to stay there. And to do that, you have to get better and better. You can never afford to relax. There are always younger, smarter players snapping at your heels."

"You always snap back!" Suzy rejoined. "None of them have beaten you yet."

"Because I never stopped working at my game. There's always a new stroke, a new way of playing, to be learned."

"I find it exhausting just to listen to you!"

"I'm finding it exhausting just to tell you!" Millie sighed. "But the odd thing is, if I had my time again, I'd still do the same. Does that surprise you?"

"Not in the least. You love your success and you have no regrets."

"I've got loads of regrets. But they don't outweigh the pleasure I've had from my career."

A question hovered on Suzy's lips and she decided to take the plunge. After all, she could not tread lightly forever.

"What about today? If Don came back into your life or if you fell in love with someone else, would you still put tennis before marriage?"

"I don't know."

It was an unsatisfactory answer and Suzy was convinced that Millie had not given it any thought.

"I'm sure Don's married by now," the girl said abruptly, once again making Suzy revise her opinion. It was as difficult to keep pace with Millie's private thoughts as it was to keep pace with her on court.

"Was he a tennis player, too?" she asked, anxious to keep the conversation in play.

"Yes. But never in the top league. To him it was a game— not a way of life. That's why he couldn't understand it when I refused to retire." Millie's voice was suddenly firm, as if to lend weight to her conviction. "But too many people had invested their time and their money in me for me to do that. I had to repay them first. That was something Don couldn't understand."

"I wouldn't have either. If you had loved him enough, you would have given up the game."

"That's a liberated way to talk! What's happened to your feminism?"

"It's still there. But I don't think it makes other feelings obsolete. Most women—at some stage of their lives—want to take time off to be broody. It's damn bad luck if their career makes it hard for them to do so, and I know several girls who've fought against it because it would mean losing their place on the promotion ladder. But if it were me . . ."

"Wait until it is," Millie said tartly. "It's easy to say what decision you'd take, so long as you know you don't have to take it."

Suzy smiled. "You've a point there." She wriggled her toes and slightly shifted her position.

"Maybe I didn't love Don enough at the time," Millie went on. "If I had, I might have thought exactly the same as you."

"Not necessarily. After all, you were only twenty. That's not quite the broody stage! It's the way you feel now that's important."

"I don't know how I feel. I'm as changeable as your damned British weather! When I knew Don I was still crazy ambitious. I wanted to win Wimbledon and once I did, I wanted to win it again."

"And Don wouldn't wait?"

"Have you ever met an Aussie male who would?"

"I don't know any Australian men."

"They're the last frontiersmen," Millie said. "Their attitude to women is archaic. When I turned Don down, he left the tennis circuit and went back to his parents' sheep station. That was the last I heard from him. As I said before, he's probably married by now with a stack of kids. He always wanted a big family."

"What about you?"

"I have my adoring public. The cheering, screaming fans who love me to distraction and who'll forget me overnight, the minute I retire."

"I'm sure that isn't true. And you don't believe it, either."

"Of course I believe it. There's nothing more fickle than public adoration. If you forget that, you're in for a big letdown. As long as I go on winning, my fans will go on loving me. But the day I start to slide, that's the day they'll start loving someone else."

"You don't wear rose-colored spectacles, do you?"

"I had them knocked off in my first match!" Millie swung her feet to the ground. "I'm twenty-seven, Suzy. At the most, I've got five years ahead of me. There are some wonderful young players catching me up fast, and the one thing I'm determined to do is to give up while I'm still champion. I hate seeing all the has-beens coming back and trying to regain their titles."

"Does that mean you're thinking of retiring?"

"Only thinking." Millie stood up and stretched, looking slimmer in a long dressing gown than she did on court.

"You're a great player, Millie," Suzy said, suddenly realizing how much she liked her. "You'll be at the top for years yet."

"Heaven spare me that!"

Suzy was startled by the vehemence, and seeing it, Millie shrugged.

"Don't take any notice of me, Suzy. I'll say anything when I'm edgy before a match." She went to the door of her bedroom. "Are you coming to watch me play tonight?"

"Of course. I find the crowds and the cheering rather exciting."

"Wait till we get to Italy. Then you'll really see some excitement. Italian crowds go absolutely wild, and their photographers are the worst in the world. They'll tear you limb from limb to get a good picture."

So would their English counterparts, Suzy thought an hour later as they left their chauffeur-driven limousine and dashed toward the stadium entrance, chased by a crowd of men brandishing flashlights.

"Do you think you'll beat Jean Elder in straight sets?" one of them shouted at Millie.

"I'll do my best."

"Don't you get bored playing her?" someone else demanded. "You've already beaten her eight times."

"I'm never bored playing tennis," Millie replied. "It's all a question of concentration, and so far I haven't lost mine."

"Do you think you're the female tennis robot?"

"There's only one tennis robot," Millie grinned, "and that's Craig Dickson."

Suzy pulled a face. One did not need to be a tennis fan to have heard of the great Craig. A year older than Millie, he had been undisputed champion of the world since winning the American junior title twelve years ago. He still seemed to be unbeatable and there was no one playing the circuit or coming up on the horizon who looked capable of taking away any of his titles.

Occasionally she had watched him play on television and had admired his agility and grace. Not for nothing had he been likened to Nijinski. But off the court he had the reputation of being a womanizer, and his name had been linked with nearly all of the young and pretty girls in the tennis world. Millie too had been favored with his attentions, and Suzy asked her about it as they entered the small but well-furnished dressing room where they were to wait until her match was due to commence.

"There was never any romance between Craig and myself," Millie said laconically. "That was all newspaper talk. He likes tall, slinky girls who never lose control of themselves—except when he presses the right buttons!"

"Is he a genuine playboy or is that newspaper talk too?"

"I'll leave you to find out for yourself! You're bound to meet him in Rome. I'm surprised he isn't playing here, as a matter of fact. He usually enters everything."

"Maybe he's decided to take things easy."

"Craig? That'll be the day. If you think *I've* got drive and determination, you should study *his* lifestyle. He's a human dynamo. No matter what profession he'd taken up, he would have reached the top. He's that sort of person."

"Then he's a very lucky one. I hope he realizes it."

"Craig doesn't believe in luck. He says it's a question of a little talent and a lot of hard work."

Suzy agreed with this only in part. She firmly believed that luck had a great deal to do with one's success. But it seemed typical of Craig Dickson to discount it. He was obviously the sort of man who believed he made his own destiny.

"From the way your eyes are sparkling, I can see you don't agree with what Craig says," Millie chuckled. "But don't judge him until you've met him. I bet you'll be as bowled over by him as the rest of us."

Suzy doubted it but knew she would not be believed if she said so. Silently she watched Millie change from her tailored suit into a pretty concoction of lemon silk, its pleated skirt fluttering gracefully below her thighs. Though the girl took little interest in fashion in her everyday life, on court she was noted for her dress, and always wore a new outfit for each big tournament.

"My fans like me to look glamorous," she had confided a few days ago, "and since it's tax deductible, I oblige them!"

Now she surveyed herself in the mirror and quickly added a tortoise-shell comb to her wind-tousled hair.

"Will I do?" she asked, swinging around.

"If you do as well on court, you'll have a walkover."

"I don't want it to be too easy."

"You mean you might lose your concentration?"

"Don't even suggest it!" Millie looked humorously aghast, though Suzy had the feeling that this was indeed the champion's fear. Was it something that most top-class players were afraid of? Before she could ask, there was a knock at the door and a tall slim girl came in.

Suzy had not seen her before, though she had met quite a few tennis players since she had started to spend her time with Millie. But Millie apparently knew her, for she gave her a casual smile and then bent to re-tie the laces of one of her shoes.

"I thought you were still in the States."

"Acapulco," the girl corrected. "We flew in this afternoon."

"You and Craig?"

"Who else?"

"Who else?" Millie echoed dryly. Straightening, she saw Suzy and made the introductions. "Suzy, this is Elaine Esterson—one of our up-and-coming players."

Suzy had not heard of the girl. But there was something in her manner that indicated she would not appreciate knowing this, and since Suzy had no wish to arouse anybody's ire, she tried to look impressed.

"When are you and Craig going to Italy?" Millie asked.

22

"At the weekend. Dad has friends in Milan and they've invited me and Craig to stay with them."

She continued to talk and Suzy watched her. Like Millie, she was dark and well coordinated, but unlike the champion she had an excellent figure and a glossy kind of beauty that came partly from her small, neat features, and mainly from her flawless grooming. There was an air of money about her that indicated more than tennis success; she had the confidence that came from being in the right social strata and knowing it. Yes indeed, Suzy thought. Miss Esterson certainly knew it.

Elaine turned to go and her eyes flickered over Suzy. There was a faint tightening of the rose-pink mouth and a narrowing of the rather prominent blue eyes, before they swung around to Millie.

"Good luck for the match. I'll be cheering you on."

The door closed behind her and Suzy raised her eyebrows. "Is that Craig Dickson's latest?"

"And hoping to be his last." Millie picked up a racket and tested it in her hands. "I doubt if he could do better."

"You like her so much?" Suzy was surprised.

"I was thinking of who she is. Her father's Harry Esterson."

"Good Lord!" The man was a Texas tycoon whose fortune was as legendary as his acumen.

"She's his only daughter," Millie went on. "By his third wife—or was it number two? Anyway, he's got five sons and Elaine, so you can imagine how he dotes on her. If Craig marries her, he'll have it made for the rest of his life."

"Why doesn't he?"

"You'd better ask him yourself!"

"I'm writing about *your* life, old dear, not his."

"Lucky for you. Most of his would be unprintable!"

Millie grabbed hold of the rest of her things and motioned Suzy to open the door for her. Side by side they walked along the corridor toward the stadium. The hard thwack of a tennis ball could be heard as well as the occasional burst of applause and Suzy saw Millie stiffen, as if she were an animal scenting man. The adrenaline was already coursing through her veins. It did not matter that she had already played and beaten her opponent four times in as many months. In tennis anything could happen and frequently did. For this reason alone it was an exciting sport.

"Wish me luck," Millie said suddenly.

"You know I do."

Suzy watched her walk over to greet her opponent who was standing beside the draped curtain that screened the entrance from the crowd. In the stadium there was another burst of applause, and a moment later two hot and perspiring players walked off the court.

Peering through a chink in the curtains, Suzy saw new linesmen take up their positions. The referee climbed down from his chair and Millie and Jean Elder walked out to greet him.

Suzy wished she had not promised to watch the match. Although she now had a better appreciation of the game, it still meant little to her. But Millie would be hurt if she didn't see her in the spectators' box and she ran swiftly up the concrete steps toward it.

The players were still warming up when Suzy entered the box and looked around for a seat. To her dismay they were all taken and she was on the verge of going out when Millie's trainer, Larry Evans, saw her and beckoned her over.

"You can squeeze in next to me," he murmured, and shuffled along the bench to make room for her.

Gratefully she sat down, jumping up with a gasp as she felt a hand beneath her buttock.

"Sorry," said a drawling male voice. "I was just removing my camera from the seat."

She sat down again and turned to see a pair of hazel eyes ranging over her. Their interest increased as they did so, itemizing her with a frankness that brought color to her face. The great Craig Dickson in person. Hastily she averted her head. Trust Fate to have her practically sit on

24

him. She stared straight in front of her, trying not to notice that she was still being appraised.

"I would have saved a seat for you if I'd known you were coming up here," a female voice said, and Suzy was obliged to turn her head again and acknowledge Elaine Esterson.

"I hadn't made up my mind whether or not to watch," she explained.

"Not watch?" Elaine said.

"Suzy doesn't like tennis," Larry Evans explained. "She finds tiddledywinks more exciting!"

Beside her she felt Craig Dickson stiffen.

"Clever girl," he said so softly that only she could hear. "What better way to attract attention than to tell tennis pros you don't like the game? It's like finding a vegetarian at a meat marketing convention!"

"I am not saying it to attract attention," she said icily.

"Then why the act?"

"It is not an act, Mr. Dickson."

"So you know who I am?"

"One doesn't have to be a tennis fan to recognize you," she said coldly. "You are as notorious for your games off court, as you are for your games on it!"

The amusement left his face and he gave her a blank stare before turning away. Annoyed that she had let herself be provoked into losing her temper, Suzy focused her attention on the court, where the match had just started.

Jean Elder was a base-line player, which made the game tedious to watch. Surreptitiously Suzy eased her weight from one buttock to the other, then glanced carefully around her. Everyone was intent on the court, following the ball as though it were a magnet drawing their eyes. Even Craig Dickson seemed totally absorbed, which surprised her, for she had assumed he would find it dull to watch women's tennis, even when it was in the championship class. But then, as Millie had said only yesterday, most players liked to watch other top-class ones; they believed they could always learn from it.

Gingerly Suzy studied him. Neither his looks nor his charisma were diminished by being seen at close range. If

25

anything, they were increased. The strength of his personality exuded from him like radiation, and his physical appearance was heightened by the reality of three dimensions. Owing nothing to the exaggeration of television color, his skin was still tanned to the shade of honey, his hair still chestnut brown with golden flecks, and swept back from a high, wide forehead.

He was so preposterously good-looking it was hard to believe he was real. But he was, and it helped to make his retinue of feminine admirers more understandable, as also his enjoyment of them. After all, what young, virile male wouldn't take advantage of peaches not only ripe for the picking, but actually falling on to his plate!

Though his eyes were turned away from her she remembered they were hazel, and that the humor that had lurked in them before they had turned cold, had been reflected by the faint quirk in his well-shaped mouth and the dimple that had come and gone in one cheek as he spoke.

There was a burst of applause as the players changed ends, and Craig Dickson flexed his body and leaned back to speak to Larry over Suzy's head.

"Millie's in great form. If she keeps this up she'll have no trouble in Rome."

"Do me a favor and tell her. One minute she's sure of her game, and the next she's getting uptight about it."

"I know the feeling."

"I doubt it. You're the most consistent player in the world."

Craig Dickson grunted, as if he had heard the remark many times before, and turned back to the court as play resumed.

Throughout the short conversation he had not once shown any awareness of Suzy. It made her feel as if she did not exist which, she knew, was exactly what he had wanted. It seemed he was as determinedly cold-blooded off the court as he was on it.

She edged closer to Larry, who gave her a warm smile.

"She'll take Jean in two straight sets," he whispered

happily. "I think that calls for the three of us to have a celebration dinner, don't you?" He glanced over Suzy's shoulder. "Care to join us, Craig?"

Craig's eyes flickered over Suzy and then away. "No thanks, Larry."

Suzy's cheeks flamed and, as if aware of her discomfiture, Larry said hastily: "The invitation included Elaine."

"Some other time, huh? We only got in from Acapulco this afternoon and I'm whacked."

Again he turned his attention to the court and immediately became absorbed, which made Suzy, seething with chagrin, long to kick him.

II

Millie was in extremely high spirits after her easy victory and was delighted at the prospect of a night on the town.

"It'll be better for you than for us," she quipped to her manager. "Two gorgeous young dolly birds vying for the attention of a middle-aged man with no hair!"

"There's no shortage of hairy young men willing to take you out," Larry retorted. "I can easily fix it."

"The way you always fix my love life?"

Suzy sensed an undercurrent beneath Millie's comment and had it confirmed when she saw Larry's face tighten. As a journalist she knew she should try to find out what lay behind the remark, but she was strangely reluctant to try. Yet if she allowed her personal liking for Millie to prevent her from getting the full story about her, she was failing in her job and letting down her editor.

For this reason she tackled Larry as soon as Millie went off to change, knowing that if she didn't do it now, she never would.

"Does Millie blame *you* for the fact that she's still single?"

"Only when she gets tired of blaming herself."

Suzy tried to digest this, but it was too condensed an answer to be swallowed without being chewed over. "Are you saying that Millie makes the rod for her own back?"

"I'm saying that she's a determined little lady who knows exactly what she wants and where she's going. Don't believe all that guff she gives you about my running her life. I manage her tennis career—full stop. And even then, I only arrange things after she's agreed to them."

"But I get the impression she's tired of the competitiveness. That she'd like to retire and do something else with her life."

"No way. You've caught her on a downward spiral. Believe me, I know what I'm saying. Wait a few days and you'll catch her going up again. Then you'll see for yourself that tennis is the only thing she cares about."

"I know it used to be." Suzy was still unconvinced. "But I'm not so sure it still is. I don't think that the Millie of today would break off her engagement, the way she did years ago."

"So she told you about it?" Larry looked surprised. "Did she also tell you that Don flew back to see her six months later and begged her to change her mind? Huh! I thought not. Well, he did. Begged and pleaded. But she wouldn't listen to him."

"I bet *he* wouldn't have retired if he'd been as big a success as she was." Suzy was outraged. "Some men take a lot of stomaching! If he'd been Wimbledon champion instead of her, he'd have expected her to follow him around the circuit until the babies came, then she'd have had to go home and wait for him to drop by between tournaments!"

"That's what lots of wives do," Larry said. "With tennis the way it is—and golf too—you have to travel around the world if you want to earn big money. But Don didn't want that for Millie. He wanted them both to stop at home."

"You can't blame her for refusing."

"Who says I blame her?" Larry looked put out by the suggestion. "I'm merely telling you the way it was. The way it still is."

"He could still have given her a chance to work for a few more years." Suzy felt she had to defend Millie. "If he'd agreed to wait. . . ."

"He wasn't the waiting type. He was a man's man. Knew his own mind and couldn't be ordered around. Which was why he appealed to Millie. Give her a weak man, and she'd walk all over him."

Suzy deemed it wiser not to pursue the subject. Her belief that the tennis champion was harboring regrets for what she had done years ago stemmed from nothing more tangible than feminine intuition. In the not-too-distant future she would ask Millie outright if she still loved Don, and whether she had tried to find out if he was married. It was difficult to credit that someone with her determination would not have done so.

They dined in one of London's most expensive night spots, a private club off Berkeley Square where the customers seemed to be as high as the prices. The food was excellent and so was the music of a quintet that made Suzy itch to dance.

"I think I'll pay for you to have dancing lessons," Millie informed Larry as a particularly lively tune vibrated around them. "Old age and no hair I can cope with, but flat feet on the floor—never!"

"No one will get me on a floor," Larry said emphatically. "My wife used to love dancing, and I wouldn't even do it for *her*."

"But I'm your bread and butter," Millie said. "And the jam too."

"I'm getting to the age where I need to start thinking of dieting," he said easily.

Suzy tensed. Millie was pulling at her lower lip and scowling, and an angry comment seemed imminent.

"I'm a cow!" she blurted out. "Forgive me, Larry."

"There's nothing to forgive." He grinned as he eyed her piled plate. "Anyway, you're no cow. You're a pig! Have you forgotten you're still in training?"

"Not for tonight. I deserve to relax after my victory." Vigorously she dug her spoon into the creamy dessert in front of her. "One day I'll quit tennis and eat myself silly!"

"You'll never quit until you start to slide."

"Don't bet on it. Just because you can't change, doesn't mean other people can't."

"People don't change," he said flatly. "They only think they do."

Millie was about to reply when she was attracted by a flurry at the entrance. Following her gaze, Suzy saw Craig Dickson come in with Elaine Esterson. So he'd been too tired to join them for dinner! Her anger simmered. His refusal had obviously stemmed from his reluctance to be in her company, even though Larry had asked him to bring his girl friend along.

As he was led past their table to his own, he saw them and waved a greeting, in no way perturbed at being discovered in a lie.

"I thought you were too tired to go out?" Larry teased.

"I got my second wind." Craig bent to kiss Millie's cheek. "Congratulations. You played a great game."

"Thanks. How come you aren't playing?"

"I thought I'd let someone else win some money for a change!"

His eyes rested momentarily on Suzy and then slid away as he went on to his table.

"Well?" Millie questioned. "What do you think of the great Craig?"

"Not so great—at least off the court," Suzy replied. "I met him this afternoon."

"Don't you think he's good-looking?"

"Extremely. He's also rude, conceited and opinionated."

"Love at first sight," Millie said emphatically, looking from Suzy to her manager. "That's what she's suffering from. If she weren't, she wouldn't be putting up such a fight!"

Suzy burst out laughing. "I make it sound that way, don't I? But it doesn't happen to be true. I really did find him dislikeable."

"He can be overpowering," Millie agreed. "But you'll soon get used to it. He wasn't putting on an act for your

31

benefit. Craig is always Craig. Sure of himself and confident of his judgment. He's got a first-class brain."

Remembering his assertion that her dislike of tennis was an act calculated to arouse interest, Suzy bristled.

"Well he didn't like *me* either! So where does that leave us?"

"Both in your own corner of the ring!" Millie chuckled. "And it's a match I'm going to enjoy watching."

"He's playing it with Elaine Esterson," Suzy said coolly.

"That's no fight. It's a walkover. Or should I perhaps say a lie-in?"

"Either way, he looks as if he's enjoying himself," Larry put in, and they all turned to watch Craig on the dance floor, holding Elaine close and smiling down into her eyes.

Suzy watched them, at the same time admitting to herself that her comments about Craig Dickson had played her right into Millie's hands.

Of course I'm piqued by his behavior, she thought. I'm a good-looking girl and he didn't even seem to notice. Well, maybe he did, but it didn't stop him from practically calling me a liar. Why shouldn't I find tennis a bore? I'm sure lots of people do. But probably most of them would deny it, if they were with Golden Boy. I'm damn sure all the girls would. They'd be only too happy to crawl all over the court on their hands and knees if he asked them.

Stop it, she warned herself. The more you keep thinking about him, the more life you'll breathe into him. And he's only a dummy. No matter what Millie says, all his brains are in his hands and feet. Remember that, and you'll be able to forget him.

It was past midnight when Suzy returned to her mews house. She would not be seeing Millie for the next few days, having decided to stay home and pound out her first installment of the biography. She knew she would be able to do it satisfactorily, but she wanted to do it better than that.

"You're still coming with us to Rome, aren't you?" Millie had asked anxiously.

"You sound as if you want me to." Suzy had not been

able to hide her amusement. "I'm the girl you call Snoopy Sue, remember?"

"I'm trying to forget it." Millie smiled back. "You're far too nice to be a journalist, you know. When you've finished my life story, you should stay on and work for me."

"I like my present job."

Millie had looked ready to argue, but Larry's hand, tugging at her arm had made her desist.

Suzy closed the front door and slowly went up to her bedroom. It was fun sharing Millie's life but she doubted if she would enjoy doing it on a permanent basis. It was a frenetic existence that would inevitably pall for her. She preferred a more stable way of living.

She glanced around her room. There was a contentment in the atmosphere that she found nowhere else. Yet it was a doll's house rather than a real home capable of holding a husband and family. She slipped off her dress, sat down at the dressing table and began to brush her hair. It was odd that she should think of a husband when, for as long as she could remember, she had thought only of her freedom. She set down her brush with a clatter. Perhaps girls inevitably became broody at a certain age. If so, she must guard against it. She still had too much to do before she could consider settling for domesticity. Journalism and marriage did not mix. She had to be free to travel; to keep odd hours; to give her first loyalty to her career.

For the next few days she worked diligently at the typewriter, setting down all her impressions of Millie. To begin with it was difficult. The words in her head appeared as a jumble on paper, and the wastebasket was full to overflowing before she was able to write with any genuine fluidity. From then on the words poured forth, and on the third day she took the first installment of the story to her editor.

"How's it going?" he asked.

"Read it and judge for yourself."

"I haven't got time." He picked up the first page and cast a quick look at it. "I'll call you later when..." His voice trailed away as his attention was caught, and he set down the first page and picked up another and then another.

"This is good," he said finally. "Bloody good. I must say I never thought you had it in you. You've made the girl come alive."

"She *is* alive!"

"You know what I mean." He half-read another page. "Until now, I've only thought of her as a machine, but you're making me see all the nuts and bolts! You should write a novel, Suzy."

"I would if I had something to write about."

"Don't give me that! There's a million stories around you. Even Millie's life would make the basis of one."

"I can't write about people I know. It gets in the way of my imagination."

"It wouldn't once you started. Novelists always use real people—often without knowing it."

Suzy remembered this when she resumed her daily life with Millie. If Bill Walters was right, she should find a book coming out of her experiences in this strange new world. But it wouldn't be about Millie, of that she was sure.

On Sunday they flew to Rome and were met at the Leonardo da Vinci Airport by a hail of flashing light bulbs. The tough reputation of the photographers was well deserved, Suzy thought as they fought their way across the marble floor, getting their hair tousled and their clothes pulled in the process.

Larry had arrived a day earlier to make sure all the arrangements were in order for the tour, and the young man he had sent to deputize for him was no match for the determined newshounds, who rounded on Suzy when Millie managed to escape their clutches. Only by pretending a total ignorance of Italian, French and English, was she finally able to join the tennis star in the back of the car, when they were then whisked off at breakneck pace for the hotel.

To Suzy's disappointment they were staying at the Rome Hilton. Like its namesakes, this one could have been in any part of the world, so little did it remind her of the grandeur of the Eternal City. There was the same piped music in the corridors and elevators; the same expensive menus with American-sounding names for the dishes, and ice water taps in every bathroom. But the magnificent view of Rome that Suzy discovered from her bedroom window was almost compensation enough, and she unpacked with a little more contentment.

But contentment was not the order of the day. Work was. Long grueling hours of practice sessions on the tennis court, with Millie sweating profusely as she dived and darted in front of the nets, and Suzy doing the same as she watched her.

Only now was she beginning to appreciate the enormous amount of effort that went into keeping a tennis champion a champion. Everything was geared to obtain the maximum out of her and to give her the minimum of trouble. No telephone calls were put through to her without Larry first vetting them; no interview granted without his ensuring what the questions would be; no meal served without his approving the protein content. Nothing and no one were allowed to interfere with his star's regime, which was five hours of daily practice followed by massage, special exercises and plenty of rest. It was like watching a world-class racehorse in training, and Suzy acknowledged that the same amount of detail and precision went into producing both types of winner.

It was not the kind of life she personally could have lived, and she marveled that Millie had been able to do it for so many years. What was the use of earning vast sums of money if you could not spend it the way you liked? If you had to watch what you ate, how many hours you slept? If your horizon was bounded by other tennis players whose horizons were equally as limited? Yet this was the life Millie had chosen—had preferred—in place of Don. It was a chastening realization; this knowledge that ambition could be strong enough to drive out all other emotions and desires. It was not only Craig Dickson who was a tennis robot, she thought. That title applied to Millie too.

Yet in this assumption she was unexpectedly proved wrong, for on Friday afternoon, in the middle of a practice session, Millie stalked off the court.

"I'm going shopping," she announced to her manager.

"Sure," he said easily and placed a cardigan over her sweating shoulders. "What do you want to buy?"

"Clothes."

"You've a stack of them you haven't worn yet!"

"They were clothes *you* chose for me," Millie said. "Now I want to buy some for myself." Her brown eyes fixed themselves on Suzy. "Will you come with me?"

Suzy nodded, but as she made to follow the girl, Larry's hand caught hold of her arm.

"I'll meet you in the foyer, Millie," she said. "I don't need to change."

"Give me fifteen minutes to shower. Then I'll be right down."

As she went out of earshot, Larry spoke.

"What's got into her, Suzy? I've never known her to behave like this."

"She's a woman. And sometimes they're illogical."

"Not Millie."

"Why not Millie?"

"Because staying at the top is too important to her. She's never missed a practice before—not when it's so near a tournament."

"There's always a first time," Suzy said, "and if you want my opinion—" Abruptly she stopped and started to walk away.

"Don't go," Larry said quickly. "Finish what you were saying."

"I'd rather not. It isn't my business."

"You like Millie, don't you?"

"Of course I like her. I like her very much."

"Then finish what you were saying. I like Millie too," he added. "I've been with her since she was fourteen and I feel as if she's my daughter."

"But she isn't," Suzy replied. "I don't think she feels she's anyone's daughter. That's the trouble. Let her go shopping, Larry. Let her ease up, if that's what she wants to do. She's a twenty-seven-year-old schoolgirl who wants to grow up."

Pulling free of Larry's restraining hand, Suzy headed for the hotel.

For the rest of the afternoon Millie indulged in an orgy of shopping, rushing from one fashion house to another, and spending money with the happy abandon of a child in a toy store. She bought anything and everything that took her fancy, and insisted on buying Suzy a couple of dresses too.

They were the two most expensive garments Suzy had owned, and later that day she hung them carefully in her wardrobe and tried not to feel she should have been firmer in refusing them. It was a pity she did not have an opportunity of wearing one of them tonight, but Millie was back on her training schedule, as though compensating Larry for having run off the rails earlier that afternoon, and all Suzy could look forward to was supper in the suite and a game of cards.

"We'll have to give our clothes an airing soon," Millie said later that evening, enviously eyeing the spaghetti heaped on to Suzy's plate. "I'd have gone out tonight except that I didn't want to give Larry a heart attack! He's had enough of a shock for one day."

"You didn't do anything so terrible." Suzy ignored Millie's greedy eyes and dug her fork happily into the pasta. "You're entitled to a normal life, you know."

"My normal life is tennis."

"For how much longer? The other day you as good as said you wanted to get married and have children."

"I've changed my mind. I'm not cut out for marriage. I'm too bossy and ambitious. It's better for me to knock the hell out of a ball than out of a man!"

There was a tense look on Millie's face that warned Suzy to hold her tongue. It was a pity that the girl's moments of soul-baring always seemed to take place before a big match. To take her up on what she had said might disturb her so much that it would have an effect on her game. In fact the game might even be responsible for her emotional outburst. It was not unheard of for a sports star—or anyone in the public eye for that matter—to use confession as a means of releasing tension, and if this were the case with Millie, then it would be wiser to discount all she said on these occasions.

Suzy's appetite vanished. That could mean that a great many of her impressions about the champion would have to be revised; to say nothing of the installments already written.

"What's wrong?" Millie asked. "You look sick."

"I've got writer's cramp."

"In your stomach?" Millie stared at Suzy's full plate. "Don't kid me. Something's upset you."

"You," Suzy stated baldly. "I don't know whether to feel sorry for you when you're sorry for yourself, or tell you to snap out of it. Do you *ever* mean what you say?"

Millie dug into her salad, stared at a tomato in disgust and set her fork on her plate. "One more steak and salad, and I'll throw up!"

She pushed her chair away from the trolley and flung herself down on the settee. In a cotton dressing gown and with her hair still damp from a shower, she almost looked like the schoolgirl Suzy believed her to be.

"I mean everything I say to you, Suzy—when I say it. But that doesn't mean I go on feeling it. I've made my bed and I'm happy to lie in it—alone."

"Beds can be remade," Suzy replied and then quickly changed the subject as Larry came in. If only he had arrived ten minutes later.

"You look very smart," Millie said, eyeing him. "Got a date?"

"At my time of age? Why do I need more aggravation when I've got you?" He ruffled her hair. "I'm having dinner with Frank Ellman, Craig's manager," he added for Suzy's benefit.

"That should make you appreciate *me*," Millie commented. "Compared with Craig, I'm as soft as a coddled egg!"

"Where's the tennis robot himself?" Suzy asked, deeming it wiser to refer to him. At least then, no one would think she was avoiding mentioning his name.

38

"Nightclubbing with Elaine, according to Frank. I must say I wouldn't manage that boy if he were the last player on earth."

"Nobody manages him," Millie said. "He knows exactly where he's going and doesn't need anyone to tell him how to get there."

Larry shrugged and went out, but Millie continued the conversation.

"Craig's like me in a way. We both put tennis before anything else."

"It hasn't affected his love life. From what I've read about him, he changes his girl friends as regularly as his shirts!"

"There's safety in numbers. Anyway, that sort of thing can be fun when you're young."

"He's not so young and he still seems to find it fun," Suzy said. "He obviously doesn't want a lasting relationship. I doubt if he's capable of having one."

"I wonder." Millie looked speculative. "Perhaps if you have enough confidence in yourself, you don't need to be close to anyone else. And Craig's certainly got confidence." A twinkle grew in the brown eyes. "You could write a far better biography about him than you can about me. If you think I've been ambitious, you should talk to him—and not only about his past—but about all the things he still wants to do."

"I'd never be able to write about a man like Craig Dickson," Suzy said. "I dislike everything he stands for."

"Then you dislike handsome men with sex appeal!"

"There's more to a man than looks and sex appeal."

"But you've got to admit it's a great beginning!"

Suzy could not help laughing. "A beginning and a swift end as far as I'm concerned. I really do find him a bore. I'd have nothing to talk about with a man who finds total satisfaction in patting a ball across a tennis court!"

"You find plenty to talk about with me."

"You've got far more depth than he has. He's so puffed up with his own ego he doesn't even need a plane to fly!"

"You're too hard on him, Suzy. He isn't like that at all."

39

"Let's agree to differ, shall we? I'm here to write about you, and I'd rather concentrate on *that*."

"You know all there is to know about me."

"I know about Millie Queen the tennis champion. But what I still have to discover, is the woman who's trying to take her over."

"Trying and failing," came the somber reply. "She's been denied existence so long, she may have atrophied."

Had Millie made this comment tomorrow after the tournament, nothing would have stopped Suzy from dissecting it. But, still fearful of unnerving her, she was forced to keep quiet. Tonight it was her duty to keep Millie away from any thoughts that might lead her into introspection and a lowering of her mood.

"Are you annoyed because Craig hasn't noticed you?" Millie asked unexpectedly.

Suzy was so deeply immersed in Millie's emotions that it took her a few seconds to return to her own.

"Why in heaven's name should he be interested in me?" she asked. "He's already got a girl friend."

"That's never stopped him before."

"Maybe Elaine is special."

"I wonder if—"

"How about a game of cards?" Suzy cut in, determined not to continue talking of Craig.

Happily Millie allowed herself to be sidetracked, and for the next couple of hours they played gin rummy. Millie brought the same competitive spirit to it that she did to her tournaments, and Suzy was blitzed repeatedly.

"The trouble with you is that you don't concentrate," the tennis star complained. "Don't you mind if you lose?"

"Not a bit. It's only a game."

"My God, what a thing to say to me, of all people!"

"Maybe I should say it to you more often." Not waiting for a reply, Suzy triumphantly called "gin" for the first time that evening, then announced that victory was the best moment for stopping play.

"I don't need to be up early tomorrow," Millie said. "I rarely do more than an hour's workout on a Sunday."

"Then I'll meet you by the pool and bag us a good position."

"Why not have a game of tennis yourself first?"

"That would give everybody a real laugh," Suzy grinned. "I play like a hippopotamus."

"That's only because you haven't tried."

"I spent my schooldays trying."

"Trying to avoid playing," Millie teased. "I'm not the only one who's confessed their sins! I remember everything you've told me about your love of sport."

Suzy giggled. "So we meet by the pool, right?"

"Right. If you don't mind bulging in all the wrong places, why should I worry for you."

"I don't bulge," Suzy protested, then glanced down at her slender body. "Do I?" she asked doubtfully.

"You sure do. Every skinny curve of you!" Avoiding the pillow thrown in her direction, Millie dived for her bedroom, leaving Suzy to go to her own.

The next morning Millie had a change of heart, and no sooner had Suzy settled down by the edge of the sparkling blue water, when the girl sought her out and dragged her off to the tennis courts.

"Can't you find anyone else to play with?" Suzy protested.

"Masses of people. But I intend to have a game with you."

It couldn't have been a more appropriate statement, for during the next fifteen minutes Suzy was rushed off her feet desperately trying to return Millie's shots. But every single one of them went smack into the net.

"Why don't you play with your feet?" Suzy called finally, wiping the sweat from her brow. "It's the only chance I'll ever get to win a point!"

Millie laughed and gently bounced a ball across to her. By dint of great effort Suzy returned it and when it came back, only slightly more quickly, she muffed the reply.

"You really are a lousy player," Millie called.

"And I don't even care! Let's give it up and go and sunbathe."

"You've talked me into it." Millie came around the side of the net. "Do you really play so badly, or were you putting me on?"

"I don't normally miss quite as many shots," Suzy said candidly, "but I'm not wearing my contact lenses, and without them I can't see a thing."

"For goodness sake! Why didn't you go get them? I never even knew you wore any."

"That's the purpose of them!"

"Then why aren't you wearing them today?"

"Because I intended sunbathing, and they're not comfortable when you have to keep your eyes closed for a long period of time."

Millie put her arm through Suzy's. "I'm glad there was a reason for you playing so dreadfully. I didn't think it was quite normal!"

"I'm not much better when I can see," Suzy confessed.

They reached the edge of the court and a tall, brown-haired man came into Suzy's focus. Her heart thumped and she hoped Millie did not notice the involuntary jerk her body gave as she recognized Craig Dickson. He was smiling broadly in her direction.

"If they ever decide to have a clown play on court between tennis matches," he said, "you'd be ideal for the job!"

Scarlet-cheeked, she ignored the comment, but Millie laughed.

"She was dreadful, wasn't she? But she hates the game."

"Still continuing with that line?" Craig Dickson said to Suzy. "I've got to admit it's a very novel one."

Suzy's color intensified. Once more this man was inferring she was putting on an act in order to make herself noticed. Or did he think she was doing it to make herself noticed only to him? The thought was so unpleasant that she pulled free of Millie and began to walk quickly away. But Craig had other ideas, for he swung around and kept up with her.

"Have you ever thought of taking lessons?"

"Only in how to avoid you."

"There's no problem about that," he assured her, and instantly wheeled away in the opposite direction.

Disconcerted, Suzy stopped walking, and Millie caught up with her.

"Whatever made you say a thing like that to him?" she demanded, having heard the conversation.

It was impossible for Suzy to explain why Craig made her so angry, since she could not logically explain it to herself, and she shrugged and continued on her way to the pool.

The two chairs she had commandeered earlier were still vacant, and she collapsed onto the first one and fanned her face. Millie seemed uninterested in sunbathing, and doffing her tennis dress to disclose a one-piece bathing suit, headed for the pool.

"Coming in?" she called.

"Later," Suzy replied, and watched the girl dive neatly into the water and swim to the far side.

Only then did Suzy take off her own sun dress, wishing ruefully that her editor had sent her into a less energetic world. The biography of a centenarian now—that would have been right up her street!

It was only as she bent to spread her towel over her mattress that she noticed Craig and Elaine sitting a few feet away from her. Her cheeks flamed again but she managed to continue her movement down to the mattress and hoped she had not given away her agitation. Of all the places where Craig and Elaine could have sat, what unkind Fate had placed them a hand's distance away?

Careful to avoid their eyes, she lay back and tried to relax. But no amount of concentration could make her forget the man lying so close to her, nor forget that he appeared totally unaware of her existence. If only she could say the same about herself!

"Do come in for a swim, Suzy!" Millie called from the water.

"In a moment," Suzy said and, sliding forward, dangled her feet over the edge of the pool.

Not being able to swim well was the only thing she

43

regretted. But for as long as she could remember she had had a phobia about going out of her depth. She supposed it came from being thrown into the deep end by a boy cousin when she was a toddler. She could not remember the incident, though she had repeatedly tried, nor could she overcome the horror. Somewhere deep in her subconscious it still tormented her, making it impossible for her to swim if she knew she could not reach down with her toes and touch terra firma. Even swimming lessons from a professional coach had not helped her to overcome her fear, so she had accepted it and, in the main, forgot it.

"Do come in," Millie repeated plaintively, and though Suzy wanted to oblige, she was unwilling to explain the reason for her reluctance with Craig and Elaine sitting within earshot. She could imagine what amusement Elaine would cull from the story, and knew even without being told that the American girl was a wonderful swimmer.

"I'll come in shortly," she prevaricated, and closing her eyes, tilted her face up to the warm rays of the sun.

"Afraid to get your hair wet?" a voice said in her ear, and without lifting her lids Suzy knew who had made the comment.

"Or maybe those lovely golden locks aren't real," the lazy drawl continued. "Perhaps it's a wig."

She opened her eyes and glared at him. "I find your humor extremely childish, Mr. Dickson. Nor can I understand why you bother to make conversation with someone who puts on an act."

"Puts on an act?"

"*Pretending* not to like tennis."

"Oh, that." He squatted beside her, golden-skinned and close enough to touch. "Maybe it wasn't such a bad idea after all. It was one way of getting me to notice you."

Her chest heaved with indignation and, aware of it and not wanting to act out the cliché of the outraged female, she let out a hot breath and cooled herself down.

"Surprising though it may seem to you, Mr. Dickson, I have no desire whatever to attract your attention. I find you a bore both on and off the court."

44

"Well, well," he murmured, "if your arms and legs were as skillful as your tongue, you'd be gold medalist in the decathlon!"

Too infuriated to speak, Suzy slid back on her mattress and closed her eyes, trying to pretend that a man called Craig Dickson had disappeared from the face of the earth.

"You don't need to do anything to attract my attention, you know." He was still speaking, his voice so low that only she could hear it. "You're beautiful enough for me to notice you if you just stand still."

"Thank you," she said coldly, lifting her lids. "Coming from such a connoisseur of females, I suppose I should be flattered."

"Aren't you?"

"No. You're too shop-soiled for my taste."

For a brief instant his eyes gazed into hers, then he gave a laconic nod and moved back to his own mattress.

Without meaning to do so, Suzy watched him. In brief swimming trunks there was not much of his tanned body left to the imagination. He was exceptionally good to look at. Six-foot-two of superbly coordinated bone and muscle, covered by golden skin as smooth as silk. He had the strong forearms of a tennis player and his shoulders were well-developed, too, with a sprinkling of hair—several shades lighter than that on his head—splaying out across his chest.

As she watched him, he went to stand by the edge of the water. Because he was in profile she had a chance to study his face, and critically decided that his features were too perfect; so classically chiseled that they could have belonged to a statue. But a Michelangelo statue, she admitted: one that combined strength with beauty; sinewy muscles allied to grace. His nose was firm and straight and his eyebrows well-shaped crescents above eyes that were more green than gray in the bright sunshine. His mouth looked as if it had been molded by an artist, so clearly defined was the curve of the upper lip, so sensual the lower one.

All the gods in Christendom must have graced the christening of this lucky young man, she thought dispassionately, acknowledging that he had all he needed to make his life perfect. It would be interesting to know why he still put himself through the strain of playing competitive tennis. It couldn't be for the money. He must have earned enough to live like a millionaire for the rest of his life. Could it be a desire to remain in the limelight? To hear the applause and see the adulation? Or was he driven by a restlessness that made it impossible for him to relax? If one could decipher the mechanism that made him tick, one could get a marvelous story. If she did not dislike him so much she would have suggested to Bill Walters that they follow Millie's biography by one about Craig Dickson. Hastily she dismissed the idea. It would be disastrous to spend any time in his company. They would end up murdering each other!

She became aware of him slanting a sardonic look in her direction and knew he had been fully aware of her watching him. He straightened his shoulders and the muscles rippled across his chest.

"Care to wet that golden head of yours after all?" he asked.

"My wig will go straight," she said sarcastically.

"As long as your figure doesn't—why care?"

Without waiting for her to reply he did a neat dive into the pool.

Quickly Suzy got to her feet. Slipping her sunglasses onto her small nose—glad that they were sighted ones so that she could at least see where she was going—she went in search of somewhere more secluded, finally ending up on a small stretch of lawn on the far side of the hotel.

It was far duller here than by the pool, and in the distance she could hear the occasional splash of water and the sounds of laughter and playful screams. But at least she was not being watched by a pair of all-knowing hazel eyes that saw her and misjudged her. Craig Dickson was so used to girls falling over themselves to get his attention that he couldn't believe he had met someone who wasn't doing the same. Leaving the poolside had been the best way of showing him how wrong he was. If she never saw him again it would be too soon.

Closing her eyes she tilted her face up to the sunlight again and made another effort to put him from her mind. But though the rays warmed her body she could not relax, and kept thinking of all the witty retorts she could have made to his snide remarks.

"Drat the man!" she muttered angrily, and hearing herself say the words aloud, suddenly saw the humor of the situation and was able to stop thinking of him.

III

One could not be part of the tennis scene, as Suzy was, and not get caught up in the frenzy of excitement engendered by a major tournament. This was particularly true on the day Craig Dickson played Alfredo Martelli.

At the best of times Martelli was a noteworthy opponent, but in Rome he was not only on his home ground but also in his home city, and the Romans turned out in force to cheer him to victory.

It was a daunting prospect for his opponent, but Craig Dickson seemed completely unaware of it as he sauntered onto the court, deliberately allowing Martelli to walk ahead of him and get most of the applause. It was almost as if he were silently saying to the crowd: "Cheer your boy while you can, because soon you won't have anything to cheer about!"

Suzy could not but help admire Craig's cool nonchalance in the face of the very faint smattering of applause that followed him as he crossed the clay and draped his sweater around the back of his chair. Looking at his bland expression she searched for some sign of emotion and, seeing the slight smile that curved his mouth, and the arrogant tilt of his head as he tested first one racket and then another, considered him to be incapable of feeling.

"If that were me," Millie said beside her, "I'd be so angry I wouldn't be able to hide it. I hate a partisan crowd."

"Maybe he doesn't mind what people think."

"I doubt it. But one will never know for sure. Craig doesn't just play his cards close to his chest, he plays them on it!"

Another roar from the crowd made Suzy turn quickly back to the court, and she saw that Martelli had taken his place at the base line. The two men started their warm-up, Craig tall and supple, his hair gleaming chestnut brown in the sunshine, one lock already falling over his forehead in the inimitable way that his women fans found so sexually stimulating.

He played superb tennis too, she conceded as the game got under way. He made difficult shots look easy and spanned the court with such effortless grace that one saw, almost with a sense of disbelief, that in a matter of seconds he had crossed from one side of it to the other. Lobbing brilliantly, he kept the Italian firmly at the base line, then made a series of gentle returns that forced his opponent to come to the net, where he was again destroyed by a lob.

With one brilliant stroke after another, Craig upstaged Martelli, but the more pyrotechnics he displayed, the more hostile the crowd became. But he was able to disregard it, almost to use it as another spur in his determination to win. Nothing and no one was going to prevent that from happening.

At the end of each game he changed sides without looking to the right or the left. His face was completely serious, his lids lowered and his mouth set in a firm line. He also appeared unaffected by the sun blazing down upon his head, and though he took salt tablets he showed no sign of fatigue.

There was little doubt in Suzy's mind that if the game continued like this, Craig would be a comfortable winner. But as if to show he had other tricks up his sleeve, he began

49

to play with increased speed and agility, taking many unnecessary chances in order to win spectacular points that he could have gained with ease. It was as if he wanted the crowd to know that he did not need their approbation in order to give of his best. As a gesture, it was a thumb to the nose, and several onlookers were quick to realize it.

"Not only can I win against your national hero," he seemed to be saying, "I'll also show you how easily I can destroy him."

"That's Craig all over," Millie said, her eyes never leaving the tall figure on the court. "No wonder they queue up to see him play. They can't make up their minds whether they love him or hate him!"

Suzy knew only too well what Millie meant, for she was experiencing the same mixture of emotions. Tearing her eyes away from Craig Dickson's figure, she focused on Martelli. His shirt was drenched with sweat and his hair clung wetly down the sides of his face. But he was still putting up a fight, and each time he managed to save a point, the crowd roared approval.

"Nothing can save him," Millie said. "Craig's won hands down."

As if to reinforce her statement, Martelli began to limp. A murmur of sympathy went up from the crowd, wafting over the court like perfume. To Craig it was the scent of victory. Suzy could almost feel him marshaling his strength for the final onslaught, digging deep within himself to refire his concentration. Having expected him to ease up on his game, she was astonished to see him play with increased ferocity, and his opponent, unable to run, allowed several shots to go unreturned. Whereas before he had been outclassed by Craig's virtuosity, Martelli was now physically at a disadvantage.

Suzy was overcome by shame that Craig made no concession to the Italian's valiant attempt to overcome his handicap. Why was he deliberately trying to antagonize the crowd? Didn't he know he was going to win? Watching his stony face she instinctively felt that he was playing for himself, obsessed by a demon that made him totally unaware of anyone around him. Two more fast, backhanded returns of serves and the game was over.

Only then did Craig leap over the net and look in any way concerned about Martelli, a fact which did nothing to appease the anger of the crowd.

"What an unsporting player he is," Suzy said in disgust. "Why didn't he slow down when he saw Martelli was hurt?"

"Because he—"

"—can't bear not to show off," Suzy finished for her, and turned away. Even thinking of Craig nauseated her.

"We're all having lunch at the tennis club," Millie murmured behind her as they eased their way through the crowd.

"I think I'll skip lunch and go for a drive." Suzy made the decision on the spur of the moment. "I haven't seen anything of Rome yet."

"Wait until after lunch and I'll come with you."

"You have to practice and I may be late returning."

"In other words, you want to be on your own?"

"Right." Suzy's smile took all the sting out of her reply. "It's always good for two girls to get out of each other's hair from time to time."

"You're never in mine," Millie said. "But I'm obviously in yours!"

"Don't be silly. It's just that I'd like to get away from the whole tennis scene. You're used to this kind of tension, Millie. I'm not. I want to go in the country, park the car and lie in a field somewhere."

"Look out for the Italian bulls."

"I assume you mean the two-legged kind?"

"What else!"

Suzy laughed and headed toward one of the exits. She was lucky enough to flag down a taxi to take her back to the hotel, where she knew she could borrow the little Fiat that Larry had put at her and Millie's disposal during their stay here.

Changing into a cool linen dress and donning a wide-brimmed hat, she set out in the direction of the sea, deciding that a vista of ocean would be more therapeutic than the rolling hills that surrounded the city.

The roads were not as crowded as she had expected and she made excellent time. She had no precise idea where she was going and when she came to the coast she was disappointed at the flatness of the scenery. It reminded her of the British east coast, except that here the sky was bright blue and the sun extremely hot.

Ahead of her lay a single-storied restaurant: all white wood and plate glass and seemingly built directly upon the sandy shore. She parked the car under a grass mat awning and went in search of some coffee and a sandwich. There were no other customers and, from the pristine state of the sparsely furnished room, there had not been any for some time. The menu was nonexistent and she had to settle for spaghetti. It was surprisingly good, and she washed it down with a small carafe of rough red wine.

Only when the meal was over and she wandered barefoot along the edge of the sea, shoes in hand, did she realize how strung-up she had been during the match she had just watched. She had wanted Craig Dickson to win; the more so when she had sensed the antagonism of the crowd. But when Martelli had strained a muscle and Craig had refused to lessen his attack, she had reacted violently against him.

How could he have been so vengeful and unsporting? As long as he had won, would it have mattered to him if the scoreboard had not shown every single point in his favor?

She trod on some seaweed and stopped to look at it. It was still damp and gave off a not unpleasant smell. She pushed it over the sand for a few yards, then left it by the water's edge and walked on, her thoughts reverting to the afternoon's match which she had wanted to forget.

It was strange that Millie had not been equally disgusted by Craig's behavior. Yet perhaps here lay the difference between herself and the girl champion. In order to get to the top you had to eschew sentiment and pity. Had to be positive in what you did and convinced you were always

52

right. There was no room for self-doubt. That was the biggest weakness of all. You played to win—regardless.

On that basis, I'll never be a success, Suzy decided ruefully, and quickened her pace along the shore.

A slight breeze had sprung up and it tugged at her skirts and flattened the material against her thighs. The sand was warm underfoot and she was glad she was not wearing stockings. The grains rasped her feet in a rather pleasant way and she wandered closer to the sea's edge and let the water lap against her toes. It was cold and refreshing, and she ventured in up to her ankles, then stepped back and played a game of trying to avoid the spume, awarding herself points each time she did.

At five o'clock she knew it was time to return to the city. It had been foolish to stay so long, for she was bound to meet the rush-hour traffic. But short of staying here for considerably longer there was no way she could miss it. Still, the road should be clear until she reached the suburbs. From then on she would relax and not try to fight the excitable Italian temperament.

For the next half hour she bowled contentedly along the highway, and was congratulating herself on the good time she was making when the little car shuddered like a bucking bronco and came to a jerky halt. Warning herself not to panic she pressed the starter. It wheezed obligingly but did nothing else. She repeated this action a couple of times and so did the car. There was nothing for it but to take a look inside the bonnet; except that if there was anything wrong, she would still have no idea what to do. However, if there was a loose wire or a plug had come undone, she would at least know what it was.

In no way heartened by this thought, she opened the bonnet and peered inside. The engine was still there. So far, so good. She touched a few wires. They seemed firm enough. Then a plug. She jumped back, rubbing at her burned fingers. Could the fault be caused by overheating? Feeling very incompetent, she put down the bonnet and stood by the side of the door. She would have to signal for help.

This proved embarrassingly easy. Hardly had the thought entered her head when a low-slung white roadster purred to a stop and a swarthy-faced man in his fifties beamed at her. In a spate of Italian, which she could not follow but which she vaguely took to be commiseration at her plight, he offered her the use of his car. There was something in the boldness of his eyes as they raked her that she did not like, and she shook her head and went on shaking it until he shrugged and drove off.

The second man who stopped to help her re-enacted the role of the first, and Suzy decided it would be safer to get inside her Fiat and wave for help from there. At least behind a door, and with a wide-brimmed hat covering her corn-gold hair, she would make a far less glamorous picture than she did standing by the side of the road, with the breeze playfully flattening her dress against her body and whipping friskily around her legs.

No sooner had she settled herself behind the wheel when a limousine slowed down alongside of her and then spurted past without stopping. Three more cars did the same and, with a sigh of despair, she climbed out and stood beside the door again.

Almost at once, a silver-gray roadster slid to a stop beside her.

"Are you in trouble?" a young man asked in mellifluous Italian.

In carefully enunciated English she explained that the Fiat had incomprehensibly broken down and asked if she could be taken to Rome, or as near to it as he was going.

"No problem," he said in excellent English, and leaned forward to open the door. His eyes moved boldly down the length of her body and Suzy, in the act of stepping into his car, hesitated.

"Perhaps it might be better if you took a look at the Fiat for me," she said. "If it were only a small thing—"

"I know nothing about cars," he cut in smoothly.

Silently she looked at the intricate dashboard in front of him. There could not have been more switches, dials and levers, had it been the Concorde.

"I just drive it," he explained with a supple movement of his hands. Roving ones, she was sure. "My chauffeur attends to the innards." Again his eyes admired her. "Please get in, signorina. First I must make a little detour and then we will go to Rome."

"A detour?"

"To my home. It is only a few kilometers from here."

"You mean you weren't going into Rome?"

"No. But I will be happy to take you there afterward."

"After what?"

"After we have had a drink."

"No thank you, signor. I don't want to take you out of your way. I'll wait here for another car."

"That is foolish and unnecessary."

He slid swiftly forward and caught her hand as she went to lift it from the door. His grip had the strength of twine and it tightened painfully as she tried to pull away.

"P-please, signor," she stammered. "L-let me go."

"You have no need to be frightened, signorina. Please come into the car."

"No!" She glanced around her but there were no cars approaching in either direction; just a great stretch of tarmac and the darkening sky above it.

"Please let go of my hand, signor," she said firmly. "I would prefer to wait here."

"I have no intention of leaving you. You have no need to be frightened of me. Get into the car."

"No."

Without any further pretense of nonchalance she tried to pull free of his grip, and without any pretense of courtesy, he refused to let her go.

She was wondering whether to move closer to him and resort to jujitsu, when she saw a bright red car moving steadily toward her. With her free hand she waved vigorously. She was sure the car was going too fast to stop and her gesture was purely instinctive. There was a sharp squeal of brakes and the red monster halted, then reversed swiftly. Overwhelmed with relief she waited for the driver to reach her eye level. He did so and her breath expelled in a gasp.

Craig Dickson: the man from whom sensible girls like Suzy ran away. But only when there was no amorous Italian from whom a sensible girl would want to run even farther.

"Craig!" she cried, giving him a wide but wavering smile. "How wonderful to see you."

His glance went from her to the man, and the Italian released her hand quickly, slammed his door and drove off in a burst of exhaust fumes.

"Thank heaven you arrived when you did." She was too relieved to monitor what she said. "If you hadn't, I think he'd have abducted me."

"What did you expect if you stand there looking like that?"

"I can't help the way I look." She was angry at his unfeeling attitude. "The car broke down and I had to get a lift."

"There's a garage half a mile back. Why didn't you walk there?"

"Was there a garage?" she asked, astonished.

"Do you drive with your eyes closed?"

With an effort she controlled her temper, afraid that unless she did, he would drive off without her. Craig Dickson—as he had shown this afternoon—was not a man given to kindness.

"I'm afraid I didn't notice a garage," she replied quietly. "But if you'd be kind enough to drive me back to it, I may be able to get someone to come along and see what's wrong with the car."

"I'll have a look first."

He sauntered over, lifted the bonnet and peered into the interior. He turned a knob, tapped at another one and then climbed into the car and switched on the ignition. The engine wheezed into life, turned over for a few seconds and then stopped.

"No petrol," he said.

Her mouth dropped open and he smiled wickedly.

"If I ever had any doubts about you being a woman," he went on, "you've now proved it conclusively!"

56

"And you are an authority on women, of course."

"Of course. They go out without money in their purses and without petrol in their cars."

Before she could guess what he was going to do, he plucked her bag from her grasp and tipped its contents onto the seat beside him. A lipstick, compact, handkerchief and purse tumbled out, and he swooped down on the purse and opened it.

"As I thought," he said triumphantly. "Empty—except for ten-pence and a hundred lira!"

"Of all the—" Furiously she gathered her things together and stuffed them into her bag.

"I was only making my point," he explained.

"I came out with more than enough money," she rasped. "But I happened to buy myself lunch, which I hadn't anticipated doing."

"So how do you hope to buy petrol?"

With a determined effort she hung onto the last thread of her control and, enunciating her words, said: "Will you kindly drive me to the garage and pay them for a gallon of petrol?"

"And then you would like me to drive you back here and put the petrol in the engine for you. Is that it?"

"Yes, please."

He regarded her thoughtfully and she braced herself for his next thrust. But it did not come. Instead he returned to his own car and nodded.

"Wait here, blondie. I won't be gone long."

"I'll feel safer if I came with you," she said hastily and climbed in beside him.

Swinging the car around, he set off in the direction from which he had come. For several moments they drove in silence, then Suzy spoke.

"We've come more than a kilometer."

"So?"

"I am merely reminding you that you said the garage was a kilometer back along the road."

"So I'm out by a few hundred yards. But it was still

57

walking distance away from where you broke down. Look, there it is."

A large garage, festooned with flags, stood to one side of the highway. He stopped in the forecourt and jumped out as a plump young man came from the side of a truck, wiping his hands on a rag. Suzy remained in the car. She could not hear what the two men were saying, but the plump one looked in her direction and then started to laugh. Trust Craig Dickson to make capital out of her discomfiture. Her temper quietly simmered.

"All fixed." Craig was at the wheel again, a can of petrol stowed in the boot. "What made you drive all the way out here?" he asked as they headed for the Fiat. "I thought you'd be lunching at the club."

"I wanted to be by myself."

"How come?"

"How come what?"

"That you wanted to be by yourself. Most girls don't."

"You do love to generalize, don't you, Mr. Dickson."

"Make it Craig, Suzy. It sounds more friendly."

"I came out by myself," she said in an expressionless tone, "because I was bored to death with the tennis crowd and wanted to be alone."

"I know the feeling," he smiled. "I get that way, too. Generally before and after a match. Being alone helps me to unwind."

"I wouldn't have thought you needed to unwind after your match today. It was a walkover for you."

"No match is a walkover. Martelli's a good player."

"You outclassed him long before he hurt his leg. Once he did, it was no contest."

"Think so?"

"Wasn't it obvious?"

"Not to me."

"Is that why you played twice as hard once he was injured?"

"Martelli wasn't injured." There was a bite to Craig's voice. "If you're accusing me of being unsportsmanlike,
58

which you obviously are, I suggest you learn more about the game before you start giving your opinion."

"I don't need to be an expert to know when I'm seeing rotten sportsmanship!"

With a jerk on the brakes that almost shot Suzy through the windscreen, Craig stopped the car. Afraid he was going to abandon her in the middle of the road, she was relieved to see they were beside the Fiat, and she quickly scrambled out.

"If you had an ounce of brain in that empty head of yours," he stormed, jumping out with her, "you'd know that Martelli is renowned for his playacting on court. He won his last match by pretending he had a cramp and then getting in a sneak win because his opponent let up. It's his favorite trick. But I didn't think he'd pull it today; not when he was playing me and not in front of his own people. When he did—because he knew he was going to lose and he wanted to get sympathy—I decided to teach him a lesson. That's why I made him run around the court. Anyone with half a brain would have known immediately that if he'd really pulled a muscle—the way he pretended—he couldn't have got back three-quarters of the shots I threw at him. *If* his injury had been genuine, he would have had to abandon the match completely."

Both the tone and substance of Craig's words told Suzy he was speaking the truth. She was overwhelmed with shame, and wished Millie had told her about Martelli's reputation.

"I'm sorry, Craig. You've every right to be annoyed. I don't know much about the game and I should have kept quiet."

"That'll be the day!"

"Must you be so rude?"

"Me? Be rude to you!" He glared at her. "That's a laugh."

With a quick gesture he opened the can and slurped petrol into the tank. She watched him, wanting to apologize again but afraid that if she did, and said the wrong thing, they might come to blows.

Still in silence he put the lid back on the now-empty can and returned it to the boot of his car. Then he handed her the keys of her Fiat.

With burning cheeks she climbed in and switched on the engine. It turned over at once and he stepped back.

"I think you'll be all right now," he said, and without another word returned to his own car and drove away.

IV

Suzy was still feeling discomfited when she reached the hotel, a fact which Millie was quick to notice and remark on.

"I ran out of petrol," Suzy explained, "and if ever you're in the same predicament, don't try and flag down an Italian motorist."

"Wouldn't one stop?"

"They're only too willing. Honestly Millie, Italian men are the absolute bottoms!" She stopped as she heard her words, laughed, and then continued: "They think women have been put into the world solely for their convenience. If you say no to them, they merely see it as a come-on."

"Poor dear," Millie commiserated. "No wonder you look as if you want to bite someone! Mind you, I can understand them making a pass at you. You look so helplessly female. If *my* car broke down, all I'd get is a spanner to change my own wheel!"

"I wish you wouldn't keep putting yourself down," Suzy said promptly and wondered why Millie did it. If she could discover the reason, she would be halfway to knowing the girl behind the amazon mask.

"What say we go dancing tonight?" Millie suggested. "It will give us a chance to wear our new clothes and put you in a better mood."

"Don't bank on it," Suzy said darkly. "If I get an Italian octopus asking me to dance, I'll cut off his feelers! Anyway, you've got your big match tomorrow. Larry will have a fit if we go out."

"He's my manager, not my boss. And we needn't stay up late. I can be in bed by midnight. Come on, Suzy, say yes."

"Not unless you get Larry's permission."

Millie danced over to the telephone and dialed her manager's room. When she put down the receiver she was chuckling.

"He insists on joining us. Says he doesn't trust us on our own." She waltzed around the room, her short curls bobbing. "We might as well go to the nightclub in the hotel. It's supposed to be very good. And there won't be any photographers there either, which is always a pleasure."

Suzy nodded. Without knowing why, she could not summon up any enthusiasm for the evening ahead. Perhaps it was the idea of spending it solely in the company of Millie and Larry, and knowing that if anyone else broke into the threesome it would only be someone from the tennis fraternity. Good-looking young men all, but, to her way of thinking, infinitely boring.

Their lives were as closed as that of novice nuns, though their morals were anything but! Everywhere they traveled they met the same sort of people: the rich, the elite; the men and women who made the news and thought they were important because of it. The professional tennis circuit spanned the world, yet it made no difference to the players whether they were in London or Lima, Paris or Perth. One court and one crowd was much the same as another. Nothing was allowed to interfere with the game. If the stakes were high enough, they would play regardless of the politics, mindless of the policies. It was no wonder that all these superstars looked so young. Mentally they were.

Suzy knew she was being overly critical; and unjust too.

But to admit her prejudice was one thing; to change it was another. She could not afford to be unbiased. She needed to keep up her defenses in case, coming down, they brought her down with it.

She was wearing her contact lenses tonight and her eyes sparkled like amethysts. Her dress was starkly simple. Black and tight-fitting, its narrow shoulder straps held up a bodice cut so low that it was impossible to wear a brassiere underneath it.

The restaurant, like most Italian ones, was noisy, but the atmosphere was festive, and with a good meal inside her and several glasses of Asti Spumante, which she found too sweet for her taste, but which Millie and Larry both liked, her earlier despondency vanished. Even the popeyed stare of a young Italian sitting at a table a few yards to her left, failed to arouse her ire.

"Let's go into the nightclub," Millie said as they sipped their coffee.

"Why not leave it till tomorrow?" Larry suggested.

"Because I want to go tonight. Be a sport," she wheedled. "I'll be in bed by midnight. I swear it."

"Diana didn't even come down for dinner," Larry said, referring to Millie's opponent in the championship match the following day. "And she can give you eight years."

"At nineteen she needs all the rest she can get." Millie's reply was prompt. "I'm an old war-horse, remember, and they never get tired! They go on as strong as ever and then drop dead between the traces."

"You aren't dropping dead on me yet, kiddo."

Larry's eyes crinkled with amusement though there was a tension in his manner that made Suzy wonder how real his humor was. When Millie went to the cloakroom, she asked him.

"Does it show?" he asked in dismay.

"Millie doesn't notice it," she replied, "but it's very obvious to me. You're worried about her, aren't you?"

"Yes." He eyed her suspiciously. "This is off the record, Suzy. If she found out . . ."

"She won't. Not from me."

Suzy stopped, waiting for him to continue. He remained silent and she wondered if she would succeed in getting an answer to her question before Millie returned. If she didn't, and had to tackle him again tomorrow, he was likely to be in better control of himself and less forthcoming.

"Please tell me why you're worried about Millie," she said, deciding there was nothing to be lost by prompting him. "I'm not her enemy, Larry. I've become fond of her and I'd like to help her."

"I doubt if anyone can help her at this stage," came the bleak reply. "It's all in her own mind. She feels she's getting stale and she's scared that it'll affect her play."

"But she's playing superbly. No one's noticed anything."

"They don't know her the way I do. She's a mass of nerves when she comes off the court after each match, and even worse when she has to go out there again."

Suzy thought of Millie's lightheartedness before her tournament in London, and shook her head in disbelief. "She must be a great actress then. That's all I can say."

"She's a highly professional performer," Larry corrected. "But one day she'll go pop—unless she gets back her confidence."

"But she won against Jean Elder in two straight sets. What else does she need to give her confidence?"

"I'm darned if I know."

"Maybe she's bored and needs a holiday."

"A couple of months ago I would have laughed at anyone who said that," Larry replied, "but now I think you're right. After Wimbledon, I'm going to suggest she knocks off for a few months. It won't be easy, right in the middle of the season, but she has to let up sooner or later, and I'd rather it was sooner than too late."

"Maybe if she had a boy friend she wouldn't feel so jaded," Suzy said. "There's nothing better than old-fashioned admiration for making a girl regain her confidence."

Larry did not answer. His eyes had moved to the far side of the restaurant where two men and a woman had just come in.

"Well I'll be damned," he muttered, and flung Suzy a

sharp look. "Were you ever a witch in another life?"

"Not that I can remember! Why?"

"Because the answer to your suggestion has just walked in."

He turned his attention back to the threesome and Suzy did the same. The woman and one of the men were in their fifties, while the younger of the two bore such a resemblance to them—the features of the woman and the coloring of the man—that he must have been their son.

He was short and stocky and had the faintly belligerent air of a young bull. His aggressive strength was accentuated by bright red hair which, though cut short, bristled on his head like a wary porcupine. By no stretch of the imagination could he be called good-looking, but there was an arresting quality about him that everyone noticed, and his progress was followed as he came across the room and seated himself at a table only a few yards away.

Almost at once he rose again and came over to Larry.

"Hello," he said in a marked Australian accent, "surprised to see me?"

"Very," said Larry. "But I can see you aren't surprised to see *me*."

The younger man said nothing, though a half smile turned up the corners of his mouth.

"Where's Millie?"

"What makes you think I know?"

"Stuff that! You're still her manager. I've been following her career all along."

"I wondered if you did."

"Well, now you know."

There was no mistaking the antagonism between the two men, and Suzy knew that a wrong word could cause an explosion.

"Here's Millie now," she said breathlessly.

The girl was some five yards from the table when she noticed the man standing beside it. For an instant she stopped in full stride, all the color leaving her face, then she marched forward, color back again and her control with it.

65

"Hi, Don," she said easily. "They always say that if you stay at the Rome Hilton long enough you meet everyone you know." She sat down, as if glad to take the weight off her legs. "What brought you away from the cows?"

"Sheep," he corrected. "Even farmers need a holiday."

"You look the picture of health." Millie gave him a steady look.

"You look pretty good yourself."

"Thanks." She smiled and turned to Larry. "Have you signed the check? I want to go."

"When can I talk to you?" Don asked, leaning toward her.

"What about?"

"Old times."

"Old times are best forgotten."

"New times then."

Millie's smile faltered, though her tongue didn't. "New times need new girls. Look somewhere else, Don."

"I tried. But there was something wrong with my sight. All I could see was you."

"So you came here?"

"Yes."

"After seven years?"

"My second name is Jacob."

"Mine isn't Rachel."

"I love you," he said, giving her the travesty of a smile. "If you want a razor to cut me, I'll give you that, too. Though you're doing so well without it that . . ."

His voice cracked but the grin stayed firm, and Suzy, watching them both, felt her sympathies go out to this brash young man who suddenly didn't seem brash at all.

"Go back to your table, Don," Millie said. "My mother always told me never to talk seriously to a man when he was hungry."

"Do you think food will satisfy me?"

"Get them to roast you a sheep. They've satisfied you for seven years."

He wheeled around and went to his table, and Millie looked at Suzy. "That was Don," she said. "Now you know."

66

"Do *you?*"

"I'm not sure."

Suzy said nothing. Millie could not be the reigning world tennis champion as well as a wife and mother; not if Don were to be the husband and father. Something had to give, and until the girl had decided what, no one could help her.

Suzy glanced at Larry. From the way he was looking at Millie, she knew he was thinking the same. No wonder he was frowning. Millie was exceptionally important to him. She had been his meal ticket for the past thirteen years and would continue to be for a long while to come—if she went on playing. He would be the last person in the world to want her to give it up.

"Do come on," Millie urged, standing. "I want to dance."

The nightclub was small but so noisy that it made the restaurant seem quiet by comparison. The tables were crowded together and every one of them seemed occupied. But the head waiter recognized Millie and immediately a table was found for them at the far side of the room.

"You should have invited a couple of the boys along," Larry shouted above the din as he looked at the gyrating couples on the floor. "You girls won't want to sit and watch."

"I thought we might get picked up," Millie quipped. "It'll be more fun than dancing with any of the tennis crowd. All they talk about is tennis and sex."

"What's wrong with sex?" Larry asked with unusual levity.

"Nothing—if that's all you want." Bright brown eyes fixed themselves on Suzy. "How do you feel about it?"

"I'd want more. More than sex, I mean," she added hastily, seeing Larry grin. "I'm old-fashioned, I guess."

"You wouldn't stay that way if you were in this racket," Millie replied. "And forgive me for the pun—it was unintentional. But people like us lose all our inhibitions. We're like goldfish swimming in a gigantic bowl. Our whole lives are paraded and magnified for everyone to see."

"You can get out of the bowl," Suzy said.

"I might die for want of water." Millie looked agonized with doubt. "In place of water, read fame and all the heady

67

things that go with it. Crowds, cheers, fans, worship. They've been part of my life for so long, I'm not sure I can manage without them."

Suzy looked at Larry and drew a deep breath.

"Can you manage without Don for another seven years?" she asked.

"That's all in the past."

"*He* doesn't seem to think so."

Before Millie could answer, a swarthy-faced man was bending over her hand and speaking fluently in Spanish. Millie responded equally fluently and let him lead her onto the floor.

"I didn't know Millie spoke Spanish." Suzy was surprised.

"Her mother was Puerto Rican—a real firebrand too, and her father was Greek-American."

"A combustible combination."

"The result being Millie. She was a firecracker living close to a fire. When I became her manager it was the first time that kid ever knew peace."

"Does she see her parents often?"

"Once or twice a year. She telephones them though, and sends them all her press cuttings. They like the cuttings best of all."

"Don't you think Don would be good for her?" Suzy asked deliberately. "He wanted her to give up tennis years ago, so that proves he doesn't love her for her success."

"Millie and success go hand in hand. Don can't divorce the two. If he can't accept her the way she is, then—"

"But he wants a wife, not a traveling circus!"

"Millie will always be a champion. Even when she retires, she'll never give up the game completely. She loves it too much. She'll either run tournaments or a training school. But she has to be around tennis. If Don could accept *that*, I'd push her into his arms."

It was such a long and impassioned speech from a man who was usually taciturn on the subject of his client that Suzy did not doubt his sincerity. Millie had said nothing of her future, yet Larry's prognostication for her sounded so right, that Suzy found herself agreeing with him.

"Don was wrong to walk out on her," she murmured. "He should have stayed with her and waited. Given her time."

"He wasn't the type. Still isn't, I should think. He'd have hated following her around. It's hell for the wives who do, but even worse for the husbands. Men don't like playing second fiddle to managers or fans."

"Some husbands become their wives' managers," Suzy said.

There was silence at the table.

"I didn't break them up," Larry said finally. "I didn't have any need. I let Millie's ambition do it for me. Don was young and raw. He could never have taken over her career successfully and she knew it."

"What about now?"

"Now it's quite a different ball game. Millie's such a big star that she generates her own heat. All I do is pick the best offers. But I want her to be happy," he said abruptly. "She deserves it."

"You don't always give that impression," Suzy said bluntly.

"Because I'm still not sure she knows what'll make her happy."

"What are you two talking about so seriously?" Millie demanded, returning to join them.

"This and that," Larry smiled, and glanced at the Spaniard who was moving away.

"*That* was a reporter," Millie stated flatly. "And I thought it was my sex appeal!"

"Don thinks you've got plenty," Suzy dared. "Enough for him to remember for seven years."

"Maybe he only saw sheep!"

"I doubt that." Before Millie could pursue the conversation, Suzy was asked to dance, her partner turning out to be a pleasant Englishman, in Rome with a trade delegation.

"Isn't that Millie Queen with you?" he asked.

"Yes."

"Is she a friend of yours?"

"Yes." Suzy knew she had to say more. "I travel around with her for some of the time. It's very exciting."

After several more dances, during which he valiantly resisted satisfying his rampant curiosity about the tennis star, he left her at her table, and as she took her chair she saw that Millie was on the floor with Don. She was talking to him intently, her head thrown back, her free arm, which should have been around his neck, gesticulating wildly.

Suzy wished she was within earshot, and was then annoyed by the thought. Snoopy Sue, Millie called her when she wanted to tease, and Snoopy Sue was what she seemed to be. Deliberately she turned her eyes away from them, and almost at once found them on Elaine Esterson.

She was dancing with Craig: the two of them as close as corn on the cob. Even in a confined space Craig moved with the litheness of a panther. His head was lowered and his cheek rested against the pale one tilted invitingly up to his.

The group stopped playing and the floor cleared. Elaine and Craig moved back to their table which was on the edge of the floor. She picked up her bag and left and Craig leaned an arm on the table and laconically scanned the room.

Inevitably he found Suzy. She knew it from the way his shoulders straightened; as if he were going into battle. Careful to remain motionless, she stared into space. The keys of the piano tinkled and the notes were picked up by the base guitar.

From the corner of her eyes she saw Craig rise and wend his way toward her. Every nerve in her body tingled, telling her of his intention. Then he was beside her, smiling down at her with his cat's eyes.

"You owe me a dance," he said.

"I do?"

"For coming to your rescue today."

"Then I'll pay my debt."

She followed him to the floor. His arm came around her and he drew her close. The top of her head reached to his shoulder and she refused to look up into his face. Instead

70

she let her eyes rest on his throat. The skin was bronzed and smooth and smelled faintly of after-shave lotion. His shirt collar was crisp as a cracker and she noticed with surprise that he was extremely well-dressed. Tonight he could have passed for an Italian businessman, so faultless was his suit, so well-coordinated the color of his shirt and tie.

"Say something," he murmured, "or I might start to think you're in awe of me."

"I am. And struck dumb that you asked me to dance. The last I saw of you, you were driving off in a fury."

"Not true," he corrected. "I put the petrol in your engine, made sure it was working and then waited until you got behind the wheel and switched on. What more could I have done?"

"Smiled at me as you drove off."

"After you accused me of beating Martelli into the ground?"

"I apologized for that. What more could *I* have done?"

"Smiled as you said you were sorry."

It was an effort for her not to smile now. How quickly he had thrown her words back at her. It was almost a pleasure to quarrel with him. She glanced up, saw the gleam in his eyes and knew he was thinking the same. Watch it, she warned, you're treading on dangerous ground.

"I was genuinely sorry for what I said." She spoke firmly, to leave him in no doubt. "I would never apologize if I didn't mean it."

"Then all is forgiven."

His hold on her tightened, and because she liked it, she pulled slightly back. "Where's Elaine?"

"Gone to phone her father."

"So you're temporarily off the hook while she's on it?"

"Don't make me sound like a fish," he grinned. "I've never been on the hook in my life."

This immediately brought to mind a picture of a slippery trout. He must have started taking evasive action while he was still losing his milk teeth, she thought sourly. Men like

Craig had a built-in charm which was devastating at any age.

"What's going on in that gorgeous head of yours?" he asked.

"I was thinking how resistible you are," she lied.

"Naughty, naughty." He gave her a far from gentle shake. "I thought we were going to be friends from now on, which means you have to be nice to me."

"I am being nice to you."

"God help your enemies then!"

"He generally does."

"A cynic, too. I'll have to put an end to that. Violet-eyed blondes should be soft as down and sweet as sugar."

"Bad for the posture and murder for your teeth!"

He laughed. "I like your sense of humor, Sweet Sue. We could have a lot of fun together."

"I'm sure we could."

"So?"

"So no." There was a pause. "Thanks all the same."

His hand stroked her back, sending feathery tingles along her spine.

"I'm not going to take no for an answer," he said softly. "Something happened to me the minute I saw you."

"I'm sure it did," she retorted. "And from what I know of you, it'll go on happening with monotonous regularity."

He chuckled deep in his throat. "Regular it may be— and thank the Lord for it—but monotonous, never! Which brings me right back to you."

But not for long, she thought, remembering his reputation. Love 'em and leave 'em, Craig Dickson. No, that wasn't right. Lust 'em and leave 'em. Love never came into it.

"How long will you be following Millie around?" he asked.

"I'm not sure. Another month perhaps. It may be less."

"It must be like a holiday for you."

"A working holiday."

"I don't call writing a few articles, work."

"I could say the same about patting a ball over a net."

72

"You don't mean that."

She sighed. "No, I don't. I'm sure it's a very demanding sport."

"A hundred percent demanding. Once you let up, you're finished."

"Don't you resent having to give it so much of your time?"

"Why should I? It's my job and my hobby all rolled into one."

The tempo of the music slowed and he rested his cheek upon the top of her head. She could hear the heavy beating of his heart and realized that the material of his jacket was as flimsy as that of her dress. He too seemed aware of the intimacy of their closeness, for the tips of his fingers moved across her bare shoulders. She gave a slight shiver and his hold tightened.

"Cold?" he asked whimsically.

"Trembling with passion."

"But there's still ice on your tongue! One day I'm going to melt it." They moved a few steps. "Doesn't your boy friend object to you being away from London for so long?" he asked.

"I haven't got a boy friend."

"May I apply?"

"You aren't free."

"You shouldn't believe all the gossip you hear."

"I don't. Only a quarter of it. And it still makes my ears burn."

His fingers traveled her spine as if it were a xylophone. "What is it, Sweet Sue? Don't I appeal to you?"

"Visually, yes." She favored him with a deliberate look. "But mentally, no."

"What about physically?"

"Sorry." She shook her head. "That doesn't work if the mental bit isn't there."

"I can read and write," he said helpfully. "Isn't that any good?"

She refused to answer. He was playing a game and she wanted no part in it. She wished she were tall enough to

73

stare over his shoulder. The line of his jacket obliterated her view and she had to content herself with looking at his throat. There was something intimate in the curving line of it and the way his hair lay thick on the nape of his neck, the ends curling slightly as if they had resisted the touch of the brush.

"When *I* fancy someone," he murmured in her ear, "I go strictly for eye appeal."

"Naturally. You have a butterfly mentality and you flit from flower to flower. Obviously the brightly colored ones will catch your eye."

"Most men are the same."

"When they're young and immature. Intelligent ones grow out of it."

"Don't you believe it. The only reason a man sticks with one girl is because he gets caught while he's still savoring the nectar. Marriages aren't made on earth or heaven, Sweet Sue, but in bed!"

She drew back the better to see his face. His mouth was curved in a half smile but his eyes were serious.

"Poor Craig," she cooed. "Your life will be over if you ever get a slipped disc!"

"I can see you aren't up on all the variations!"

She knew better than to reply. There were times when silence was golden, and this one was twenty-two carat.

"The trouble with you," he went on, his voice lazy, "is that like most of your sex, you can't bear the sight of a free-roaming steer. You won't rest until you've roped him in and branded him!"

"Quiet steers give the best meat!"

His laugh was uninhibited and rippled through his body, sending little shock waves through her own.

"You get better and better, Suzy *mio*. I'm going to enjoy getting to know you."

"I already know *you*," she replied. "All two pages."

"There's some invisible writing, too," he warned. "And the appendix is terrific!"

"But the prologue's so dull!"

Ignoring her comment, he pulled her head down onto

74

his shoulder. For a few moments they danced without speaking. He was light on his feet, which she had expected, and gentle in his hold, which she had not. It was a pity that the purely physical had never been enough for her. If it could have been, her whole life would have been different.

"If you're going to be around for a while," he interrupted her reverie, "that means you'll be with Millie at Wimbledon."

"I expect so."

"What will you do when you've finished her biography?"

Suzy paused before answering, not sure if Craig was going to suggest she write his. If he did, and she turned it down—as she definitely would—Bill Walters would have her guts for garters.

"I'll be going back to the paper," she said quickly. "I much prefer to work on routine stories. But what about you? Do you play all year round?"

"I generally take a couple of months off. It stops me from getting stale."

"What do you do then?"

"Gardening," he said stolidly. "I go from bed to bed. Flower beds, of course."

With relief she saw Elaine standing on the steps by the door.

"Your girl friend's back," she informed him.

"So what?"

"So you should take me to my own table and return to your own."

"I wouldn't dream of behaving like a gentleman. It would spoil your image of me!"

"My image of you is too fixed to be changed by one decent action!"

With a murmur she could not decipher, he lowered his head and wrapped his arms completely around her. It brought her face in close contact with his throat, and she was acutely aware of the silky texture of his skin. She knew it was useless to try to push him away, for his muscles, though relaxed, could become bands of steel. Besides, her treacherous senses wanted her to remain where she was;

to run her hands through his hair and press he lips to his mouth. Angered by her response to him, she stiffened in his grasp. Ignoring it, he pressed his lips to her temple.

"You're wearing a lovely scent, Suzy."

"No, I'm not. It's only me."

"Only me." He breathed in deeply. "If you could market it, you'd make a fortune." The music slowed and stopped and so did he. "Though on second thought, it might be as well if you didn't. All those free-roaming steers would know where to find you!"

His hands dropped away from her but he remained close as they returned to her table, where Larry was talking to Millie and Don. Craig greeted the Australian warmly and, as soon as Suzy was seated, moved across to his chair to chat with him.

The music started again and Suzy could only hear snatches of their conversation. But it was enough to tell her that the two had known each other well, years ago.

"So you still don't have any regrets at giving up the game?" she heard Craig ask.

"Not one," Don replied. "Anyway, I was never in your league."

"No one remains at the top forever," Craig answered, and then lowered his voice, making the rest of what he said inaudible.

Suzy forced her attention away from the two men. She did not want to continue thinking of Craig and she was relieved when he left their table and returned to Elaine.

Another moment passed and she saw him on the floor with her, his arms around the red-clad body the way they had been around her own a short while ago.

Red flowers, black flowers: it did not matter to Craig what flowers they were, as long as they were there for his picking.

V

Lying in bed that night, with images of Craig and Elaine whirling around in her head, Suzy marveled that she had succumbed so easily to his charm. Or was it Craig's fame and reputation that had bowled her over? Either way, she despised her reaction.

"He's just a good-looking hunk of muscle," she said aloud, switching on the lamp beside her bed and staring defiantly at the wall opposite. "If I got to know him, he'd bore me to death in a week."

But what a glorious week it would be. Flushing at where her thoughts had taken her, she reached for her notepad and pen. She would rough out her next installment of Millie's biography.

It was easier said than done. Don's arrival on the scene was not something that could be ignored, and she would have to mention it. But she could not do this without also mentioning the part he had once played in the tennis champion's past. Yet much of what Millie had told her about Don and her attitude to him had been told in confidence, and to breach it was not something she was prepared to do.

She frowned down at the few lines she had written. It was impossible to draw a line of distinction between the knowledge she had gained as a professional journalist and the knowledge she had gained as Millie's confidante. As a professional journalist, everything she learned was grist to the mill. Damn it all, she had said as much to Millie. Her pen hovered above the paper but no words flowed from it. They were in her brain but refused to be transmitted; blocked there by the dam of conscience. She thought of her editor's fury if he could see her now and tried to imagine what he would say to her, hoping this would release the block. But it didn't, and she tossed aside her pad and pen and switched off the light.

The hotel room was sufficiently well-insulated to turn all outside noise into a muted throb, but her senses were too alert to let her sleep. In her ears she could still hear the music from the nightclub, though she knew that in actuality this was not so. Restlessly she turned on the light again and reached for a book.

She was still reading it when she heard Millie enter the suite. The bedroom door opened and the girl came in.

"I thought you left us because you were tired," Millie said.

"I was tired of dancing," Suzy answered. "How did the rest of your evening go?"

"Fine." Millie sank down onto the bed. "Don wants me to marry him."

"I know."

"I should think everyone knows by now!"

"Will you?"

"I don't know. I'd have to give up tennis and I'm not sure I can."

"What did it feel like to see him after such a long while?"

"As if I'd seen him yesterday."

"There speaks the voice of love."

Millie ran her hands through her hair. The curls, carefully controlled by one of the Milton's hairdressers only a few hours ago, broke and parted in a riot of tendrils, giving her a cherubic look and taking years off her age. She should

78

accept Don's proposal and run, Suzy thought with instant clarity, but knew better than to say so.

"How long is Don staying in Rome?" she asked.

"A week. Then his parents go on to Paris, London and New York."

"And Don?"

"Straight back to Sydney when he leaves here."

"With or without you?"

"So it seems." Millie jumped up and walked restlessly around the room. "If only I knew what to do! My heart says one thing but my head says another." She stopped by the foot of the bed. "You were dancing a long time with Craig," she said idly. "Elaine looked as if she wanted to scratch your eyes out."

"She has nothing to fear from me," Suzy said shortly. "I'm not one of Lover Boy's fans."

"He'd like to be one of yours."

"Because I'm new on the scene."

"Girls are usually flattered by his attention."

"As he was quick to tell me."

"Don't judge him by what he says." Millie yawned. "Like most of us in this game, he has two personalities: a public one and a private one."

"I don't like either of them."

Millie wandered to the door. "I'd better get some sleep. It's my big day tomorrow."

"Today," Suzy corrected. "It's a quarter to one."

The door closed and Suzy turned off her lamp to make sure Millie did not return; it was important for the girl to have a decent night's rest, and equally important for there to be no more talk about Craig.

A public and a private personality. It was hard to envisage Craig in the latter role. He seemed to lead all his life in the limelight and to enjoy doing it. She remembered the numerous interviews he gave; all of them amusing and all reflecting the different facets of a larger-than-life character. He projected a persona so shiny and glittering that it brilliantly reflected everything around it and gave away nothing of itself. Mirroring without absorbing. Emitting,

79

but only from the surface. If there was a man within, Craig took great care that no one knew it.

The next day, Suzy and Millie went early to the tennis stadium. It was the best way to avoid the photographers who would be gathered there by lunch time: vultures with cameras, ready to pick the flesh off any celebrity.

Millie appeared unperturbed by the match ahead of her and chattered on about nothing. But Larry prowled around the dressing room, so unlike his usual calm self that Suzy wondered if he were worrying about the game or Don. The Australian had not put in an appearance, but Millie did not refer to him, nor look as if she had expected him to arrive.

"Do go away and leave us," Millie ordered her manager. "I can't relax with you wandering around like a lost ball!"

"Sorry, honey."

He went to the door and paused there, irresolute. Millie gave him an exasperated stare.

"Don't worry about the match, Larry. Diana's a good player but I'm going to beat her in two straight sets. I feel it in my bones."

"Don't make it look too easy," he warned. "The Italians enjoy a fight."

"You mean the Romans do," she corrected. "From lions and Christians to tennis players! Don't worry, I'll make it look exciting."

He left, and Millie settled down in an armchair. Suzy made herself more comfortable in her own, and waited. She knew the tennis champion found it relaxing to talk, and wondered whether she had used Larry as a confidant before she herself had come on the scene. Somehow she did not think so. Larry knew his protégée well, but only as a tennis star; the woman still eluded him. That was why he continued to see her in such stereotyped terms. Only in the past few days, when Suzy had fired questions at him, had he started to reassess his earlier opinions.

"You won't find me as relaxed as this before Wimbledon," Millie said suddenly. "That's when I really work myself up into a state of nerves."

"Because of the Royals?"

80

"You've got to be kidding! I don't mean any disrespect, Suzy, but no top-class player even gives them a thought. *We're* the royal ones these days. People pay to see *us*. No, it's Wimbledon itself that gets to you. And especially the center court. When you go out there and feel the crowd—either for you or against you—then you really know what it's like to be a top-rank player. No matter how many times you've been in the same situation, the atmosphere there always gets to you. You start remembering all the tennis greats who've played there before you and—and you sort of feel diminished by them."

"No one can diminish *you*," Suzy said sincerely. "Your name is right up there along with all the other greats."

"You think so?" There was a glitter in the brown eyes.

"You *know* so," Suzy insisted. "What's the matter with you, Millie? You're a three-time winner at Wimbledon. If that doesn't make you one of the best, what does?"

Millie ran her hands through her hair. "I'm mad," she said flatly. "Put it down to nerves."

"Millie Queen is never nervous."

"Right. Thanks for reminding me."

At twelve-thirty a luncheon hamper arrived for them: sandwiches and fruit for Suzy and specially prepared ice cream—made only from cream and eggs—for Millie. Normally a hearty eater, the girl ate sparingly before a match, and even after it—win or lose—took several hours before being able to face a proper meal.

At a quarter to two, fifteen minutes before she was due to go on court, Millie changed into her tennis outfit—a pink-and-white dress with scalloped hem and collar. She wiped all the makeup from her face explaining it would streak in the heat if she didn't, and walked briskly down the concrete-paved corridor that led to the court.

Larry joined them as they neared the entrance. He did not speak to Millie and they all stood together in silence, waiting for Diana Vox, Millie's challenger, to arrive.

She appeared within a moment, flanked by her coach and her mother. She gave them all a blank stare and then turned her back on them. Suzy knew this to be part of the routine. Opposing players, even when they were friends, rarely spoke to each other before a match. Like enemies, they secretly marshaled their inner forces and maintained their silence, afraid that speech or smiles would seep it away.

A group of senior officials arrived, plump and pale and perspiring, to lead the two girls away, and Suzy and Larry headed for the players' box.

It was crowded, but Suzy immediately saw Craig and Elaine. It was as if her eyes were radar signals that automatically homed in on him. Ignoring the way her stomach muscles had tightened, she settled next to Larry and stared at the court. A strong thigh pressed against hers and her heart almost jumped into her throat. She looked around quickly, feeling foolish at her reaction, and saw it was Don.

In an open-necked sports shirt and dark slacks, he looked far more at ease than the previous night, and there was markedly less aggression in his manner as he acknowledged Larry's greeting.

"How's Millie?" he asked.

"Fine." Larry spoke before Suzy could do so, and fell silent as the girl herself came out on court.

She looked small and defenseless down there on the clay, and without knowing why, Suzy had a premonition that this match was not going to go as planned.

Her fears were justified. Diana Vox took the first four games without losing a point, breaking Millie's serve twice in order to do so. Millie came back strongly to win the next game but Diana won the next one and, with it, the set.

"S'truth," Don muttered. "What's the matter with the old girl? She's lost all her concentration."

"That's been her trouble since Forest Hills," Larry said, lowering his head to mask his lips as he spoke. "She's been fighting against it but it's getting worse. I was hoping she could keep going until Wimbledon, but if today's anything to go by . . . Hell!"

As if she knew she was being discussed, Millie glanced upward. Her eyes scanned the players' box and found Don. Suzy felt him tense and she waited for him to smile or wave in recognition. He did neither. Instead he jumped to his feet, turned his back on the court and stomped out.

Unable to credit what she had witnessed, Suzy looked quickly at Larry. But the manager was rooting around in his holdall, looking for some chewing gum, and had not noticed Don's departure.

Quickly Suzy turned to the court. Millie was still standing in front of her chair beside the umpire's seat. Her face was blank, as though with shock, and when she picked up her towel to wipe the sweat from her forehead, her movements were jerky.

Diana Vox went back on court, ready to serve, and Millie followed slowly.

Don't give Don another thought, Suzy willed the girl below her. Show him how wrong he was to write you off like that. Darling Millie, please please show him the stuff that champions are made of.

And show him Millie did. Serving and volleying like a demon, she took the second set six-three and the final set in six straight games.

To a standing ovation, the two girls left the court, Millie carrying the exquisitely made silver trophy which, having won it for the third successive time, was now hers to keep permanently.

"Did you see the way Don walked out?" Suzy muttered fiercely as she followed Larry from the box. "It was the most disgusting behavior I . . ." She was too choked with anger to continue, and it almost throttled her as they reached the back of the stand and found Don waiting for them.

"Great, wasn't it?" he said cheerfully.

"No thanks to you."

"She got mad as hell when she thought I'd walked out, didn't she?" he went on, ignoring Suzy's comment. "It was the only way I could think of to put her back in the game. If I'd stayed to watch her, she'd have gone to pieces and lost the match."

"You went out purposely?" This seemed to be what Don was saying, but Suzy could not make any sense of it.

83

"Why else? When my old girl's in a temper all her fighting spirit comes out. I've been cricking my neck watching her from the back of the stand and"—he held out his hands to show bloodied fingertips—"biting my nails to the quick in case my behavior was too drastic."

"It may have been drastic for your future with her," Larry grunted, "but it won her the tournament."

They jostled their way through the crowd and had pushed several yards when Suzy caught Larry's arm.

"Give Don a chance to go and see Millie alone."

"But—"

"If she loves him she'll go to him eventually anyway," Suzy went on remorselessly. "So you might as well play your cards properly and remain her friend."

With a fatalistic lift of grizzled eyebrows, Larry went off in the opposite direction, and Suzy paused to watch Don move inexorably toward Millie's dressing room before going in search of an exit.

Several thousand people had the same idea, and she was shoved and pushed and kicked and squeezed until she felt like a doll in a mangle. Hot breath dampened her neck and she was mantled in the heavy odors of garlic and sweat. An extra violent shove caught her off balance, and she was only saved from falling by a firm pair of hands gripping her waist and steadying her against a rock-hard chest.

"I always knew you'd fall for me one day!" Craig whispered in her ear.

She tried to turn and look at him, but the crowd was pressing too thickly on either side of her. "Have you been following me?" she asked angrily.

"Me and five thousand others. For God's sake, how paranoid can you get!"

It was justified criticism, which did not endear him to her, and she ignored it and tried valiantly to push ahead of him.

"It's obliging of you to force a way through the crowd for me," he continued, "but if you'd let me squeeze past you, I'd do it for *you*."

84

"Oh do be quiet!" she grated. "Don't you know when you're not wanted?"

"Even if I did," he said plaintively, "I can't do much about it. I'm stuck, Sweet Sue. On you—and in the crowd."

She tried to wriggle through a gap between two people, but was caught halfway, like a cloth between wringers, and squeezed back against him.

"This is more like it," he breathed upon her hair. "When we get out of this scrum, will you have a drink with me?"

"No. Thank you," she added as an afterthought. "I'm busy."

"So am I. But I can still make time to see you."

Making time was an unfortunate phrase for him to have used, for it hardened her resolve not to become involved with him.

"I'm not free, Mr. Dickson, and even if I were, I wouldn't want to go out with you. Now be a good little boy and leave me alone!"

There was a surge from the crowd, as if a barrier had been removed, and she was propelled forward fast. Not daring to look around, she darted toward the main gate, intent on finding Millie's car and chauffeur. A row of limousines gleamed ahead of her and she nipped smartly toward them.

"Got you," said a drawling voice, and she was firmly caught and shoved toward a car parked directly in front of the main gate. An attendant was at the wheel and he jumped out as Craig pushed her onto the front seat and vaulted in to take the man's place.

"Don't you ever take no for an answer?" she stormed. "I told you I'm going out."

"I know you are. With me. Relax and get ready to enjoy yourself."

"I don't enjoy myself with other girls' toys."

"I'm not another girl's toy," he said happily, "so you can play with me all you want."

Fury made her speechless and she took several deep breaths to calm herself.

"If your conscience is bothering you," Craig said as he slowed down at some lights, "though there's no reason why it should, I'll appease it by telling you Elaine is playing in a mixed doubles this afternoon and I've no desire to watch it. I fancy a run in the country and I fancy it with you. It's as simple as that."

Simple was not the word Suzy would have used to describe his pursuit of her. But then hadn't her behavior to him encouraged such tactics? To a man used to being pursued, rather than having to be the pursuer, her exaggerated dislike of him and her continuing sarcasm had been an irresistible challenge. Had she wanted to discourage him, a swift melting in the face of his charm would more easily have done the trick. From such an admission, it was also impossible not to admit that the determination of her conscious flight from him was in inverse proportion to her subconscious desire to do the exact opposite. Damn Dr. Freud. If only she'd never read him.

With a sigh she sank back in her seat and let the breeze coming in through the open roof, cool her hot cheeks. Craig was content to drive in silence, and after they had gone a few miles she shifted her position slightly and was able to study him without turning her head. In gray silk sweater and darker slacks, he looked as if he had stepped off the cover of a male pinup magazine. The dimple she had noticed in his cheek on the first occasion she had met him, was more visible now that his face had relaxed into a whimsical half smile, and his tan was deeper after a few days in the Roman sun. No wonder he had no shortage of women. His trouble would only come in fighting them off!

She averted her eyes and concentrated on the passing scene. Was it only yesterday that he had rescued her? It seemed far longer than that. But when two people were staying in the same hotel and mixing in the same milieu, it was easy to feel you had known them for a long while. Yet with Craig there was nothing for her to know. She knew it all. His past, from newspaper cuttings; his present, from her own eyes, and his future from her own deduction. They had no common meeting ground—if one ignored sexual attraction. And she was determined to ignore it. No way was she going to add to the list of this man's scalps.

Everything he represented was anathema to her. Concerned only with the sport that was his life, he paid no heed to what went on in the world around him unless it affected his tournaments and, because of it, his pocket. But then that applied to everyone in this sport. Sport. She almost snorted at the word. It was about as sportive as piranha fish in a pool. The advent of team tennis had turned the game into a profession as hard-nosed as baseball and football. No longer was the game everything. Money made the carousel go round.

But she worked for money too. She went where Bill Walters sent her, and wrote the kind of articles Bill Walters wanted. So how did that make her any different from Craig? She was carefully probing for an answer when he spoke.

"I'm taking you to a little hideout I discovered a couple of years back. I hope you'll like it."

Immediately she pictured a small hotel with double beds and a discreet patron, and was furious when he turned his head and wagged a finger at her.

"Naughty, naughty. There's no need to jump to such assumptions. When I go in for seduction, I like everything to be prepared—including my woman!"

"You can't blame me for assuming the worst."

"Most girls would think it the best!" There was silence. "That was a joke, Sweet Sue. I'm nowhere near the libertine my publicity makes out."

"I'm glad to hear it."

"But you don't believe me?"

Only a fool would believe him. Craig Dickson might not do half the things the gossip columnists said, but if he only did a quarter, it would still qualify him to contend with Don Giovanni.

Resolutely she stared through the window. The sky was deep blue and clear, the trees bright with newly unfurled leaves not yet polluted by fumes and dirt. Even the buildings looked whiter in the early summer sunshine. She was suddenly glad to be driving into the country, and she looked at Craig and thought how well he went with his surroundings: as casually elegant as his gleaming red sports car—and equally as high powered.

Aware of her eyes on him, he smiled at her. It held no artifice and seemed to be the smile of a handsome young man who had the world at his feet and was with the girl of his choice.

Yes, she thought with a curious lift of her heart, at this precise moment she was definitely the girl of his choice. The one with whom he most wanted to be. Tomorrow it would be someone else—possibly even tonight. But now it was her, and she was going to enjoy it. After all, she was a sophisticated young woman in a profession where greater experience meant better writing. If she thought of it in those terms, her surrender to Craig's charm seemed less reprehensible.

"Have we far to go?" she asked gaily, running her hands through her hair and sounding so happy that he gave her a faintly surprised glance.

"Ten more minutes. There are cigarettes in the dashboard if you'd like one."

"I don't smoke."

"Good."

He leaned forward and switched on the radio. Music filled the air and she was disappointed that he preferred to listen rather than to talk, until she saw that he had increased speed and was concentrating on the road, his eyes narrowed as the speedometer leapt from eighty to well over a hundred.

"Why so fast?" she asked.

"I want to get there and concentrate on you instead of the car."

Higher and higher they climbed the hilly road, leaving Rome far behind them. At last they branched onto a narrow lane and bumped along for a mile or two until they reached a large stone house set in a wild-looking garden. A stream burbled its way across one side of it, and the tables set out on the terrace looked down on the water and a humpbacked stone bridge. It was unbelievably rural and difficult to credit it was so near to Rome. Difficult also to believe it was relatively undiscovered, which Craig assured her it still was.

"Undiscovered by foreigners," he added, "but known to any Italian who loves first-class pasta."

"I adore pasta," she exclaimed.

"Fancy some now?"

"For tea?"

"We'll have four o'clock dinner!"

She laughed and he caught her hand and swung it high, the gesture schoolboyish and lighthearted.

There were no other people here and they had the terrace to themselves. A table had been set for two and she wondered if he had telephoned ahead to ask for it to be prepared. Who would he have brought here if he had not persuaded her to come? She swallowed the question and went to comb her hair while he ordered some drinks.

In the mirror in the cloakroom she stared at her flushed face and overbright eyes, knowing Craig was the cause of it and wishing he wasn't. He was too dangerous a man for her to like; no good would come of it. She returned to the terrace. Her step was quiet and he did not hear her, but remained leaning against the balustrade, his body outlined by the sunlight. His short-sleeved sweater showed his bronzed arms and his trousers were cut low and fitted tightly across his hips, making her aware of their muscular strength. He looked the superb athlete that he needed to be in order to remain at the top of his profession, and she wondered how hard it was for him to keep at a physical peak when there were so many distractions around him. One day all the living and the loving would rebound on him and he would no longer be able to burn the candle at both ends. But not yet, she acknowledged wryly. Today he looked as if he had the stamina to burn it in the middle.

He moved and saw her, and she went gracefully toward him, her skirts swinging around her legs. She was glad she was wearing one of her prettiest dresses, for its ruffled neckline and cape sleeves were infinitely flattering. It was also the same color as her hair, and she was not surprised when Craig, holding out her chair, remarked on it.

"You look like a buttercup in that dress. You must have Swedish ancestry."

"Not that I'm aware of." She sipped the wine he had poured for her. "Both my parents are dark."

"Odd."

"It's not a bit odd. Lots of people have dark hair!"

"But not blond daughters." He laughed at her. "You've a droll wit. I like it almost as much as I like your coloring. Your hair was the first thing I noticed about you." There was a pause as he poured his own wine. "Aren't you going to ask me what was the second?"

"I'm sure you're going to tell me."

"Sheathe your claws, kitten. This is a friendly get-together. It's the last we'll be having for some time."

Her hands were extra still on her glass. "Don't tell me you're getting married?"

"What an outlandish question! What I meant is that I'm leaving for the States tonight. I'm playing some exhibition matches there. I could have done without it," he added, "but the money was too good to turn down."

"Is that the main reason you go on playing? You've been champion so many times it can't still be a thrill for you."

"It's always a thrill to win. Never underestimate the feeling of power that success gives you. It's like adrenaline." He eyed her. "What about you? Aren't there any ambitions in that pretty head of yours, or are you looking for a loving husband and domestic bliss?"

"You make it sound like an indictment."

"For me it would be a prison sentence."

His words chilled her but she did not show it.

"One day, Craig Dickson, you're going to come a real cropper."

"You mean I'll fall in love before I can stop myself?" His hazel eyes crinkled. "Don't hold your breath for it. I'm too wary."

"Then stay away from me," she said with mock solemnity. "I'm strictly the marrying type."

90

"You don't need to put me on my guard, Sweet Sue. It's been up from the moment I met you."

She continued to smile at him, wishing she knew of a way to wipe the complacency off his face.

"Why are we wasting time thinking of the future when we have the marvelous present?" he asked softly, and raised his glass to her. "I drink to this beautiful day that I have and the beautiful girl that I don't!"

"I'll certainly drink to that," she said, and did so, suddenly glad he was going away tonight. If he weren't, the toast could well have had a different ending. It was a salutary thought.

The patron came across the terrace bearing a large silver platter filled with steaming fettucini. Golden curls of butter were added, together with a liberal sprinkling of ground pepper, then two heaped plates were set in front of them.

"There's an art in eating this," Craig informed her, deftly twirling his fork in the glistening mound. "If you drop any on your lap you'll have to pay a forfeit. One kiss for every forkful lost."

"That isn't a forfeit," she replied calmly. "I'd have said it was a foregone conclusion!"

He looked momentarily taken aback and she took advantage of it.

"The trouble with you, Craig, is that you're too obvious. You've been using the same line for so long, that I can see every remark a mile off."

"Thanks for telling me. From now on I'll try a different approach. How about sincerity?"

"I'd love that. Then I can be sincere right back."

She blinked her long lashes at him and he laughed. But when he spoke, she was amused to note that he had changed the subject.

"I'm looking forward to seeing the biography you've done on Millie. I have a feeling you don't write the usual journalistic clap-trap."

"What a marvelous compliment! But actually you're right. I'm a factual writer and I try to be an honest one."

"I can't see you as a Fleet Street hack. You look as if you should be selling sweets to children or buying some for your own."

"Do you always judge female ability by the way the female looks?"

"It depends what I'm judging."

"I should imagine you're only interested in one thing."

"How you do malign me," he said. "I'm quite aware that beautiful girls can also have beautiful brains. But they're generally also the ones with beautiful ambitions—to become Craig Dickson's wife."

"*That* being the greatest ambition of all," she retorted.

"You said it," he said modestly. "I wouldn't dare."

She choked on her pasta and took a gulp of wine. He was taking great pleasure in teasing her and she must be careful not to let him rile her.

Their meal over, they strolled around the garden, coming to a pause by the hammock that overlooked the stream. It was cooler here and they sat down. Suzy leaned back and closed her eyes, enjoying the breeze that blew against her face and the gentle sensation of swinging as Craig sat beside her and kept the seat in motion. He was content not to talk, and after a few moments the swinging slowed and finally stopped.

Only then did Suzy open her eyes and see he had fallen asleep. One hand lay across his chest and the other was flung out, the fingers uncurled and almost touching the grass. The hand was palm up and open, the way a child's often is when it slept. But Craig was no child. He was a man, with a man's need and a man's selfishness. She went on staring at his hand, wondering how many hearts had been held in its palm.

He stirred and muttered something but did not awaken, and she was amused to find him in such a deep slumber. It was the rare woman who could—or would—be able to fall so deeply asleep in front of a comparative stranger. Women were too wary, too suspicious.

Craig's ability to sleep like this was indicative of his strong egoism. He had no concern for others and so was

92

unaware of them. People were there to suit him, and if they didn't, then he would take himself away. He would be a difficult man for any girl to cope with. One would have to be constantly on guard not to lose him. She thought of the many girls willing to share his life, and of Elaine—a beautiful heiress who could have practically any man she wanted—and who only seemed to want this one.

Craig stirred again and she moved carefully to give him more room. His face was turned toward her and she noticed the delicate curve of his mouth; too beautiful for a man, yet in no way effeminate. But that was because of the firmness of his jaw. The skin there was darker, caused by the faint shadow of emerging stubble. She resisted the urge to run her finger along it to see if it rasped. But it wouldn't; it was too downy. Tenderness flickered inside her. She was too intelligent not to know what was causing it, but all her intelligence could not make it disappear. Dismayed by her vulnerability, she looked into the sleeping face and was glad he had no idea what he was doing to her.

As if to prove her wrong, his lids lifted with startling swiftness, and green-gold eyes looked directly into hers.

"What a great way to wake up."

His voice was slurred with slumber and she found it intensely exciting. She shifted back into the corner of the hammock. The hard edge of it dug into her waist but nothing could still her trembling, and it increased as he rubbed the side of his leg against hers.

"You're beautiful," he said thickly and, reaching out for her, pulled her across him.

He moved with such speed that before she knew it, she was the one lying on the hammock with Craig gazing down at her. Even as his mouth lowered to hers, she marveled at his dexterity, bitterly reflecting that he must have had a great deal of practice. Then rational thought vanished and consciousness became Craig's mouth; the pressure of his lips, the sharp edge of his teeth and the gentle softness of his exploring tongue.

Instinctively she resisted his penetration, and was agreeably surprised when he immediately withdrew. But he did

93

not raise his lips from hers and continued to explore their surface. Despite his height and muscularity, he was light upon her. It showed his gentleness as well as his practice. It was a sour thought, reminding her that today was only a passing experience for him. As it was for her too, she reminded herself, and hoped that if she said it often enough, she would believe it.

He rubbed his cheek upon hers. His skin smelled of sunshine, as did his hair, and she reached out and touched it. It was thick beneath her fingers. She gripped a strand and used it to try to pull him away from her, but it only served to make him chuckle deep in his throat and hold her more closely.

"You can't escape now, little kitten. So don't start hissing and scratching."

She opened her eyes wide and closed them instantly as she saw how near his hazel ones were.

"Open them again," he commanded, and when she refused, rubbed his tongue upon the top of her nose. "Look at me, Sweet Sue. Let me drown in those violet waters."

Her eyes flew open. "Don't be ridiculous!"

"Ridiculous because I find you beautiful? You are, you know. Even in close-up, you're flawless."

She longed to believe him and was angry because she almost did.

"Tell me more," she said in an effort to be flippant. "How about two lips, indifferent red; two violet eyes, with lids to them; one neck, one chin—"

"Two breasts with gentle curves," he continued in the same singsong tone. "One waist, two legs, with feet to them; two—"

"Enough," she laughed. "I can't win with you."

"If only you meant that." He ran his lips along the side of her neck to her ear, where he delicately nibbled the lobe. She half turned her head and he stopped. "Don't you like it?"

"No."

"I have other tricks."

"I'm sure you have."

94

"Do you want me to show you?"

"No. Save them for your next performance."

"That's great."

"What is?"

"That you've agreed to another performance."

"I didn't say it would be with me. You're a natural performer, Craig—with any female."

"But the act would be better with you."

"Try saying it once more with feeling," she mocked. "Or maybe you should change the line completely."

"As long as you don't tell me to change the girl." His voice was sharpened by something too faint to call anger, too crisp to call humor. "Your inexperience will urge me on to greater heights!"

Indignantly she twisted up to look at him. Seeing his glinting eyes, she knew he was again teasing her. With a chuckle he pulled her sideways and slid himself down beside her, slipping his arms around her waist.

"You're the sexiest-looking bird I've seen, but when it comes to lovemaking, the Vestal Virgins could give you lessons!"

Her face flamed. "Nobody asked you to kiss me. If I'm not up to your exacting standards—"

"But you are," he cut in. "You're beautiful and bright without being too brainy! That's every man's ideal. Now if you'd only stop behaving as if I'm the Rome Rapist, I might be able to get a response out of you."

"Oh!" she gasped in fury. "You're the most—"

"*You* are the most," he said huskily and covered her mouth with his.

This time he was not gentle. Passion rose high and he did not restrain it. It drew its own response, and where experience failed her, desire came to her aid. Though innocence made her fearful, her need for him gave her the courage to meet him halfway, and he was experienced enough to take her the rest of it.

"Suzy," he whispered, and lowered his hands to her hips.

She could not stop the convulsive movement that racked

her, nor the painful desire that surged through her body. But she could stop herself from repeating it, and knew that she must. Clenching her hands, she pushed them against him, at the same time twisting back deep into the hammock to separate them.

"Please, Craig. No. I don't want . . . I can't . . ."

Only the leaves moved; only the birds sang. Slowly Craig straightened his arms and raised himself away from her. His eyes stared into hers, so empty of expression that they might have been colored glass. Then he lifted himself off her and sauntered down to the stream. He reached the humpbacked bridge that spanned it and stood there.

Suzy sat up and smoothed her dress. Thank heaven her control had saved her. Now she must also save face; must not let him guess how closely she had come to surrender. Keep it light and cool, she warned herself, and rose to follow him across the grass.

"What time does your plane go?" she asked lightly. "You don't want to miss it."

"We must leave now." He stepped back from the bridge. He looked relaxed and friendly; passion gone, though not spent. "Will you come with me to the airport? It will save me having to go back to the hotel."

"What about your luggage?"

"Frank's bringing it to the plane with him. Come and see me off?"

She nodded and they returned across the sloping ground to the car.

The journey to the airport took an hour and neither of them talked much on the way. But it was an easy silence, interspersed with the exchange of occasional smiles. There was a softness in Craig's expression that perplexed her, but she was too concerned for her own feelings to concentrate on his. A New Zealand geyser was a pool of tranquility compared with her present emotions. It was a good thing he was leaving for the States today. If he weren't, she was not sure if she would have had the strength of mind to steer clear of him.

They reached the airport with only minutes to spare.

Craig's flight had already been called and his manager, a stocky, gray-haired man in his forties, was waiting impatiently by the International Departure gates.

"I wish you wouldn't always cut it so fine," he complained.

"Have I ever missed a flight?" Craig grinned.

"There's always a first time." Frank Gerrard gave Suzy a cursory smile that relegated her to the legion of girls whom Craig had squired and left. "Come on, Craig," he ordered, and strode forward.

Craig put a hand on Suzy's arm. "When are you returning to London?"

"The day after tomorrow."

"Will you be staying with Millie?"

"No. I have my own home."

"Is your number in the book? Good. I'll call you." He turned to follow Frank, then stopped and pulled her close.

Lights flashed and he jerked back, flinging an angry scowl at the photographer scuttling away.

"The penalty of fame," he muttered, and touched his hand to Suzy's cheek. "Don't forget me, Sweet Sue."

Then he was gone, striding into the marble hall and taking too much of her away with him.

VI

"So you just had a friendly lunch with Craig and then drove him to the airport?" was Millie's greeting the following morning when Suzy went into her suite. "If that's what you call friendly," she said, pointing to a newspaper on top of a pile of others, "I'd like to know what you call loving!"

Following Millie's pointing finger, Suzy picked up the tabloid and saw what the flashing bulbs at the airport yesterday had produced: an intimate-looking picture of Craig Dickson clasping a willowy blonde.

"I photograph rather well," she managed to say casually.

"Oh sure. And the way he's holding you photographed even better! Some clinch you two must have had. Looks like he's stuck on you in more ways than one! Come on, now, don't keep things from your Aunt Millie. Tell me what's going on between you two."

"Nothing. I told you last night."

"Last night I hadn't seen this picture."

"It still means nothing. We went out for a drive, had a snack in a restaurant and I then drove with him to the airport."

"And this loving embrace was his way of saying cheerio, Miss Bedford, it was charming to make your acquaintance?"

"That's *exactly* what it was meant to be."

Suzy spoke with a firmness that brooked no argument, and busied herself collecting all the paraphernalia that Millie had scattered around the room: photographs of friends and places; menu cards; books and magazines.

"I like making the place look untidy," Millie had once explained, seeing Suzy's astonishment when she had come in and found her dropping various oddments on the settee and tables. "It makes it look more of a home and less of a hotel."

With Don's return into Millie's life, she might soon have no need to resort to such tricks.

"Elaine won't like this photograph of you and Craig," Millie commented, retrieving the newspaper and looking at it again. "She regards him as her property."

"The number of girls who do that, would make up a battalion!"

"Not since Elaine came on the scene. She's practically commandeered him for the past six months."

"Then let's hope this picture puts her wise. Any girl who takes Craig seriously should have her head examined. He's a philanderer."

"Show me a handsome young bachelor who isn't, and I'll show you a man who's got problems!" Millie's expression was considerably less humorous than her remark, as she eyed Suzy. "What's the matter with you anyway? Don't you know we're living in the age of freedom! Men don't hide their love-life the way they used to do—even married men—so why do you judge Craig so harshly? He'll probably settle down one day and make a wonderful husband."

"To lots of different wives! Let's talk about Don. He's a much more rewarding subject." Suzy whacked the conversational ball straight at Millie. "Are you going to marry him?"

"I haven't decided."

"Does that mean he's going back to Australia?"

Millie hesitated. "This is off the record?"

99

"I promise."

Millie still hesitated.

"If you don't believe me," Suzy said, "I'll put it down to your bad experiences with 'my fellow journalists!'"

"Sorry." The tennis champion looked rueful. "But you know the old saying: twice bitten—forever shy! Anyway"— she tugged at her hair, a habit she did when unsure of something—"I told Don I wasn't going to be rushed into a decision. It's too important for me—and for him too—and I need more time. He thinks I'm crazy. Says I've had seven years to make up my mind, and that if I don't know it by now, I never will. But there's more to it than that. I've thought about him a lot since we broke up, but it was in a different kind of way. Almost as if it were a story in a book. And now that he's come back into my life and wants to make it real . . . Well, I just don't know."

"I'm glad you had the courage to admit it. Don's wrong if he expects you to go back to square one. You can't. You aren't the same girl any more."

"If I'm not the same girl I was, I should say yes to him!" Millie rejoined. "My problem is that I think I *am* the same. The same ambitious female who turned him down seven years ago."

It would have been simple for Suzy to tell Millie to turn him down again; in the mood the girl was in, she would listen to her, too. But life was not simple, especially for someone like Millie, and it could not be resolved by stock answers.

"Why not ask him to come to London with you? If he loved you enough to stay single all these years, he won't give you up so easily again. Don't be scared of him, Millie; it makes you aggressive."

"That wouldn't be anything unusual!"

"Then *be* unusual. Call him up now and tell him how you feel. If—"

"I told him last night."

"Tell him again. But *gently*. With tears in your voice, if you can find any."

Millie looked so astounded that Suzy laughed.

100

"When you're dealing with a man of iron, Millie dear, there's nothing better than tears for rusting it."

"What a sly puss you are." Millie was beginning to look less upset. "But I've never put on an act with him. We've always been honest with each other."

"What did it get you? seven years' solitary!"

"You're right." Millie marched over to the telephone and Suzy tactfully retired to her own room.

"It worked!" The excited words accompanied Millie's rush into the bedroom a few minutes later. "Don's agreed to stay over for a couple more weeks. I didn't manage to cry, but I did get a sort of sob in my voice." She grinned. "Maybe if I'd met up with you years ago, my whole life would have been different."

"I doubt it. People only accept advice if they happen to agree with it! When Don first asked you to marry him you were standing at the beginning of a long straight road. Today you're at the crossroads, and ready to be directed."

"Yes, ma'am, thank you very much for telling me!"

Suzy gave her a steady look. "I'm *not* telling you what to do, Millie. All I've done, is to help you get more time to make up your mind."

"I know. And thanks a million."

The rest of their stay in Rome was frenetic.

With Millie the winner of the Italian Open, they were besieged by the press wherever they went, and when they foolishly elected to dine outside the hotel on their last night in the city, Don almost had a punch-up with a particularly pushy young photographer who tried to follow them into their car.

"Haven't they heard of the invasion of privacy?" Suzy asked angrily.

"Oh, sure," Don said, slamming the door and sending the photographer flying. "And they invade it all the time!" He looked at Millie speculatively. "When we go back to the hotel, I think you'd better leave in the car ahead of us. That way Suzy and I won't get crushed to death!"

They all laughed, which relieved their annoyance and set the mood for the rest of the evening. When they did

101

finally return to the Hilton their driver took them to a staff entrance, where they managed to mingle with some laundry workers and reach their suite undetected.

Leaving Millie and Don on their own, which they had refused to let her do earlier, when she had suggested they dine by themselves, Suzy went to bed.

But not to sleep. Thoughts of Craig kept her awake long into the night as she relived the afternoon she had spent with him. Was he thinking of it, too, as he went about his business on the other side of the world, or was she already part of the passing parade! It was not a question, because she already knew the answer.

On this singularly unpleasant admission, she fell asleep.

At noon the next day they boarded a plane for London. To Suzy's dismay Elaine was traveling with them, and was unfortunately seated directly across the aisle from her, which made it difficult to avoid their speaking.

"You and Craig made a nice picture yesterday morning," Elaine said silkily. "He's a genius at getting himself publicity. A pretty blonde is always good for a headline."

"A blond male would have got him an even bigger one!" Suzy said, straight-faced.

Elaine ignored the comment. "When are your articles about Millie going to appear?"

"The first week of Wimbledon fortnight."

"Will you have finished them all by then? I suppose you'll be glad to get back to your paper? As you don't like tennis, all this must have been a real drag for you."

"I enjoyed it. It's fun seeing new places and being part of all the excitement." Mischief made her continue: "I've half a mind to give up journalism and travel around with Millie for a few months. She's asked me if I would."

The blue eyes hardened and Suzy knew that Elaine had misjudged her reasons. Which was only to be expected.

"But I won't," she went on, taking pity on the girl. Darn it, anyone who loved Craig Dickson was deserving of pity. "If I do give up my job, it will be because I want to write a novel."

"Can't you do both at the same time?"

102

"I haven't succeeded so far. I'm always using my work as an excuse. At least if I have nothing else to do, I won't be able to plead lack of time!"

"What do you want to write?"

"A big fat best-seller!"

Elaine smiled with the complacency of a big fat bank account, and turned to talk to Millie.

Left with her own thoughts, Suzy found them centering on the Texan girl. Elaine made no effort to hide her jealousy of Craig, hence her attempt to make it seem as if he had cold-bloodedly used Suzy to get himself a picture in the tabloids. Without question, this was untrue. Craig was such a natural for the press that he had no need to court them. He had flirted with her yesterday because he had found her attractive. There had been no other reason.

She studied Elaine openly. Even in the full glare of the afternoon sun she looked as pretty as she had done in the dimness of the Hilton nightclub. Yet she still did not satisfy Craig. It seemed that no girl, however lovely, could stop him from wandering.

Arriving in London, Suzy went straight home. She had a mass of notes to put together and told Millie she would not be seeing her for a few days.

"You know where to find me when you want me," Millie replied, "but don't make it too long. I like having you around."

Suzy knew she meant this, and found it sad that someone who had so much success should have so few genuine friends. But friendship took time to cultivate before it could be left for months at a time, and Millie's lifestyle made it impossible for her to put down any roots. That applied to Craig, too. Even if he married, it was unlikely that his wife would travel with him for long. Once children started to arrive, she would have to remain at home, which would spell death to the marriage. And if they did not want children, then he probably wouldn't see the need for marriage either.

Angry that she should still be thinking of a man she had vowed to forget, she flung herself into a bout of house-

103

cleaning, and did not come to rest until much later that evening, when she collapsed, exhausted, into an armchair. How blessed this solitude was after being part of a glamorous entourage. Only now, in this peace and quiet, did she realize what a strain it was to be constantly in the limelight—even though the light had been a reflected one. So would any girl feel who was in Craig's life, she admitted on an indrawn sigh. It would be like living in a fish bowl. With more fish waiting behind the seaweed, she added grimly, to remind herself yet again, how lucky she was to be heart-whole.

Later, fresh from a bath, she sat at her desk and sorted through the notes she had made. They fell into place easily and within an hour she had put them all in order and inserted them in a large file marked "Millie Queen."

Then she went to make herself something to eat.

She was curled up on the settee, drinking an after-dinner cup of coffee and thinking longingly of going to bed, when the telephone rang. She lifted the receiver, almost dropping it as Craig's voice sounded in her ear.

"I—th-thought you were in America!" she stammered, and could have kicked herself for her naïveté. America wasn't the moon, and even if it had been, he could still have called her from it. "Did you have a good flight?" she asked quickly.

"An excellent flight and the weather is fine." There was humor in his tone. "How's my favorite girl?"

"One of your favorite girls is fine."

"I can see her tongue is! Tell me what you're doing."

"Drinking coffee and thinking of going to bed."

"I wish I could share it with you. What are you wearing?"

She made a face at the telephone. He really was lamentably predictable.

"A dressing gown," she cooed. "All pink and filmy and I know you'd like to be here with me, so that you could take it off."

The silence lasted for all of thirty seconds.

"I hope you know when *not* to be funny?" he said finally. "Humor at the wrong time can be a real passion killer."

"Thanks for letting me know. I'll make a note of it."

"I'd better make a few notes myself. I can see that if I don't change my dialogue, I'll bore you to death!"

She laughed and he joined in before speaking again.

"Have you missed me, Sweet Sue?"

"I've been too busy."

"I've missed *you*. I enjoyed our afternoon together. I got on the plane feeling more relaxed than I've been for a long while."

"Which is more than I can say for your girl friend," Suzy replied, warning herself as much as Craig.

"Which one?" he asked with an aplomb that annoyed her.

"The one with dark hair and blue eyes. She saw a picture of you kissing me good-bye and she didn't like it."

"I'm always being kissed by my fans," he said solemnly. "It doesn't mean a thing." There was a slight pause and his voice changed. "I'm sorry about the picture, Suzy. I wouldn't have kissed you if I'd seen that damned photographer."

"It didn't matter to *me*. I'll have something to show my grandchildren!"

He did not reply and she racked her brains for something else to say. But everything that came to mind seemed trite. When they were together, his magnetism made speech unnecessary, but separated by thousands of miles they had nothing with which to bridge their ignorance of each other.

"There's so much I want to know about you, Suzy." Uncannily he echoed her thoughts. "When I'm with you I seem to know everything, but with the Atlantic between us, I find I know nothing."

"That's the way I feel," she admitted.

"Tell me about yourself."

"Now?"

"Why not?"

"This call must be costing you a fortune!"

"I've got a fortune. Come on, Sweet Sue, tell me. Are there any more like you at home?"

"Two brothers—both in their teens—and both, you'll be pleased to know, real tennis buffs."

"What do your parents do?"

"Father is headmaster of a boys' school and my mother keeps house and is a part-time music teacher."

"Didn't you ever want to teach?"

"Never. As soon as I left school I went to secretarial college and then got a job on our local paper."

"How come you didn't go to college?"

"I'm not sure. I felt I'd led such a cloistered life that I couldn't face the same regimen for another three years."

"It wouldn't have been the same," he said whimsically. "Not if I know Oxbridge guys. Tell me how you got your present job."

"I was—" She stopped. "Do you really want to know all this? It's so unexciting."

"I'm finding it very exciting," he said. "If you could see me now, you'd know what I mean!"

The receiver wobbled in her hand and she was glad her voice didn't. "I think it's your turn to talk now."

"My life's an open book—or perhaps I should say newspaper! Look me up in your reference library and you'll find everything there."

"I'll do it tomorrow, since you're so reluctant to tell me."

"My life only began in Rome. Everything that went before is unimportant."

There was a sound in the distance, and she heard him give a muffled exclamation.

"I've got to go," he said hurriedly. "I'm due on court in five minutes. I'll call you the same time tomorrow."

"I may not be in."

"I'll keep trying until you are."

Long after their conversation had ended she found it impossible to relax. All she could think of was Craig. Repeatedly she told herself his call meant nothing, but it did not dim the pleasure that lingered inside her like a reverberating bell.

It's all part of the buildup, she warned herself. Once he thinks you've fallen for him, he'll go on to the next conquest.

True to his word, Craig telephoned her the following night and every night for the rest of the week. He stayed on the line for an hour or more each time, talking about everything under the sun with the exception of tennis. It was almost as if he were trying to show her that the sport she disliked so much, played no part whatever in his life.

Yet tennis had made him a world-renowned figure and she dare not forget it. To do so would be as foolish as trying to pretend that music was unimportant to a pop star.

Because she knew she was enjoying his telephone calls too much, she went to her parents' home for the weekend without telling him, then spent Friday and Saturday evening in an agony of frustration as she thought of the pealing bell in her living room.

Returning home at ten o'clock on Sunday night, she heard the bell ringing as she unlocked her front door, and rushed to answer it with a speed that was more an admission of her feelings than any of her thoughts had been.

"Did he give you a good weekend?" Craig's voice greeted her.

For an instant she was at a loss. Then she recovered.

"Extremely. We made violent love the whole time."

"Good. I'm glad you're getting in some experience!"

"I thought you would be. Especially as I'm only doing it for you!"

He laughed. "It's a good thing I'm not the jealous type."

"I thought you might be."

"No way. It's a two-edged sword and I don't want it stuck in *my* gullet. Live and let live is my motto."

Sourly she regarded the receiver. If it were his neck, she would have wrung it. Of course he wanted his girls to be fun-loving and carefree; that way there were no strings attached.

"What have you been doing with *yourself* this evening?" she asked casually.

"My evening hasn't begun yet. California time is eight hours behind yours."

"I'd forgotten. So tell me what you plan to do."

"Have an early night." He paused. "I've got a big match tomorrow."

"Will it be a hard one?"

"Do you care?"

She was surprised to find that she did. She wanted Craig to win. Those bronze and virile looks of his went so well with success, that she could not bear to think of him without it.

"I'll win," he went on confidently, as if he did not notice she had not answered him. "I'm playing well and I've already beaten Pedro twice this year. Once in South Africa and once in Mexico."

The reference to Mexico launched him into a dissection of South American policies. From this it was a short step to the problems of the Third World, and an even shorter step to philosophy, in which he had majored at college. He had such a wide range of interests and such a deep knowledge of many of them, that she found it increasingly amazing that he was so single-minded about tennis. When she had first met him she had likened him to a racehorse in blinkers. Now she was having to revise her opinion. A racehorse he might be, but in blinkers he certainly wasn't.

"Do you know you've been talking to me for an hour and a half?" she interrupted him in mid-conversation.

"If you can tell me what else we can do," he said plaintively, "I'd be happy to oblige."

"I'm sure you don't need me to tell you."

"I need you to do it with!"

Her heart thumped and then steadied. But it was enough to warn her how responsive she was to him. And he wasn't even hers!"

"Suzy? Are you still there?"

"Yes. But propping my lids open with matchsticks," she lied. "I'm a working girl, Craig. I have to get some sleep."

"I'll call you tomorrow."

"What on earth will we have to talk about!"

"Me. That's an endless source of conversation!"

She was smiling as she put down the telephone. A few days earlier she might have believed that remark of his; now she didn't. It showed her how far their relationship had progressed. If only she knew how much farther it had to go before they reached the end. That it would be a dead end, she had no doubt. Craig's ideas of their future would not be hers.

Believing this, it was foolish for her to go on accepting his calls.

The knowledge was so painful that she sat on the side of her bed and forced herself to face the truth.

She was in love with Craig.

It was not a lighthearted infatuation—she had had too many of those not to recognize them—but something far more serious. It had begun lightheartedly enough—that was the trouble—for it had put her off her guard. Had made her feel she was in control of the situation when, in reality, she was as defenseless as a three-footed doe against a four-footed hunter.

But did his chase and capture of her have to end the same way as all the others? Wouldn't it depend on the way their friendship developed? Remembering the seriousness of many of his conversations, she could not believe they did not depict the real man, and that the glittering image he projected to his fans was only a façade.

Had the other girls in his life thought the same way, and been proved wrong? This, too, was a thought that had to be faced. Elaine was no fool, and the daughter of a millionaire to boot, yet she had not succeeded in holding him.

So why should I think it will end any differently for me? Suzy wondered, and was filled with self-disgust. But not because she saw herself joining the Craig worshipers who had gone before her, but because she foolishly believed she wouldn't. Of such idiocy were dreams fashioned.

In the morning Suzy gave her editor the second and third installments of Millie's biography. He glanced through it briefly, chuckling as he spotted a turn of phrase he enjoyed.

"This would make a good book," he commented, leaning back in his chair to face her. "How would you feel if we brought it out as one?"

"And not put it in the newspaper?"

"We'd do both."

"I don't see it as a book. It isn't written that way."

"There's nothing wrong with the way it's written. You should think in book terms, Suzy. Hard-hitting biographies of some of the big names that are around. Not necessarily tennis stars, but anyone who has achieved fame and is known to the public."

"I've been thinking along those lines myself," she confessed. "Even to the extent of giving up my job and writing properly."

"Writing properly?" he grunted. "That's the trouble with you literary lot. Look down your noses at good, intelligent reporting and happy to settle for third-rate fiction!"

"That's—"

"A libelous thing to say? I know but I won't take it back! There's *some* truth in it, Suzy, and don't you forget it. Or my suggestion either."

Promising to give it some thought, she went to see Millie at the Savoy. Since she had not yet found a suitable plot for her magnum opus, Bill's suggestion was not a bad one. It would at least set her writing in a more literary style instead of the crisp journalese which she had found herself all too frequently adopting. She thought of all the people she knew who had marvelous ideas but no ability to write, and wondered whether this was better than having an ability to write but no ideas.

As soon as she saw Millie's face, Suzy forgot about her own problems. "When's the wedding?" she asked.

"Who told you? Larry swore he wouldn't—"

"He didn't." Suzy grinned. "Your face gave you away. You look as happy as a sandboy."

"I am." Millie held out her hand to show a sapphire surrounded by diamonds. "Isn't it wonderful?"

"The ring is. But I thought you weren't so sure about Don?"

"I was sure how I felt about *him*. It was tennis I couldn't make up my mind about."

"So you're going to give it all up and become a sheep farmer's wife?"

"A sheep farmer's tennis wife," she corrected. "Don's

110

going to turn part of his land into a tennis ranch. He says he knows I'll never be completely happy away from the game, and this way I can combine tennis and marriage. I'll coach all the really good players who come to stay and we'll organize our own competitions too."

"So the ultimatum he gave you in Rome wasn't quite so ultimate!"

Millie laughed and Suzy hugged her. She was convinced Millie had made the best possible decision. No career, however successful, could give a woman total happiness. But if one could combine it with the right man, then it would bring total fulfillment.

"I wish *you* could meet someone," Millie said.

Suzy chuckled. "Why is it that the minute a girl gets a husband of her own, she starts matchmaking for her friends!"

"Maybe it's because she sees other bachelors as a threat!" Millie eyed the ring on her hand. "I'm going to rustle up all Don's friends for you."

"What about your own friends?"

"They're all tennis players, and I know what you think of them!"

"As a matter of fact, Craig has—"

"Craig!" Millie said triumphantly. "I knew I had something to tell you. That good-bye kiss he gave you at Rome Airport must have given Elaine the wind up."

"Why?"

"Because she scratched all her matches and flew out to California the day before yesterday to be with him."

Suzy's newfound happiness—if happiness was the word to describe the varying emotions she had just begun to experience—disintegrated completely. What a fool she had been to read anything serious into Craig's nightly telephone calls. He needed female adoration the way a bee needed nectar. Except that nectar was part of a bee's life cycle, whereas adoration was but a massage to Craig's ego. And what a masseuse she had turned out to be! Her anger was directed inward and she stood there silently, allowing it to flagellate her.

111

"Why have you gone so quiet?" Millie asked. "You haven't fallen for Craig, have you?"

With an effort Suzy smiled. "Do I look so daft? I was trying to put myself into Elaine's mind and wondering what she hoped to achieve by running after him. Even if he marries her, she'll never be sure of him."

"He's going to be serious over a girl one day."

"I doubt it. I can't see him being faithful to any woman. He's too immature and conceited."

"You certainly aren't a fan of his," Millie said dryly. "If you—" She stopped as Don let himself into the suite and dumped a bouquet of flowers on her lap.

His arrival was opportune, for with Millie's attention given to him, Suzy was able to relax. Watching the Australian's unremarkable features, she saw only the abiding fidelity that had kept him in love with the same girl for seven years. One need have no fear in loving a man like Don. Bitterly she remembered her conversation with Craig last night. He had told her he was going to bed early and she had believed him. What he had omitted to say was that it would be with Elaine! Images too painful to picture wavered in front of her and she closed her eyes. But the images seemed painted on her lids and she opened her eyes again and forced her attention back to Millie and Don.

They were going to be married in December—summertime in Australia—which would enable Millie to finish her contractual appearances before she announced her retirement.

"Won't your parents expect you to be married in the States?" Suzy asked, and Millie's look of surprise gave away more of her attitude to her parents than a thousand words could have done.

"Don has a huge family who'd like to be at the wedding," she explained, "and I only have Mom and Dad. It'll be far easier for them to come to Sydney. I hope you'll be able to make it, too? I'd like you to be my bridesmaid."

Suzy was touched. "But we hardly know each other."

"The length of a friendship is no indication of its depth. Now try and cap that for instant psychology!"

Suzy could not laugh. Millie's words seemed to mirror her own feelings for Craig and, had Don not been there, she knew she would have blurted them out. Instead she concentrated on the idea of going to Australia, and decided that the sooner she said good-bye to the tennis scene, the quicker she would one of its leading stars.

"I'd love to be your bridesmaid, Millie, but I couldn't spare the time or the cash to be with you."

"I'll be getting you the ticket, you dope!"

"It's very generous of you to offer, but I'd never accept it." She went to the door. "I'll leave you two lovebirds alone."

"I thought you were staying with us for the rest of the day?"

"When you've just become engaged?"

"Re-engaged," Don put in. "But we appreciate your tact, and we'll take advantage of it." He put his arm around Millie's waist. "Won't we, sweetheart?"

"If you say so."

He grinned at Suzy. "See how docile she is? But I can promise you it won't last!"

"As long as you realize it!" Suzy grinned back, and closed the door behind her.

Unwilling to be alone with her thoughts, she went to her office. Her desk looked forlorn without its usual welter of papers and publicity handouts, and she wandered into the main office, which was an open plan, to talk to some of the other reporters. Most of the ones she knew were working on outside assignments, and after refusing a couple of male offers to share a drinking lunch, she returned home.

Resolutely she pulled the cover off her typewriter and set to work on the next installment of Millie's story. The adrenaline that anger had sent coursing through her blood gave her both impetus and energy and the words fairly rattled off the keys.

By six o'clock both the fourth and fifth installments were written. But the jealousy Elaine had aroused was still raging inside her and had to be released in the only way she knew how: with work.

As a child she had always scribbled away her emotion—be it joy or misery—and now she did the same. But she had nothing more to say about Millie, so she wrote about herself and Craig. It was too painful to do it in the first person—that was too much like drilling on one's own tooth—so she transcribed it into the third. In this way she managed to abstract it; to see her feelings for Craig with detachment.

Regardless of time she pounded away, and it was only the throbbing in her temples that made her drop her hands in her lap and cease work. With surprise she saw it was ten o'clock. Incredible though it was she had been sitting here, pouring out her heart for five hours. What a waste of effort! Tiredly she gathered up the typewritten sheets to dump them into the wastepaper basket. At least they had served their purpose and drained away her anger. As she started to crumple the pages she was impelled by curiosity to see what she had written—the white heat of fury that had been her inspiration had also burned out the memory of what she had put down—she began to read.

For the first few lines she felt as if she were peering into her own soul, but as the power of the words took over, her sense of involvement disappeared. She was reading about someone else; someone who moved her deeply; whose hopes she shared, whose fears she shivered with. How ingenuous this girl was; in love with a monster but unable to stop herself. Carlton Barrett was a larger-than-life version of what she knew Craig to be. He was a parody of all literature's Casanovas, a man beside whom Don Juan appeared a celibate.

Enthalled yet disbelieving, Suzy read on to the end. Was it possible that Carlton and Jill and Tommy and Ruth were her own creation? They were too alive to be imaginary characters; yet they were. Fashioned from her own fantasies, they bloomed upon the page. How clear their lives were to her. She knew everything about them. Their hopes, their fears, their motives, what they wanted and what they would get. Ah yes, that was the nicest part of it all. She knew what they would get. Carlton Barrett's future strung

114

itself out in front of her and her fingers itched to get to the typewriter.

But she resisted it. What she had to say could not be written in a matter of hours or days. It would take weeks, maybe months. Today's work had been a happy accident; the first outpouring from a disillusioned heart. Tomorrow, work had to come from the brain, and that would make the creation more difficult.

She clipped the pages together and put them in the drawer of her desk. At last, when she had almost despaired of it happening, she had the story that she wanted to write; had possibly known it subconsciously from the moment she had met Craig. If only he had not had to shatter her illusions before she could wake up and see them for the dream they were; the nightmare they could have become.

But now the disillusionment was for her heroine Jill, and she herself was, in some magic way, free of it.

The peal of the telephone bell made her reach for it. It was Craig, as she had known it would be, and her hand trembled.

"I'm glad you're in," he said, before she could do more than say hello. "I had to make the call early because I'm leaving for New York in ten minutes."

Alone? The word was so loud in her head that she was astonished he could not hear it.

"Rather sudden, isn't it?" was what she said.

"Jack Reikel, my opponent, scratched from this afternoon's game, and Frank managed to get me on the Manderson show."

"A chat show?"

"Why not? I can talk as well as play tennis! Surely you know that by now?"

She certainly did. He could talk the wings off an angel; a bird from a tree; a heart from a girl.

"Have a good flight," she burbled cheerily.

"Is that all you can say?"

"And safe landing." But men like Craig always did. "I've a stack of work to do, Craig. I can't think clearly."

"Okay, Sweet Sue. I'll call you tomorrow, when we'll

115

both have more time." His voice deepened. "I miss you, Suzy."

"You don't know me enough to miss me."

"That's what I miss. We'll have to put it right when we meet."

She counted to ten. How could he say such things when he was with Elaine, who had flown six thousand miles to be with him?

"I don't believe you're pining for me," she mocked. "I'm sure you've been surrounded by girls since you got to the States."

"Hordes of them," he agreed, "but no one I want."

"Poor Craig."

Against her better judgment she could not keep the edge from her voice and he heard it.

"You sound angry, Sue."

"Angry and jealous." She was still cooing, though the sugar was turning to acid. "I just found out that Elaine is with you, and I'm gnashing my teeth into powder."

He chuckled. "I wish I could believe you meant that."

Ruefully she realized the difference between the male and female mind. Testosterone did more than increase aggression and abstract thinking; it obviously diminished perception and subtlety. Suddenly it was impossible for her to continue with this pretense.

"I must go, Craig. I've a deadline to meet."

"Okay. But keep the end of next week free for me."

"I may be away on an assignment."

"Then I'll come and join you."

"You'd hate Manchester on a rainy weekend!"

"Not if I'm singing in the rain with you!" His voice thinned as if he had turned away from the receiver, then it came back strong. "Frank's getting impatient. I must go. Think of me."

It was an unnecessary admonition. Long after the call was over, she could do nothing else. For hours he remained in front of her, and at four A.M. she retreated to the kitchen. There was nothing like hot milk for putting tormenting thoughts to rest.

116

Craig was determined to make her his girl friend and would continue to pursue her until he had made her change her mind. Or another woman changed his.

It would not be Elaine, though. She had obviously lost her lure for him. It seemed that conquests always did. Which is the best reason I know for never becoming one, Suzy thought savagely, banging her cup on the Formica part of the sink. Yet how close she had come to it. She looked upward and thanked Someone for small mercies.

VII

Suzy thought long and hard how to tell Craig she did not want to see him. No matter what way she phrased it in her mind, it always came out sounding as if she were jealous of Elaine. So far she had managed to make him believe she was not, and since this was the impression she wished to retain, she finally decided it would be better to see him once—possibly even twice if need be—before making him believe she had met someone else whom she preferred.

But did such a man exist? The possibility seemed so unlikely that it bitterly confirmed her love for Craig. With hindsight she blamed their nightly telephone calls. They had given her a deeper insight into his character and had made her believe that the man he appeared to be during their long and absorbing conversations, was the man he really was. Instead of which it was yet another façade. One face among the many.

For Craig, the physical would always be of supreme importance. He was the hunter personified. The man who never tired of the chase—only of the catch.

His opening sentence when he called the following night exemplified this.

118

"You're a real gadabout, Suzy. I've had this call in for two hours. Why don't you stay home and pine for me?"

"I planned on doing so," she quipped, "but something else came up."

"What's his name?"

"Tommy," she lied, wondering what he would say if she told him she had been working on her novel and had forced herself not to answer the telephone each time it had rung.

"Soon there'll be no more dates with anyone except me," he said.

"How many more days of freedom do I have?"

"Four. I'm playing a match in Holland on Saturday and flying to London on Sunday. You wouldn't like to join me in Rotterdam, I suppose?"

"You suppose right," she replied, wishing she could accept Craig as he was and have fun with him for however long it lasted.

"Pity," he murmured. "I had a feeling you weren't that sort of girl."

"It doesn't stop you from trying to change me."

"Naturally not. You know I can't resist a challenge."

"Is that all I am to you?" She heard the longing in her voice and spoke again quickly, before he had a chance to analyze it. "It's about time someone resisted you, Mr. Dickson. You've had your way with us females for far too long."

"Right now I'm only interested in one way with one female. I'll catch the first flight out of Rotterdam on Sunday," he continued. "I should be with you around eleven."

"That's awfully early."

"We've been invited to spend the day in the country with some friends of mine. Bring your costume and a racket."

"I hate playing tennis."

"I know," he said sympathetically. "Sometimes I feel the same."

After the call was over she sat woodenly in front of her typewriter, unable to write. Excitement at the prospect of seeing Craig dulled the thoughts that tumbled from her imagination. Reality had so much more to offer! But for so

119

short a time. She wondered how Elaine could bear his philandering. Perhaps if one were the pampered daughter of a tycoon, one believed that sooner or later money could buy everything.

On Saturday evening she had dinner with her editor and his wife. He had enjoyed her biography of Millie so much that he had taken it home for his wife to read before publication. Anne Walters was a literary agent and her interest had been sufficiently aroused for her to call Suzy and invite her around.

"You made the whole tennis scene so alive for me," was her comment as they relaxed in the garden with a pre-dinner drink. "Have you ever considered writing a novel?"

"Many times," Suzy confessed. "And now I've actually got down to doing it."

"I hope you will let me see it when it's finished?"

"You'll probably be the only person willing to read it!"

"How much of it have you done?"

"About a fifth."

"You've kept it pretty dark," Bill Walters said. "How long have you been working on it?"

"A week."

"And you've done a fifth! You're a damn quick writer then. Is it one of these arty-farty type books—all brain and no bed?"

"Dear Bill," his wife remonstrated kindly. "Can't you at least *pretend* that you're the editor of *The Times?*"

He grinned, unabashed. "What's wrong with plain speaking? If Suzy wants to be a success she's got to know the ingredients that make for it. And a book without sex is like—" He saw his wife's eyes flash and finished good-humoredly: "Like soup without salt!"

"This particular soup has got lots of salt," Suzy smiled, answering his question. "But it isn't sprinkled in freely. It's a necessary part of the seasoning."

"I've heard that one before!"

"What's it about?" Anne Walters asked. "Or are you the sort of author who likes to keep the plot a secret until the book is completed?"

120

"I'm not any sort of author yet, so I haven't decided what kind to be! But I don't think I'm too superstitious to tell you about the plot. It's concerned with the sports world and the way success is built up by the media, and blows people into such an enlargement of themselves that they lose all sense of proportion."

"Are you taking the lid off Fleet Street?" Bill Walters asked. "Because if you are, I'll fire you!"

"I'm trying to show what pressures sports people have to live with."

"You mean you're using Millie Queen to—"

"It isn't about a woman," Suzy interrupted. "The main character is a man."

"I bet you're going to make him a real bastard."

"Why do you say that?"

"Women novelists never write about a man otherwise!"

"I hate that expression—women novelists. It's so . . ."

"All right, I apologize. But any novelists who aren't male, always make their heroes into saints or sinners. They can never accept that we're both!"

"*I* accept that you're both, darling," his wife said, and grinned at her guest. "I hope you will let me see your book when it's finished. If you don't have an agent, perhaps you would consider . . ."

"You may not want to act for me once you've read the manuscript."

"Then I'll tell you so."

"Good."

"But I'm sure there won't be any need. You're a born writer. I said as much to Bill when I read those articles of yours."

"You've given me the impetus to carry on," Suzy said gratefully.

"I should think so too! Never stop anything halfway through. Always finish what you start."

It seemed like a prophetic remark, in view of her decision to end her association with Craig. Association. What an odd word that was. Yet no other applied. She certainly didn't have a relationship with him.

121

On Sunday morning Suzy was up with the dawn. The day was set fair, as it generally was before Wimbledon began. Craig had said they would be spending the day in the country and she dressed accordingly, in pale green cotton that complemented the faint tan she had acquired in Rome. Checking herself in the mirror, she wondered if she was as Craig remembered her.

Her mind went back to the gently rocking hammock in the Italian garden, and she wished she had not allowed him to hold her and kiss her the way he had done. No doubt when he had thought of her during these past few weeks, his imagination had taken him several steps further.

It was with this uncomfortable thought in mind that she opened the door to him shortly after eleven. They stared at one another in silence, then she stepped back, faintly flustered without knowing why.

"You're different from the way I remembered you," he said softly.

"In what way?"

"Less pretty and more beautiful."

This was better. Compliments she could deal with.

"*You* are exactly the way I remember," she countered. "The Greatest Playboy in the Western World."

"Back on form again, I see. I'll have to change Sweet Sue to Sour!"

She laughed and he reached out and pulled her close. She stiffened and momentarily he hesitated.

"Shy?" he asked, and before she could answer, blotted out the room with his head.

His lips were firm but grew more persuasive as he felt her tenseness. His arms came more closely around her body to press it to his. She tried to remain aloof but it was impossible, and her lips softened and parted. He made no attempt to take advantage of her surrender but went on holding her close, so that she could hear the firm, slow beat of his heart. The heart of an athlete, she knew, that could stand up to pressure without increasing in tempo. It made him seem alien and increased her sense of vulnerability. She shivered, knowing how much he could hurt her.

122

"Darling," he said, feeling the movement. "You don't know how much I've wanted to hold you like this."

How well she did know it, but never would she tell him.

Trying to be casual, she wriggled free of him and stepped back to look into his face. If only she could find something to fault. But it was impossible.

He was better-looking than ever. The California sun had deepened the bronze of his skin and lightened his hair, particularly the front strand that always fell across his forehead when he played on court. He wore bottle green slacks, belted low on his hips, and a gray silk shirt with short sleeves that showed his muscular arms.

He wore no vest and her attention was caught by the soft tangle of hair on his chest. She longed to put her lips to it and she turned away quickly, aware of his eyes, more gray than hazel this morning, watching her.

"I'm all set to go," she said, moving into the sitting room to collect her bag.

"So am I, Sweet Sue, though I doubt if we mean the same thing!"

There was amusement in his voice and she knew he saw her haste to leave as fear of being alone with him.

"You're not going to escape me so easily," he said with a shake of his head and, taking her bag from her unresisting hands, dropped it on the chair and pulled her back into his arms.

This time he did not attempt to hide his desire, and his kiss was a deep one that awakened her own need of him; as he had known it would.

"Did I say you couldn't kiss?" he whispered. "I must have been crazy!" His breath was like a caress on her skin, his mouth so close to hers that his words formed a movement on them. "I guess wanting someone is the best teacher of all. You do want me, Suzy, don't you? The way I want you?"

Suzy knew that if she said yes it would take her along a path that could lead to total surrender. And she dare not let that happen; not if she valued her pride and self-preservation. Yet it was equally impossible to deny what she

123

felt, and she resorted to exaggeration, as she had done with him once before.

"Of course I want you," she whispered. "Does grass need the sun; does bread need butter; does—"

"Try saying does Suzy need Craig."

"The way Romeo needed Juliet and Dante needed Beatrice?"

"Our ending will be better."

"Will it?" she asked, and wished with all her heart that she could believe him. But then if things went as he planned, they would be all right. All right for Craig.

"I think my literary choice will be better than yours," he countered. "How about Portia and Antonio or Petruchio and Kate?"

"I definitely feel a Kate."

"I've felt it, too," he said, "and I've got the lacerations to prove it!"

"In a few more days they'll heal and disappear."

"But you won't." He nuzzled her ear, sending tingles down her spine. "You're going to spend tomorrow and tomorrow and tomorrow with me."

"Signifying nothing," she retorted.

"Is that so?"

"Don't you know your Shakespeare?" she questioned.

"I wish I knew *you* as well!"

She reached for her handbag again. "You told me to be ready by eleven."

"I didn't say ready for what."

"Yes you did. A day in the country with tennis and swimming."

He eyed her straw bag. "I can't see your racket."

"I can't play."

"Even when you try?"

She knew he still thought she was pretending to be a duffer at sports, and with a shrug she walked ahead of him to the door.

He had a car parked by the curb: a silver-gray Porsche, docile as a miniature Doberman. And docile it remained as he drove leisurely through the suburban streets and equally leisurely along the highway.

"I'm the steady type," he said dryly, intercepting her surprised glance at the speedometer. "I spend so much of my life dashing from one place to another, that it makes a change for me to set my own pace."

"It's probably the best way for you to relax."

"I have other ways, too."

They were set sail on his favorite subject, and all she could do was to try to change tack.

"Have you always been so single-minded, Craig?"

"You have to be, if you want to be a success. And that doesn't only apply to tennis. It's the same in every profession; whatever you do."

"Some people find success isn't enough. They start missing other things: the loss of friends, of privacy."

"Then they won't remain at the top for long," he stated.

She was quiet for a couple of miles before speaking again.

"Is being at the top as important to you now as it was at the beginning of your career? What I mean is, has the getting there—the loss of friends and privacy—been worthwhile?"

"I'm still a tennis pro," he said, as if that answered the question. And of course it did. More than answered it. Said a whole world more, in fact.

"You're still seeing it from a woman's point of view," he went on. "Being the creatures they are, they want the best of both worlds. I think they always will. The liberated woman can never come to terms with the mother in herself. It's biologically impossible."

"Naturally men are different," she said, not wanting him to feel he had sole command of triteness.

"Naturally." He refused to see, or would not recognize, her sarcasm. "They find it easy to compartmentalize their lives. Awful word, but it's the only one that will do. And equally important, they can also enjoy things even when they know they aren't going to last. Women can't do that. They have to believe that everything will go on forever."

125

Tomorrow and tomorrow and tomorrow, Suzy thought in silence, and wondered if Craig knew he was building the coffin in which to bury their relationship.

"If you take men and women in the same profession," he went on, "you'll always find that the men have a higher proportion of successful marriages behind them."

"Behind, being the operative word," Suzy countered. "Too many women are still satisfied to let their horizons be bounded by their homes."

"You're misunderstanding me," he said. "I don't want to start an argument about the role of women in society; we can do that another time, when we've a few weeks to spare. All I'm saying now is that a man with a demanding career is more able to sustain a happy marriage than a woman in the same position."

"Because women don't compartmentalize?" she asked sarcastically.

"Exactly! Men can love and leave and then return to love again. But women always have to be in possession. I'm not knocking your sex, Suzy, merely stating the case the way I see it."

"And you see it so clearly."

"It's a problem I've studied." He half glanced her way, then gave his attention to the road again.

"If successful women have a high rate of failure in their marriages," Suzy said, "and I'm not saying they do, merely *if*, then surely it can be blamed on their husbands? Men don't mind having working wives, but only so long as it doesn't prevent them from having a housekeeper and a constantly available bedmate!"

"A successful woman should have enough sense not to marry that sort of man."

"Honestly, Craig, you can't believe the rubbish you're talking? Don't you know how easy it is for people to pretend to be what they think their partner wants? Haven't you found the same with your girl friends?"

"That's why I'm not married! Well," he said softly, "haven't you any comment to make?"

"Like what?"

126

"Like the terrible or wonderful life a girl would have if she married someone like me?"

"It would probably be a mixture of both," she said in an expressionless voice. "Fun when you were together and loneliness when you were apart."

"Some wives follow their husbands around all the time. But it doesn't work for long. They find they can't take the constant travel and living in hotels and out of suitcases."

She made her voice suitably tender. "You mean it's compassion for our fair sex that's kept you single?"

"Only partly," he grinned. "Why cherish a pot plant when you can cultivate a whole garden!"

"There's no answer to that."

"I felt sure you'd find one!"

"Five years ago I might have tried. But not now. Today I've learned it's impossible to convince a happy young bachelor that he won't be a happy old one!"

"How old is old?"

She let the question go unanswered and a few more miles wheeled past.

"What about *your* future, Sweet Sue? Sometimes you give the impression of being a hard-boiled journalist—in love with her career—and other times I get the feeling you want to bind a man to you with your long golden tresses.

"I rather see it as a mutual binding," she replied. "But then my idea of marriage is different from yours. In your case, you're wise to steer clear of commitment." She spoke in her most conversational tone, as if she were talking without personal involvement. "You're rather like a racing driver. You are always the center of attraction, surrounded by hordes of pretty girls and never staying anywhere long enough to put down roots. You obviously enjoy that kind of life—if you didn't, you wouldn't do it—and trying to make a marriage work in those circumstances would be impossible."

"If you say so, Suzy dear."

"But that's your lifestyle. I'm not making it up."

"Too true." He increased speed. "I've enjoyed every minute of my career to date. Playing at the top has never

127

been an effort for me. The bigger the challenge, the better I respond to it."

"The tennis robot," she exclaimed.

"I deserve that title. I refuse to let anything bother me or worry me when I'm on court. In this game, you can all too easily be your own worst enemy."

"You won't be able to stay at the top indefinitely."

"I intend to retire long before I go over the hill."

She held her breath, hoping he would say more about his plans for the future. But he remained silent, and she wondered if it was because he had no plans or did not wish to discuss them with her. It was hard to believe he had played a grueling two weeks of commercial, highly competitive tennis. He looked as fit and relaxed as if he had stepped off a cruise ship. The Golden Boy of Tennis. How well the name suited him.

"Have you thought what you'll do when you give up competitive tennis?" she asked, risking the question by making it sound businesslike.

"Financially I won't need to do anything."

"I can't see you in a rocking chair!"

"Nor will you. I'll go into business."

"You mean a tennis ranch or organizing other players?"

"God forbid! Once I quit, I quit the entire scene."

It was on the tip of her tongue to ask if Elaine's father had offered him a job, but not only would this expose her feelings, it would shine a searchlight on them.

"I'm in business already with my brother," he added. "He has a boat-building yard down the coast from San Diego. It doesn't bring him in a fortune, but it's a wonderful life."

Suzy tried, and failed to see Craig sharing in it. But when she said so, he only smiled, as if the subject, or her opinion of it, was not worth discussing.

By now they had turned off the highway and onto a secondary road which led them through winding country lanes. Sweet-smelling hedgerows grew high on either side of them, broken occasionally by wooden farm gates that afforded them a view of bright green and gold fields, with

128

the occasional shimmer of water in the distance.

A fifteen-minute drive brought them to a Queen Anne house in a sylvan setting. The Old World charm of the atmosphere was in contrast with the owners, a sophisticated couple in their early forties. But here again there was a discrepancy, for appearance was at variance with character, and within moments of meeting them, Suzy was charmed by the warm naturalness of Marvin Harris and his wife Lydia, who turned out to be an anglophile American.

"Mind you, the only thing that's still American about her," Craig informed Suzy with a sly smile in his hostess's direction, "is the food she serves. In all other respects she's gone over to the enemy!"

"British food is something I still can't get used to," Lydia confessed. "Though things are getting better here all the time. Do you know we can even buy American lettuce!"

As she spoke she led them around the side of the house and across the lawn to a large, free-form swimming pool. Its edges were softened by trailing carnations, and a huge weeping willow which dipped its silvery fronds into the water every time a breeze ruffled its leaves. The changing rooms, built to resemble an Edwardian gazebo, did not spoil the rustic setting, nor did the lounging chairs, which were of bamboo and waterproof chintz; one more example of the skilled coordination for which North American decorators were famous.

"I expect you'd like to change into your swimsuit," her hostess said, and Suzy nodded and glanced at Craig.

He was talking to Marvin and made no attempt to follow them, and when she turned back to Lydia, the woman was looking at her with a curious expression.

"Are you a tennis player, too?"

"I'm a journalist on the *Sunday Digest*."

"Oh. Does that mean you're writing about Craig?"

"No. I've been doing Millie Queen's biography. That's how I met him."

Lydia opened the door of a changing room. "I'm glad he was able to get away for the day. From tomorrow he'll be so busy practicing and playing that we won't get a chance to see him down here." She stepped back. "We'll be by the pool. Can I get you a drink meanwhile?"

"Something long and fruity," Suzy smiled, then said in a rush: "I'm not sure I want to swim. Is your pool deep?"

"Oh, yes. You'll be able to dive easily."

"That's what I was afraid of. I really wanted to know if you have a shallow end."

"It's about four feet on the far side. But it soon gets much deeper."

Nervously Suzy changed into a one-piece swimsuit. It was in yellow silk jersey and clung to her body like a second skin. She could visualize Craig's searchlight gaze and was glad of the sighted sunglasses she had brought with her. They were a far better protection than contact lenses.

Looking far more at ease than she felt, she sauntered to the poolside where Craig and his friends were lounging. He must have changed in double-quick time, for he was in briefs with a silly little denim hat perched on top of his head to shade his eyes.

Suzy went to lie on the mattress beside him, but before she could do so, he rose and caught her arm.

"Let's have a swim first."

"You go ahead," she said quickly. "I'll follow later."

"Suzy's a great swimmer," Craig explained at large. "She's in the Olympic class."

"That's great," Marvin said.

"He's kidding," Suzy protested. "I'm a rotten swimmer."

With a shake of his head Craig did a neat dive into the pool and swam below the surface to the far end. It was a long way and required excellent breath control, but hardly had he reached the side when he submerged again and swam back to his starting point. He broke the water with barely a ripple and climbed up on the side without any visible loss of breath.

Without asking, Suzy knew that Elaine was also an excellent swimmer. She probably had a twelve handicap at golf, an excellent seat on a horse and was a dab hand at trimming sail. All that and a tennis player too!

If I were colored by my thoughts, Suzy admitted dis-

mally, tilting her face to the sun, I'd be green as grass!
Willing herself to relax, she gradually did so. The mattress
was soft beneath her body and the sun warm upon it. A
soft breeze lifted her hair and blew a tendril against her
cheek. Then the breeze died and the warmth increased,
the light beating golden upon her closed lids. This was
more like it. She sighed contentedly. Let other hardier
spirits dive into the water or perspire after a tennis ball.
Each to their own, and hers was definitely time and no
motion.

"Come on, lazybones!" Craig's voice was insistent in her
ear, and unwilling to have him look down at her, which
made her feel vulnerable, she sat up quickly. To her dismay
he was close beside her and her shoulder brushed against
his chest. The hair on it was still wet, coiled in tight little
curls, and she resisted the urge to gather a fistful and pull
it. But he had no inhibitions, and before she should stop
him he swung her up in his arms, padded with her over
to the edge of the water and dropped her in.

She parted her lips to scream and swallowed a mouthful
of water. Down below the surface she went and the terror
that always gripped her when she was out of her depth,
caught hold of her now, making her fling her arms wide
and thrash her legs like a turtle gone berserk. She rose to
the surface but was too far from the edge to reach it. A
single breast stroke would have brought her to the side but
fear had taken away reason and she flung her arms above
her head, gurgled helplessly and sank below the surface
again.

Her lungs were full to bursting and there was a singing
sensation in her ears. The redness in front of her eyes
deepened to crimson, as if the water was turning to blood.
My blood, she thought in panic, and thrashed more wildly
still. Then hands were upon her, heavy as clamps as they
brought her swiftly to the surface. She felt herself being
dragged upward and out of the water, then placed gently
on tiles that bordered the poolside.

Her body heaved and she retched, vomiting water from
her mouth and hot tears from her eyes. Again and again

131

she shook with nauseous spasms, until suddenly, they ceased and she was overcome by a lethargy that made it impossible for her to do anything except lie inert. Only then did hands fasten themselves upon her again, and Craig was dragging her up and holding her against his chest.

"You'll be fine in a moment," he said. "Stay still."

What a silly thing to say, she thought, when all she wanted to do was to stay where she was forever. She drew a deep breath and oxygen flowed through her blood. With it came sanity, and she struggled to move away from him. He let her go at once and she sank back on her heels. Able to see Craig, she was surprised by his pallor, then belatedly realized she must have given him a fright by her stupid, panic-stricken behavior.

"Why the hell didn't you say you can't swim?" he demanded.

"But I can."

He gaped at her. "Then why in God's name didn't you swim to the side?"

"I—I'd forgotten how."

He stared at her as if she had gone out of her mind, and resisting the urge to laugh—it was only nervous hysteria that was making her feel she was going to explode into giggles—she made an effort to explain.

"I'm afraid I got into a panic. I always get that way when I'm out of my depth."

"But it wasn't more than a foot above your head. You could have walked to the edge!"

"I could have sat on my bottom and slid along, too," she flared, suddenly furious. "Except that I was out of my mind with fear!"

Craig went on looking at her. His mouth started to twitch and his eyes, so like the color of the trees behind him, narrowed at the edges. Quietly he began to laugh, the sound building up until it roared out of him.

"One foot above your head and you couldn't . . . A single stroke from the side and . . ."

More laughter boomed and Suzy glared at him in fury.

"It's not a bit funny," she stormed. "How would *you* like

to think you were drowning? You should be jolly thankful I didn't have a heart attack from fright!"

"How could you have drowned when I was next to you?" He stopped laughing sufficiently to answer her question, and then dissolved into laughter again. "If you could have seen your face as you came up for air. You looked as if you were stranded in the middle of the Atlantic instead of in a swimming pool six feet deep and three inches from the side!"

"Very funny."

Furiously she jumped to her feet. Only then did she see her host and hostess watching the little scene with an amusement they were striving to hide. She did her best to see some humor in the situation but the fear she had experienced was still too close.

Recognizing the hysterical edge to Suzy's faltering smile, Lydia came across to her.

"I have a phobia about flying," she sympathized, "so I know how you feel. I've gone to the airport on innumerable occasions and had to chicken out. It's something one can't control."

"Lots of people don't like flying," Suzy muttered, "but it's nowhere near as irrational as being afraid to go out of your depth in a swimming pool!"

"A bit odd, I agree," Lydia conceded, "but I'm sure there's a reason for it. If you swam more often, it might lessen your fear."

"I keep saying I will, but I don't."

"It's just a matter of getting used to having your head under water," Marvin put in. "Come in the pool with me and I'll show you what I mean."

"No thanks." Suzy backed away from him smartly. "I think I'll go back to the cabin and make myself tidy."

"Not yet you won't," Craig said behind her. "You're coming into the water with me."

She spun around indignantly but before she could speak he had lifted her into his arms and walked with her to the pool.

"If you drop me in again," she said in a very low voice,

133

"I will never speak to you nor forgive you—*ever*."

"I have no intention of dropping you in," he said calmly. "But I won't let you go running away from your fear. At least try to see if you can conquer it."

Still keeping tight hold of her, he crouched down on the side. "Now will you be a brave girl and get in on your own, or must I climb down the ladder holding you? If I do that, I might slip."

She looked into his face. It was resolute. She struggled to speak but no words came.

"It will be better if you get in the water on your own," he said softly. "I'll be right beside you and I won't let anything happen to you."

She nodded and he set her down. Gingerly she climbed onto the ladder and dropped down several rungs. The water reached to her breasts and she stood still, watching as he slipped in beside her.

"All the way down," he ordered. "You're not out of your depth here."

"But—"

"I'm going to show you how to put your head under water and open your eyes at the same time. It's all a matter of practice. But once you can do it, half your fear will have gone."

For the next hour Suzy was astonished by the patience Craig displayed in his effort to help her overcome her phobia. When they finally emerged she could not in all honesty say she would have dived into the deep end, but she could at least view the prospect of doing so without her skin coming out in goose bumps.

"A great swimmer you'll never be," Craig said as he padded beside her to the changing cabins. "But I bet you don't go berserk next time some"—he hesitated—"some bloody fool throws you in!"

She half smiled but he did not reflect it.

"I'm terribly sorry, Suzy. I had no idea you were scared of the water. And then I had to go and make things worse by laughing at you."

"That *was* rather tactless. I was so cross I could have murdered you."

134

"For one dreadful moment this afternoon that was what I thought I'd done to *you*. When I hauled you out of the pool, you looked half dead."

"Like a stranded fish," she replied, embarrassed by the memory.

"A very pathetic one. Darling . . ."

Without finishing he gathered her close. Their bodies were still wet and there was a sucking sound as their skins touched.

"I'm really stuck on you," he teased. "It can't be the way you swim, so it must be the way you play tennis!"

She giggled and remained in his arms. She knew she should pull away but could not bear to do so. This was the only day she would spend with him and she might as well make it as perfect as possible: a jewel to store in the empty box which would contain her happy memories. Don't be melodramatic, she chided herself. You won't stay in love with him forever. A year from now, you'll be wondering what there was about him that attracted you.

"Darling girl," he said against her cheek. "I want to love you so much. I've never felt like this before."

"I didn't know you suffered from amnesia," she commiserated.

"Stop that!" His grip was tight. "Of course I've wanted to make love to other girls, but with you it's different."

"It's always different the first time."

"I mean it, Suzy."

Today he did, and tomorrow, perhaps. But after that? Unable to stop herself she shivered.

"I'm cold, Craig. Please let me get dressed."

He released her and she hurried into her cabin. Craig went into the next one and she heard the little intimate sounds as he changed: the rattle of coins in his pocket, the trouser zip being fastened, the clatter of sandals.

Anxious to be away before he emerged, she dressed quickly, but as she came out he was waiting for her, and he clasped her hand and led her across the lawn to the house.

When lunch was over they lounged in deck chairs. As the day grew more sultry, conversation languished. Marvin went to sleep, Lydia retired to meditate and Craig dozed. Suzy watched him; she could not bear to sleep away the short, precious time she had with him. Even with his eyes closed he looked on the alert, but she knew this was merely the aura of vitality he exuded.

With predictable lack of warning he opened his eyes and saw her watching him.

"What a lousy date I am," he said, without sounding in any way apologetic. "Still, I'll always be able to say I've been to sleep with a beautiful blonde."

"*Beside* a blonde," she corrected.

"There's still time!"

"You shouldn't have gone to Holland from America," she admonished, ignoring his remark. "With Wimbledon beginning tomorrow, you should have had more than one day's rest."

"The first week of Wimbledon is no sweat. Nor the second," he added.

"It isn't good to be so sure of yourself."

"I know my ability. That isn't smugness—it's confidence."

She was sorry she had spoken. Craig was the champion and a better judge of the tournament than she could ever be.

"I'm sorry," she said. "It was presumptuous of me to pass an opinion."

"It shows you care, and for that reason I'm glad you said it."

He held out his hand and kept it there until she placed hers in it. Then his figners curled over hers and he squeezed them.

"Happy to be with me, Sweet Sue?"

"Delirious."

"You and your jokes," he grumbled, and closed his eyes again.

He did not release her hand and she made no effort to free it, wondering what he would say if he knew she had not been joking.

136

VIII

It was after seven when they returned to London. Instead of taking her home, Craig drove straight to the Savoy Hotel, saying he wanted to change into a suit before taking her to dinner, and ignoring her own protest that she couldn't go anywhere smart in a cotton sun dress.

He took it for granted she would accompany him to his room and she self-consciously followed him to the elevator, wondering if it was imagination that made her think the desk clerk followed her with lascivious eyes.

Whistling below his breath Craig unlocked a door half-way down the corridor. Bracing herself for the intimacy of his bedroom, she was relieved to enter a well-furnished sitting room. It was empty though a pile of crumpled Sunday papers and a cardigan on the floor indicated recent occupancy.

"That Frank." Craig shook his head. "He's the most untidy guy I know."

"Do you always share a suite with him?"

"Yes."

"Don't you find that curtailing?"

137

His eyes glinted. "We have our own bedrooms."

She reddened, knowing she had led with her chin.

"Help yourself to a drink," he said. "I won't be long."

Restlessly she wandered around the room, switching on the television and then turning it off again before settling for the radio.

In five minutes Craig returned, unexpectedly conservative in dark blue.

"It's the executive look," he explained, reading her expression as he came toward her.

She backed away from him but he sidestepped her and opened the door into the corridor, which made her feel a fool, as he had intended.

"I may be a wolf," he drawled, leading her to the elevator, "but I'm not a big bad one!"

He had booked a table in a restaurant overlooking the Thames. It was an ideal June evening, the air soft and clear and the river resembling a sheet of dark glass that mirrored the purple-blue sky and the twinkling stars.

"This is the first time we've had dinner together," she told him.

"I'd like to make it a first for breakfast, too." His mouth quirked. "You look adorable when you blush." He reached across the table for her hand. "I'd like us to be together the whole time, Suzy. I've hated these past two weeks away from you. I kept thinking what a waste it was for me to be on one side of the world and you on the other."

"We spoke to each other every night."

"Have you ever tried to eat the picture on a can of spaghetti?" he countered. "My God, Suzy, don't you know what I'm trying to tell you?"

She looked down at her plate, hoping to control the turmoil that was threatening to destroy the aloofness which was her only defense. Could Craig be asking her to marry him? Keep calm, she told herself. Don't say a word.

"We can't go on like this," he said. "I'm only in England for Wimbledon, and if we can only meet when I'm here, we'll never get a chance to know each other. That's why I want you to be with me."

138

"Be with you?"

"Yes. It's the best way. I work hard during the tournaments; even when I'm playing team tennis I have to practice two or three hours a day. But I do get the odd day off—remember Rome?—and we could be together evenings and weekends. Say yes, Suzy."

A camp follower, Suzy thought bitterly. That's what he wants me to be. A camp follower. And she had thought he had wanted her to be his wife! A proposition instead of a proposal. Well, it served her right for seeing him again after she had discovered that Elaine had been with him in California. That was when she should have stopped taking his nightly calls.

But no, she had wanted to leave him in her own time; to make it look as if she had found someone else. And where did all this leave her now? With her pride in the dust, where her heart was.

"I'm flattered by your offer, Craig, but I can't accept it. I like my job too much to leave it."

"You can still go on writing. When you've finished your articles on Millie you can write about me. Newspapers are always pestering me for stories." His fingers tightened their grip on hers. "You can have the exclusive on Craig Dickson—in every way you want."

Except the way I want, she thought bleakly as anger dissolved into mortification. How glib he was, showing the same delicate touch with words as he did with the ball. But when his desire for her faded and he grew tired of the play, would he deliver the *coup de grâce* in the same devastating way he had destroyed Martelli? That was something she would never know, because she did not intend to be around to find out.

"I don't want to go on writing about tennis," she said. "Millie was a one of a kind for me, and I wouldn't want to repeat it."

"Then come with me and look on it as a holiday."

"Why don't *you* take a holiday and stay in England?"

"My work is different from—" He stopped, contrite and faintly flustered. "I'm putting both feet in it, aren't I? I'm

139

sorry, Suzy. I didn't realize that writing is as important to you as tennis is to me."

"There are lots of things you don't realize about me, Craig. But the most important one is that I have no intention of following you around like a groupie."

He let go of her hand with an angry exclamation. "That's a damn fool thing to say! Don't insult yourself, Suzy. You know damn well I've never seen you like that."

"Haven't you?" she said raggedly. "Don't you? Or have I imagined the way you've just propositioned me?"

"I didn't proposition you," he said swiftly. "All I said was that I'd like us to be together."

"What sort of togetherness did you have in mind?"

He paused and looked at her with frankness.

"You know you turn me on. I wouldn't attempt to deny it. But that isn't why I asked you to give up your job and travel around with me. I meant it when I said I wanted us to get to know each other."

"I have no intention of following you around the tennis circuit like a lapdog."

"How else can we be together?"

"We can't. You have your life and I have mine."

"So what do we do? Meet for the odd weekend; take a holiday together in between tournaments? Do you know what my schedule is like after Wimbledon? Six weeks touring the States, then Japan, South Africa and Australia. It will be months before I'm back here."

"I'm sure you won't miss me."

"Are you asking me or telling me?" He was furious and did not hide it.

"Neither. I'm stating a fact."

"Based on what? The rubbish you've read about me? Christ! You don't believe that, do you?"

"I believe you like lots of pretty girls around you and that you frequently change the faces."

"I do what most normal young males would do if they were given the opportunity. But it isn't the way I see *you*."

Once again he had placed himself in a position where,

140

had he loved her, a proposal of marriage would have been his next logical step. Tensely, she waited.

"Like most girls, you want everything cut and dried," he said in a hard tone.

"I thought you said you didn't see me the way you see most girls?"

He frowned, then ran the flat of his hand across the top of his head. "This conversation isn't going the way I planned. I never imagined you'd react like this."

He stared moodily through the window and she studied his profile. Was he annoyed because she had rebuffed him, the great Craig Dickson whom no girl turned down? If it was more than hurt pride, why didn't he say so?

"I'm sorry, Suzy," he said at last. "I guess I didn't make myself clear. Sure we can meet from time to time. I can work things so that I'll be able to spend a couple of days here with you and I can even scratch a few matches. But we'd still be meeting in a rush. Our time together would still be full of phony glamour and excitement—a sort of holiday." He turned and looked her fully in the face. "It would be romantic but it wouldn't be real. Six months from now we wouldn't know each other any better than we do today. Do you understand what I'm trying to say?"

All she could understand was that she was afraid of being hurt, and self-preservation was still uppermost in her mind when she answered him.

"Where does Elaine fit into all this?"

"She doesn't. So why bring her into it?"

Suzy remembered California and was filled with towering rage.

"Your name has been linked with hers for months," she managed to say.

"Before that it was linked with Anne Gelder." He named another tennis player. "And before that it was June Rugg and Christine Bell."

"And now?"

"Now it will be linked with yours."

"A long chain," she replied, "and I'm the newest link.

141

It might be better if it broke off right here."

"Do you want a man with no experience?" he asked flatly.

"I want a man who'll make me his last one." Quickly she reached for the wine she did not want, and sipped it. Why had she made that last remark? Didn't she know it was as good as an open admission that she would accept nothing less than marriage? Or didn't she care any longer if he knew how she felt?

"Right," he said. "You've made yourself very clear."

Abruptly he rose. His chair rocked but did not topple. Like his temper, it maintained its equilibrium. But only just.

"Let's get out of here," he said. "I fancy a walk."

Quickly she followed on his heels, half running to keep pace with him. She wanted to remain angry but all she felt was doubt. Would it have been so foolish to have accepted his suggestion and gone with him? She wasn't a teenage innocent who didn't know the facts of life. Hell, most teenagers today were far more worldly than she would ever be. So what had stopped her from saying yes? Romeo and Juliet. The two names flashed into her mind, legacy of one of her long transatlantic conversations with Craig. Had Juliet demanded stipulations of undying love and faithfulness before committing herself to the man she loved? But I'm no Juliet, she admitted sadly, and I wouldn't believe Craig even if he made me such a promise. I gave up illusions when I gave up wearing socks. I know Craig for what he is, and I don't trust him. There speaks age, if not wisdom, she thought bleakly. She was as much a prisoner of her upbringing as of her intellect, and both told her that a man should do the chasing; that there should be only one rabbit in the field.

How adroitly he had sidestepped the issue of Elaine. Even now she did not know if his affair with her was over.

He stopped walking and she saw they had made a wide detour but had now reached his car. He looked more relaxed and there was a half smile on his lips as he unlocked the door and helped her in.

142

She wished she could find something inconsequential to say but none of her thoughts seemed to fit, and they were both silent as they drove through the deserted Sunday streets to her mews house.

"It's cute," he commented as he slowed to a halt by the gaily painted front door. "You sometimes see places like these in Cape Cod."

"Do you have a home in the States?" She was determined to be as casual as he was.

"I have some land next to my brother and I'm in the middle of building a house on it."

"You won't get much time to live there."

"It's an investment," he shrugged. "I can always sell it if I've no use for it."

He climbed out and waited for her to unlock the front door. She hesitated, not sure whether to ask him in, but he took the decision away from her by moving back to the car.

"Thanks for today," he said lightly. "Good-bye, Suzy."

The door closed, his hand waved, and he was gone. It was over. Finished. But with a whisper instead of the big bang she had anticipated.

She tried to be glad but failed. Craig had occupied her thoughts so exclusively that to tear him out of them would leave black holes of despair. Even the book she was writing, that great, supposedly cathartic exercise, was an anguished cry for him.

Knowing it, she was unable to face the typewriter. She put the cover on it and bundled the pile of manuscript into her desk drawer. She would pretend the story did not exist. That was by far the best way to forget Craig. Writing about him had been a stupid idea anyway.

Two days went by. There was no word from him and though she kept telling herself she did not expect to hear—had never thought he would call her now that she had made it clear she did not want to be his current girl friend—she almost jumped out of her skin each time the telephone rang.

By Wednesday she was convinced she would never see

143

him again. Free of fear—how could she be afraid of giving in to him when he was not going to ask her anymore—she was almost able to think of him with regret.

Had she misjudged him, as he had said? Was she so blinded by his publicity that she had failed to see the real man? Doubt nagged at her resolution, and was finally so strong that she dialed the Savoy and gave his room number.

The bell rang. Once. Twice. Three times. Her heart was hammering so loudly that she pressed the receiver hard against her ear. The bell was still ringing and she knew he was out. Relieved, she put down the telephone. Her heart resumed its usual beat, her brain its usual logic. Thank heaven he hadn't been in.

On Thursday she saw Millie. There was the final installment to write and she needed a few more facts to bring it up to date.

Millie was still in bed when she entered her suite, yawning and looking with jaundiced eyes at boiled eggs and buttered toast.

"I drank too much last night," she said gloomily. "Larry would kill me if he knew."

"Where was Don?"

"Celebrating *with* me." The girl smiled. "Craig and Elaine took us out to dinner and we didn't get back till four this morning."

Suzy waited to feel some reaction. None came. She was numb.

"You should spend the day resting," she said briskly.

"There's no need. I'll be fine once I'm up. Anyway, I'm booked for a practice session at Queens this afternoon. I'm playing Diana tomorrow and she's always more of a threat to me on grass."

"You'll win," Suzy said.

"I hope so. I'd like to retire while I'm still champion." She pushed aside the bedcovers and walked about the room, a sturdy figure in blue pajamas. "I expected Craig to bring *you* along last night. I was disappointed when I saw Elaine."

144

"I was with him on Sunday," Suzy said casually, "but I don't think he enjoyed the end of the evening."

Millie's face crinkled with amusement and Suzy wished she had kept quiet. But it was too late now.

"Give with the rest," Millie pleaded. "What did you say and how was it left?"

"He said will you? I said I wouldn't, and it wasn't left anywhere. It's over."

"There's got to be more to it than that. Come on, Suzy, tell me all the details. After all, I feel responsible for the whole thing. I practically threw you together."

"There isn't much more to tell."

Briefly she recounted Craig's offer and had the satisfaction of hearing Millie gasp.

"I don't believe it. Craig couldn't be such a damn fool. Not with a girl like you."

Millie's words were liniment on Suzy's bruised feelings, though her next comment was like Swedish massage, pummeling her into the painful awareness that her judgment of him could have been wrong.

"Are you quite sure you didn't misunderstand him? I've known Craig for years and he's never asked a girl to travel around with him. It's been a standing joke among his friends that he won't even commit himself from one date to another!"

"What does that make Elaine—apart from unique! Or wouldn't you call *her* a commitment?"

"No, I wouldn't. She does all the running, Suzy. She always has. Now tell me again. Did he come right out and ask you to give up your job and go with him on all his trips?"

"Yes. He said I should regard it as a holiday. It wasn't a commitment on his part. Nothing like it."

"I'm not so sure. I think he genuinely wanted to get to know you."

"Even when he's been genuinely getting to know Elaine at the same time?"

"Maybe he's using her as a second string."

"Then it doesn't say much for the strength of the first one!"

"What do you expect him to do? Be content to see you for a weekend every couple of months? And what does he do in the interim?"

"For sex, you mean?" Suzy asked bluntly. "The same thing he would have had to do if I had followed him around! I wouldn't have gone to bed with him."

"You don't believe that." Millie was exasperated. "That's why you turned him down: because you were scared of yourself. If you were more sure of Craig, you wouldn't be so moral. You still see sex as cheese in the mousetrap."

"That isn't true."

"Yes it is. But I won't argue with you about it. You're lying to yourself, Suzy, so I don't expect you to be honest with *me*."

Suzy sat down and got out her notebook. A lot of reporters used tape recorders these days, but she had always found them to be inhibiting. Besides, they recorded everything, and one was then faced with the mammoth task of extricating the gold from the dross. Or the coal from the rock. That was a more realistic description. I'm running away from what Millie's said, Suzy thought, because I can't bear to think she may be right.

"Let's stop talking about Craig and get down to work," she said. "This may be the only free time you'll have."

"Will you come to Queens with me this afternoon?"

"No."

"Craig will think you're avoiding him."

"If I come, he'll think I'm running after him. Either way, I'll be doing the wrong thing."

"Then at least come and keep me company."

Suzy laughed. "When you're surrounded by friends, and have Don, too? Stop acting like a marriage broker. Craig and I are too ill-matched."

"I still think you should have agreed to his suggestion," Millie stated. "What was the worst that could have happened to you?"

"You're being too simplistic," Suzy countered. "It's not
146

just a question of will I or won't I go to bed with him. It's more than that. It always has been."

"Has been what? I don't follow you."

"Love," Suzy said in a miserable voice. "I love that— that . . ." She swallowed hard. "That tennis Casanova! That's why I turned down his offer. I don't want to get hurt more than I am already."

"Does Craig know how you feel?"

"Of course not. It's still a game to him. And he's a far better player than I'll ever be."

"I see." Millie sounded as if she did. "Well, in that case, I don't blame you for not wanting to play." She tugged at the side of her head, pulling at a strand of hair, which she always did when she was perplexed. "On the other hand, how will he ever know if he feels seriously about you, if he doesn't have a chance to know you properly?"

"*I* know."

"Women are different."

"You sound like Craig," Suzy said bitterly. "Do you mind if we change the subject?"

Millie did so, but neither she nor Suzy was able to concentrate on tennis, and finally Suzy gave up and returned home.

She was fumbling for her key when she heard the telephone ring. Hurriedly, she opened the front door and dashed into the sitting room in time to catch the final peal. But even as she lifted the receiver off the hook, the dial tone sounded.

"Damn!" she said with feeling, and turned away.

The telephone rang again, choked off in mid-peal as she almost throttled it in her hurry to lift it off the hook.

"About time, too," Bill Walters muttered. "I've been trying to get you for hours. Why don't you have someone take your messages, so I'll know to call you wherever you've gone?"

"You knew I was with Millie."

"I forgot. Anyway, she's the reason I'm calling. We're running the first installment on Sunday. His Nibs has seen it and is very impressed. You've made a hit there, my old dear. He's actually asked for a rundown on you."

"Praise indeed."

Craig or no Craig, she was delighted by the news. Perhaps she was a career woman after all. A single-minded, single career woman.

"Don't be surprised if he offers you a job on our daily," Bill went on peevishly. "They only manage to exist by pinching the talent *I* find."

"I know," she said sympathetically, "and if I remain in Fleet Street I promise I won't leave you, as long as you give me the same salary they'll offer!"

"What do you mean by *if* you remain? No, don't bother answering that. I knew I shouldn't have introduced you to Anne. Which reminds me, she wants to know how the book is coming along."

"Quite well," she lied.

"Is that why you're late with the last installment on Millie?"

"I'm not late," she protested. "You'll have it the day after tomorrow."

The promise sent Suzy directly to her typewriter. It was an effort to concentrate on the biography when all her thoughts centered on Craig. If his desire to know her better had been genuine, he would never have walked out on her the way he had done. He had wanted an easy conquest and became angry when his charm had failed to get it for him. She stared at the blank page, then forced herself to type. Nonsense flowed from her fingers but the movements helped her brain to coordinate. She pulled out the sheet, crumpled it up and inserted a new one.

She was a quarter way through her work when her mother telephoned her, asking if she were coming home for her younger brother's birthday that weekend.

"I'm not sure," she hedged. "I may be busy on a story."

"Can't you get down for the day? I'm sure you could do with a break."

"I'll try," Suzy promised, but knew she would do no such thing. She wanted to be here in case Craig asked to see her. So much for her staunch belief that she had done

148

the right thing; that she was her own mistress. One look from Craig's hazel eyes and she would become his.

For the rest of the day she hovered close to the telephone, willing it to ring and for Craig to be at the other end. But it remained obstinately silent and the next morning she went to her office to write, determined not to be at home if, by any remote chance, Craig did call.

Roger Paxton, the features editor, greeted her with mild sarcasm and pretended not to recognize her after her long absence from the office.

"I was here the other day," she protested.

"But to see Bill Walters, not me. I'm only the one who put up the idea for the Millie Queen story," he grumbled, "and now he's going around saying what a great idea he had!"

Suzy laughed. She had long since learned not to get involved in interoffice feuds.

"What's scheduled for me after I've done this?" she asked.

"Back to general features. Unless our editor thinks of another great idea all by himself!"

Suzy retired to her office and tapped away the best part of the day. One of the other reporters in the room turned on a transistor radio during Millie's match and she was delighted when the girl won it easily. Then Craig's drawling voice sounded in the room and she hastily stacked her article together and took it to Roger.

He also had his television set switched on—though with the sound turned down—and the sight of Craig's face on the screen gave her such a jolt that she was hard put not to turn tail and run.

"It's finished," she stated, keeping her eyes from the set and placing the pile of paper on the desk. "I'm going home."

"Wait here while I read it."

Roger picked up the first page and, as always, Suzy experienced a niggle of fear. Would she still have it when she was pushing forty and an experienced journalist, or would it disappear as her bylines grew bigger? She sat in a chair and waited. A darting glance at the television screen

149

showed her that Craig was still on it, and she moved her chair closer to the desk.

"There's a call for you, Suzy."

One of the girls with whom she shared her office put her head around the door, and with a murmur of apology to Roger, Suzy went to take it.

"Hi," Craig said. "How are you?"

"I—I—" Astonishment made her incoherent. "You're—on television—I've just seen you!"

"It's a recording. I did it an hour ago. I'm at my hotel now. When can I see you?"

"I'm working."

"I was thinking of this evening. I'm free and—"

"I'm not," she said coolly. "I have a date." How dare he think he could ring her like this and expect her to be available for him?

"Tomorrow, then?"

And now he was making it worse by not even asking her if she could break it!

"I'm afraid not."

"Playing hard to get?"

"I'm not playing."

"That much I've already realized." He paused. "You're annoyed with me for not calling you before."

"You flatter yourself."

"You obviously won't do it for me!"

"I'm sure there are plenty of others who will."

"You're so jealous," he said in such a contented voice that it was only by a great effort that she refrained from hanging up on him.

"I didn't call earlier," he explained, "because I wanted to give you time to calm down and see things in perspective."

"I do. But I haven't changed my mind."

"I figured you wouldn't. I know when I'm beaten."

She was about to ask what he meant when Roger came in waving the last page of her article.

"I have to go," she said into the receiver, and put it down before Craig could reply.

150

"What's the matter with you?" Roger asked. "You look as if you've lost a diamond and found a zircon!"

"I have."

Bitterly regretting that she had refused to go out with Craig tonight—the least she could do was to see him again and hear what else he had to say—she toyed with the idea of calling him back and saying she had made a mistake and that her date was for tomorrow. She discarded this idea at once. Craig was too well-versed in the ways of women not to see through such an excuse. He might even see her change of mind as a weakening of her intent, and this was something she dare not encourage.

"Damn," she said aloud.

"It's not much of a rewrite." Roger misunderstood her and apologized. "Just the last page."

"Sure." Suzy took it from him. "I'll have it done in fifteen minutes."

He went to the door. "I have a couple of tickets for a first night. If you're free by any chance . . ."

He had asked her out once before and she had refused, unwilling to encourage a personal relationship. But the prospect of a solitary evening was unbearable, and she nodded.

"Good." He looked pleased. "We'll have a drink around the corner first and supper after the show."

"I'd like to go home and change."

"Fine. Do you want me to pick you up?"

"It would be rather nice."

"I knew you'd say that!"

"You don't know my address," she called after him.

"Yes I do. I've had it in my diary since the day I hired you!"

IX

A bad conscience—it was underhanded to make use of Roger—made Suzy take extra care with her appearance. If she looked beautiful, he might also fail to notice that her thoughts were elsewhere.

Yet to her surprise, once she was in his company she found herself enjoying it. They had a great deal in common apart from both being journalists, for he had grown up in a small town, too, was still close to his family and had ambitions to return to his roots and run a provincial newspaper. Only where his last wish was concerned did Suzy's own ambitions digress. To be tied to the daily grind of reporting for the rest of her life was more than she could stomach; not even the thought of her own byline, once so important, could excite her now. She wanted to write novels. That much, at least, Craig had helped her to confirm.

The play was amusing and sufficiently cerebral to take her mind off her own problems. She could also keep them at bay as the curtain came down for the first act, and she happily let Roger hold her hand as he led her to the bar. Perhaps finishing the Millie Queen story was all she had needed to help her finish with Craig.

"Champagne," said Roger, waving a half bottle in front of her. "In celebration."

"Of what?"

"Our first evening together."

"I didn't know you were so romantic."

"Try me." He poured the champagne, and raised his glass to hers. "To us."

She smiled but did not echo the phrase, which he noticed with a lift of one shaggy eyebrow. He was an attractive man with a thatch of dark hair that always looked untidy, due partly to the way it grew and partly to the way he ran his fingers through it when he was exasperated—which he frequently was. He was a pipe holder—having given up the habit though not the pipe—and used it the way a conductor would a baton. Tonight, she was glad to see, he was pipeless.

"What's amusing you?" he asked.

"I was wondering what you've done with your pipe."

"I left it in the office. I know all my faults, Suzy, though I don't always try to correct them."

She recollected a divorced wife and wondered if he had learned of his faults from her. Unwilling to pry, she talked about the play.

"I can't imagine how it's going to end. Lily is such an impossible woman to love."

"It's wedding bells at finale time," Roger said. "But I won't say whose wedding."

"Are you guessing?"

"I saw the play when I was in New York. It's a smash hit there."

"It'll be a hit here, too."

"I know one of the backers," he added. "That's how I got tickets for tonight."

"Who?" she asked, to keep the conversation going.

"Harry Esterson. You've heard of him?"

"The man who owns Texas! You do mix in illustrious circles."

"Working ones," he grinned. "I did a stint on one of his papers when I lived in the States."

153

"I didn't know you'd been there."

"I spent a couple of years there after my divorce. You knew I was married?"

"Yes. Was it for long?"

"It seemed long once it started to go sour. But that's all water under the bridge. Which reminds me . . ." He poured the rest of their champagne. "Mr. Esterson wanted me to stay in Texas permanently but at the time I was too restless. Sometimes I regret that I didn't. There's a lot to be said for being a big fish in a little pond."

"Not such a little pond."

"I was thinking of his newspaper interests. His main ones are oil and politics."

"I bet they mix well!"

"And how. If you think some of our Westminster lobbying can be strong, you should spend some time in Esterson's entourage. The way he manipulates those men in Washington has to be seen to be believed."

"I thought Watergate had put an end to that sort of thing."

"Did Canute turn back the tide? All Watergate did was to make the carpet bigger."

"Bigger?"

"So that more dirt could be brushed under it! Anyway, Watergate wasn't about lobbying."

"I know. But it did cause a general cleanup and—"

"You need to have a cleanup every year, which is impossible. No, Suzy, politics is a dirty business, whichever way you look at it."

She looked at him with a knowing smile. "Would I be wrong in thinking *we'll* be looking at it for a possible series?"

"I'm afraid not. It would make a damn good one, but not enough people over here care about American shenanigans, and our own are too tame." He glanced around. "Esterson is here tonight. He flew over for the premiere."

The glass shook in Suzy's hands and she lifted it hastily to her lips. "I know his daughter. I met her when I was with Millie."

"Of course. I keep forgetting she's a professional tennis
154

player. Beats me why she does it. She has enough money to buy out everyone and still only use her petty cash."

"I don't think she's in it for the money." Suzy kept her voice level. "She's in love with Craig Dickson."

Roger nodded, as if he had heard this before. "It's all coming back to me. I saw him just now, by the way, when I was at the bar collecting our champagne. I suppose he must have come here with them tonight."

Accepting the inevitable, Suzy knew that before the evening was over she would come face to face with the one man she did not want to see. It looked as if Craig was doomed to haunt her like a recurring nightmare.

A burly figure loomed down on them, massive shoulders appearing constricted in the formality of a dinner jacket. Like a lumberjack, Suzy decided, until she saw the shrewd eyes behind steel-rimmed glasses and the small, neat features with the dominant chin. She did not need his Texas drawl to tell her who he was either; Craig and Elaine, walking beside him, did that.

"Glad you were able to make it, Roger," Mr. Esterson said. "My secretary called yours to say I wanted to get together with you during the intermission, but you had already left the office."

"I went to collect Suzy."

"Well worth collecting, if I may say so." The Texan beamed and caught hold of her hand.

His look reminded Suzy that he had already married and discarded three wives, and from the way he was keeping hold of her fingers she had the distinct impression he might be thinking of discarding his fourth.

"Nice to see you again, Suzy." Elaine's cool greeting had the desired effect, and her father let go of Suzy's hand and eyed his daughter.

"You two know each other?"

"Suzy's writing Millie Queen's life story."

"Is that so?" Mr. Esterson was quick to jump to the wrong conclusion as he wagged his finger in Suzy's direction. "What can be nicer than an evening out with the boss!"

"I daren't say an evening without him!" Suzy smiled, and from the corner of her eye saw Craig glance at Roger.

What a stroke of luck that they had met here tonight. At least he would not be able to think she had been lying when she had said she had a previous engagement. She inched closer to Roger and wondered what he would say if she slipped her hand through his arm. She toyed with the idea and then discarded it. She did not want to give Craig the impression that she was trying too hard. She took another sip from her glass. Elaine and her father were talking to Roger and Craig was standing idly by. He looked relaxed and uncaring. Hard to believe that only a few days ago he had propositioned her so blantantly. What would Elaine say if she found out?

Craig moved back a step and drew Suzy to one side with him.

"No wonder you didn't offer to get out of your date for tonight. No career girl can afford to antagonize her boss."

So he had been waiting for her to make the offer, had he? Of all the conceited, thick-skinned men she had met, he was the thickest. She gave him a warm smile.

"It didn't take you long to find someone to take my place."

"What place?" he asked blandly.

Giving him the victory of this round, she turned and edged closer to Roger. He was reminiscing about Texas with Elaine, who tonight had lost some of her hard gloss and looked exceptionally pretty. It was probably her chiffon dress that did it. Pink was a color that could soften the appearance of a stone. It was a wry way of putting it. Diamond would have been more apt. A very big, blue-white diamond; there for Craig's taking. Elaine was leaning toward him as she included him in the conversation, slipping her arm through his as if to establish her ownership of him. Suzy could have ignored it—for she knew Elaine was recklessly flaunting her aces—had it not been for the way Mr. Esterson himself was treating Craig: displaying the same proprietary attitude toward him that he might have shown to a son.

156

It was with great relief that she heard the intermission bell ring, and was able to follow Roger to their seats.

"Mr. Esterson suggested we join them for dinner," he murmured as they sat down. "I said I'd let him know."

"Do you want to go?"

"That means you don't."

"I'd rather have dinner alone with you."

"You don't like Elaine, do you?"

"Let's say I like you more!"

"I'll accept that reason." He took her hand in his and kept hold of it throughout the next act.

During the second intermission she remained in her seat, leaving Roger to see the Estersons on his own. When the curtain came down on the last act she dawdled in the claokroom until she was sure the party of three had left the theater, and played it so safe that Roger was the only person in the foyer by the time she joined him.

"I hope you like Indian food?" he asked as they drove along the Strand.

"Which kind?" she questioned. "Mogul, Kashmiri—"

"Okay, okay. You've convinced me you're an expert! It's Kashmiri, as a matter of fact."

"Then I like it very much."

But so preoccupied was she with images of Craig and Elaine, that even the exotic flavors of the lightly spiced curries, with their mixtures of fruits and meats, were as tasteless to her as the conversation was meaningless. How could anything hold her interest when her interest centered upon a lithe-limbed athlete with a roving eye?

The effort to hide her thoughts was so exhausting that she sighed with relief when Roger finally took her home. She braced herself to ask him in for a nightcap, and was delighted when he kept the taxi running as he jumped out and escorted her to her front door.

"You'll see me again?" he asked, giving her a light kiss on her lips.

"At the office tomorrow."

"Clever girl," he reproved, and climbed back into the taxi.

157

Alone at last, Suzy gave way to tears. But like a stream in a drought, they soon dried up. Instead of feeling sorry for herself, she felt furious with Craig. He must have known she would turn down his suggestion for seeing her tonight. She could not believe that Elaine, besotted though she was with him, would have given him the chance to refuse a first-night ticket from her, and more importantly, an evening with her father at the last moment. He had obviously arranged to go with her days ago. But if he hadn't, that would have made things worse; for one had to be extremely sure of his position in a girl's life to use her when the mood struck him or when no one else was available.

Poor Elaine. Suzy waited to feel sympathy but none came. She kicked off her shoes, wishing she could kick Craig instead. She remembered the way he had looked at her when they had returned to the auditorium after the intermission. His eyes had glittered more green than gray and his mouth had been tight with suppressed anger. The gall of him. "Hoist with his own petard," was a proverb he had obviously not encountered until tonight.

Anxious to avoid being in London for the weekend, Suzy decided to do as her mother had asked and go home for her brother's birthday. A telephone call from Millie to say that Larry was giving her an engagement party nearly made her change her mind. But the knowledge that she would see Craig there acted as a brake, and pretending it was a family convention never to miss one another's birthdays, she refused Millie's invitation.

Once home, she was glad of her decision. She had returned to the nest and she was able to relax accordingly. Her parents were young-minded enough to understand all her problems; but though she wanted to tell them about Craig, she found she could not bear to discuss him with anyone. Later, perhaps, when day-to-day living had revitalized her, she would be able to talk of him without pain. She knew her mother saw through her brittle chatter and was thankful to have a parent sensitive enough not to try to force a confidence.

"I'm glad you've finished the Millie Queen biography," was her mother's only comment on the situation. "Tennis players live such an artificial life that they must lose all contact with reality."

"That applies to film stars, too."

"And football players," young Bobby put in.

"Not quite," Suzy said. "Footballers manage to live at home and have some sort of private life. But tennis stars, like top golfers, spend three-quarters of their lives traveling the world. They have no privacy whatever."

"I still wouldn't mind changing shoes with Craig Dickson," Bobby commented. "Is he as randy as they say he is?"

"Bobby!" his mother remonstrated. "Must you be so explicit?"

"That isn't explicit," her young son said. "You should hear what some of the other boys say!"

"No thank you."

"Well, is he?" Bobby persisted, looking at his sister.

"I wouldn't know."

"Then why were you kissing him at Rome Airport?" Bobby asked, with all the enjoyment of a thirteen-year-old out to shock. "One of the chaps at school was in Rome at the time, and saw it in the papers."

Suzy drew a deep breath. "Craig Dickson kisses girls as casually as other people shake hands. He makes a wolf seem like a—like a—"

"Wolves are the most faithful of all animals," her brother said. "If he loses his mate, he never takes another one. Often he pines and dies."

"That's not Craig," Suzy said shortly, and muttering about seeing to the dishes, went into the kitchen.

"How about making us one of your special trifles?" her mother commented behind her, her tone conveying what her words did not.

"Sure." Suzy bent her head to the sink, then swung around and gave her mother a hug. "I do love you, darling. I don't often say it, but . . . ."

"Love doesn't need words, darling, nor even kisses."

Suzy turned back to the sink. "I'll tell you about Craig one day. Not that there's much to tell."

"He must be a remarkable young man, though," her

159

mother commented. "He's the first one to take the glow from your face."

"It'll come back. All I need is time."

"As long as you remember that, darling."

Greatly refreshed from her visit, Suzy returned to London on Tuesday and the following day took an engagement present to Millie.

"I wish you'd come to the party," Millie said, admiring the delicate watercolor of Kew Gardens which Suzy had bought her. "Larry really did me proud." She set the picture on top of the television set in her suite and stepped back to admire it.

"Craig asked after you. He expected you to come to the party with your boss."

"I suppose he was there with Elaine?" Suzy said tartly.

"What did you expect?" Millie faced her. "You're crazy if you think he'll go on pining for you. But he did ask about you, which struck me as rather odd after the way you treated him."

"The way *I* treated *him!* Honestly, if you think . . ."

"I think he's still stuck on you."

"Then he'd better get himself unstuck! Nothing has changed since I last spoke to you."

"Things won't change unless you make them. You're behaving like an idiot. Craig fancied you and he wanted to get to know you better. You can't blame him for trying, nor for giving up if he doesn't succeed."

"He gave up very quickly."

"That shows how strongly you came across! At least he gave you the benefit of believing you were a girl who knew her own mind!"

"I didn't say I wouldn't see him again," Suzy stated.

"So what did you do when he rang you? You turned him down and went out with someone else. If you hadn't told me you loved him, I could see some sense in what you're doing, but as you're crazy about him . . ."

"I'm not."

"Okay, you're not. You hate him and you never want to see him again."

160

The exasperation in Millie's voice made Suzy smile. Viewed from the brink of marital bliss, she and Craig were behaving like a couple of adolescents. She thought of his suite, several floors above her, and wondered if he were there.

"Craig comes back to the hotel for a bath and a sleep after he's played a match," Millie said, displaying one of her rare moments of divination.

Suzy ignored it. "Where's Don?"

"Buying himself some clothes. My folks flew in for the party and we're going out to dinner with them."

"Are they pleased about your engagement? That's a private question, Millie, I've finished writing about you."

"Have you really? That's great." The girl beamed. "Pa didn't say much, but my mother thinks I should go on playing for as long as my game holds up."

"What did you say to that?"

"That *I'd* give up long before my game did! I've *had* championship tennis, Suzy. I can't wait to quit; to say good-bye forever to the three P's."

"The what?"

"Publicity, people, pressure."

"I wish you'd mentioned that before. It would have made a good heading."

"Use it in a book."

"I may well do that."

"It's one of the reasons that makes me understand the suggestion that Craig put to you. He has far bigger P's than I do. Beats me the way he stands it, year after year. But if you were with him, if he could relax with you, Suzy, I'm sure he'd realize he couldn't go on without you."

"You do make your point," Suzy said, her voice thick. "You're beginning to make me feel a fool for turning him down."

"You were. Why don't you go and tell him?"

On the verge of saying she would do no such thing, Suzy stopped. Why shouldn't she? Lord knows she had often enough condemned pride in other people.

"What can I say to him?"

161

"That you're using a woman's prerogative and changing your mind! He'll appreciate that."

"I bet he will." Suzy stood up, but could go no farther. "I hate running after a man."

"Why? Are you so special that they always have to run after *you*?"

"I didn't mean that!"

"Then go see him."

Buoyed by Millie's determination, as much as her own, Suzy went up to the sixth floor. It was a good thing she had remembered the number of Craig's suite. It was only as she was walking along the corridor that she wondered if she should have telephoned him first to say she was on her way. But it was too late to do it now. Anyway, it would be nice to see his face when he opened his door and saw her.

She reached his suite and stopped. The palms of her hands were damp and her throat was dry. She swallowed, lifted her arm and knocked. There was no answer and she knocked again. Craig was either still in his bath or sleeping. It might be better to go back to Millie and telephone him from there. She had already turned to go when she heard a faint sound behind her. She swung around, her breath coming fast.

The door opened and her heart thumped and began to race as she saw the person standing there. Idiot, she berated herself. Sentimental, softhearted idiot. Why did I have to listen to Millie? Why didn't I rely on my own antenna? I was right when I said no and I should have stuck to it.

"Well, well," Elaine murmured, opening the door a little wider and smiling at her with undisguised dislike. "I don't need to ask what makes Suzy run, do I? It's Craig!"

"I—I—" Suzy could not continue and Elaine took advantage of it.

"I'm afraid you can't see him. He's sleeping. May I help you instead?"

"No!"

"What a pity."

"Suzy turned to run but Elaine's hand came out and

caught her, the fingers as hard as her voice.

"Keep away from Craig, do you hear? He's mine and I'm not going to let him go."

"You don't need to state the obvious."

"Normally I don't. But you're so dumb, you don't seem to understand it."

"I do now." Wrenching herself free, Suzy ran down the corridor.

"I won't tell him you've called." Elaine's voice mocked her. "I never like making another woman look a fool!"

The words seared through Suzy like a blowtorch. How well she deserved them. She should never have listened to Millie. But no, it was wrong to blame anyone except herself. It was her own desire to see Craig that had brought her here. Her own need of him that had made her believe his need was as great. She put a clenched hand to her mouth. She must not cry. She had to control herself until she was out of the hotel.

By the time she reached home, anger was her predominant emotion. Anger and relief. She was quite sure that Elaine would keep her word and not tell Craig she had come in search of him. The offer did not stem from the girl's good nature but from the fear that Craig's desire for novelty might still make him seek Suzy out. But if he did not know she had called to see him, he would go on believing that she was the one girl who had managed to resist his charm. Well, almost, she thought bitterly, remembering that long ago day in Rome when they had swung together on the hammock and he had kissed her until the very world had rocked.

What would have happened to her if she had accepted the offer Craig had made to her a week ago? Would his feelings for her have deepened or would they have faded with the fading newness? It was something she would never know. All she did know was that it had not taken him long to find other compensation.

It was a mortifying admission.

X

When she arrived at the office on Thursday, Roger asked
her if she would like to go with him to Wimbledon to watch
the men's semifinals. It was all Suzy could do not to laugh
in his face, though the excuse she manufactured satisfied
him. Her refusal to have dinner with him that night, did
not.

"What about tomorrow, then?"

"I'll be with Millie," she lied, unable to face going out
with any other man. "Take a rain check on it, and leave it
for a few days."

"All right. But tell me when you *are* free, Suzy. It's
better that way. I'm always available for *you*."

She left his office, hoping she had not hurt him, and
promptly forgot him as she sat down at her desk. It was
not as easy to forget Craig. Everyone seemed to be listening
to Wimbledon, where Craig was having an unusually stiff
fight against another seeded American. After losing the first
set four-one, he took second and third on a tie-break, then
convincingly won the fourth, to put him in line for the final
against the number two seed from Denmark.

"That will be a real killer," said Jane, who worked at the next desk. "But my money's on the Robot. He never gives up, even when he's down. That's the sort of spirit that separates the men from the boys."

"Must you talk like an old Huston movie?" Suzy asked in irritation. "And how can I be expected to work with these bloody transistors blaring in my ears?"

"Sorry." Jane was astounded by the attack. Suzy was normally the easiest girl with whom to share an office. "If you'd said so before, I'd have sat in the loo and listened!"

Suzy laughed, her humor restored. But she knew she had to be careful. One more explosion from her when Craig was in the news, and Jane would start to remember that he had telephoned the office a few days ago to speak to her. From then on, the girl would have no difficulty in putting two and two together and making them a coupling!

For the remainder of the afternoon Suzy went out of her way to retain an air of calm and cheerfulness, and even went with Jane to the coffee shop across the street from the office, where she ate a toasted bun she did not want and drank coffee she could not bear.

It was a blessed relief when she could finally leave for home, and she drove her car slowly up the ramp from the underground garage to street level.

She paused to let a large BMW motorcycle move past her, as black and shiny as the proud young owner who was riding it. He whistled at her and she glowered at him. Unabashed he whistled again and this time she smiled.

What the hell! Craig was not going to sour her life. He was not the only fish in the sea, nor was he the only one she wanted. No sir. She was a red-blooded woman and she would prove it.

She was still buoyant with these thoughts, even though she knew them to be lies, when she reached the mews. A taxi was parked halfway inside it, making it difficult for her to maneuver her car in front of her house.

She switched off her engine and jumped out, fighting mad. Someone was going to pay for her mood.

"Do you have to park right in front of..." Her voice

165

trailed away as the taxi door opened and Craig stepped out from it.

"Hello, Suzy."

She stared at him. The blood seemed to drain from her head and her scalp tingled. Had Elaine broken her word and told him she had gone to his suite to try to see him? It was impossible for her to guess what thoughts were going on behind those glinting yellow-green eyes. All she knew was that he looked as handsome as ever and, as ever, she wanted to throw herself into his arms and tell him he could take her anywhere he wanted.

But then logic took over and she gave him a cool stare.

"I didn't expect to see you here, Craig."

"I came direct from Wimbledon. I was afraid that if I called you first, you would make some excuse not to see me."

"How right you were."

"Why are you still angry with me? I know I didn't endear myself to you the other night, but that's still no reason for you to look at me as if I've just crawled out from under a stone."

"If I remember correctly," she said, still cool, "you were the one who walked off in a huff."

"I wasn't in a huff."

"You could have fooled me. I had the distinct impression you were not going to see me again."

"I had some thinking to do first. And now I've thought and . . . Well, maybe your idea isn't such a bad one after all. At least we can try it for a while and see how it goes. I'll fly over whenever I can and—"

"Thanks," she said with heavy sarcasm. "That's really wonderful."

"What's wrong now? Damnit, Suzy, surely we can start again?"

"There's nothing to start."

"Oh, come on. There's been something between us from the moment we met."

"Sexual attraction. Nothing more."

166

"We could make it more."

"For how long? Until the next time we had a quarrel and you crawled into somebody else's bed?"

He reddened with anger. "That's a foul thing to say."

"I can't help it if you don't like the truth."

"It's a distorted truth. You've got some image of me that . . ."

"It's nothing compared with the image you've got of yourself! Invincible Craig Dickson. The man for whom every girl would lie down and . . ." She swallowed hard. "I do wish you would realize that I no longer care what you do with your life, nor with whom and how many. I'm not interested in you."

"You're lying."

She dug her nails into the palms of her hands. She had to convince him she was speaking the truth, and she had to do it quickly, before she broke down and said she would take him on any terms, short or long.

"Poor Craig." She made her voice as scornful as she knew how. "You can't believe a girl would get bored with you. Well, in this case I'm afraid it's happened. You don't amuse me anymore. I liked you to begin with, I won't deny that, but it hasn't lasted. I find you too limited intellectually and rather obvious. If—"

"There's no need to continue," Craig cut in, opening the door of the taxi. "You've made yourself more than clear. Happy hunting for your cerebral boy friend, Suzy. I only hope that when you find him, he won't find you a bore too!"

She turned her back on him and fumbled in her bag for her keys. Her fingers were nerveless and the keys fell to the ground. She bent to pick them up, her eyes too blinded by tears to see what she was doing.

Behind her the taxi wheezed into life. Simultaneously she found the bunch of keys and inserted the Yale one into the lock, stumbling into the hall as the taxi reached the end of the mews and disappeared.

How easy it was to send someone out of your life. Phys-

167

ically. If only she could do it mentally too. But she knew, without being told, that this was not going to be so easy. She had fallen in love with Craig quickly, but it would take her a long time to forget him.

That night, for the first time in months, she took two sleeping pills, switched off the telephone bell to make sure no one could disturb her, and went to bed.

Partly because of the pills and partly because of the depression that had swamped her immediately after seeing Craig, she slept around the clock and it was half-past nine in the morning before she surfaced. Head throbbing like an engine she made some coffee and gulped down a couple of aspirins.

It was not until she had had her bath that she began to feel human again, and she surveyed herself in the mirror, surprised that her misery had not left its mark on her face. Her skin was smooth and pink, her eyes bright and innocent. Innocent! Perhaps if she had been less innocent she would have accepted Craig as he was. But she had to forget him. He had gone from her life and was now only a name she knew; she had certainly never known the man.

"I do not, repeat not, not, not, love him!" She stared at her reflection. "I was bowled over by his looks. That's all it was. By his golden hair and his bronze skin, by his gray-green eyes and sexy-looking mouth."

Her own mouth trembled and tears glittered in her eyes. What was the use of pretending? She loved a heel. She might as well admit it.

She arrived at the office late and was greeted tersely by Roger.

"I've been trying to get you since ten. Where have you been?"

"At home. I crashed out," she apologized.

He eyed her. "Feeling better?"

"Much. Did you want me for anything special?"

"I wanted you to go to Southampton to interview a clairvoyant."

"I'd like that."

168

"It's too late. I've sent Jane."

"Is there anything else I can do?"

He shook his head and she went into her office, wondering how to fill in the day.

The telephone rang and she lifted it up and automatically gave her name.

"I could kill you," Millie said plaintively. "I've been trying to get you for two days but your phone didn't answer. You weren't with Craig, were you?"

"With Craig?" Suzy asked blankly.

"Where else? For goodness sake, Suzy, don't you think you could have rung me and told me how the big scene went?"

Suzy was full of contrition. No wonder Millie was agog to speak to her. Here she was, expecting to hear about the grand reunion, and all she would get was the big letdown.

"Well?" Millie said impatiently. "Is everything patched up between you?"

"I didn't see him."

"*What?* You don't mean you left me and then chickened out? Oh Suzy, you—"

"No, no, I didn't change my mind," Suzy said hurriedly. "I—I did go to see him but Elaine was there. Sh—she . . . He's still having an affair with her, Millie. All the time he's been seeing me and telephoning me, he's still been with Elaine."

"What do you mean by 'all the time'? You've only dated him twice, and the last time you sent him packing!"

"That has nothing to do with it. If I'd meant anything to him, he wouldn't want to make love to another girl."

An angry snort resounded in Suzy's eardrum. "You're talking like a child. No, you're not—I take that back. Children are more realistic than you are. Craig's a virile man and you hurt him. When that happens, it's on the cards that he'll search out the nearest pair of sympathetic arms. Considering he was having an affair with Elaine before he met you, I can't understand why you're so surprised that he went back to her."

169

"I couldn't have meant much to him."

"Haven't you heard a word I said?" Millie exclaimed. "All he did was what *you* did."

"What I did?"

"Sure. Rush back to familiar security and comfort. In your case it was your family. With Craig it was Elaine."

"There's a world of difference between my mother and Elaine," Suzy retorted.

"I know that. But in essence, they both represent the same thing. If you've let Elaine talk you out of seeing him, you're a fool!"

"I've already seen him. He came here yesterday." Suzy paused, then decided her friendship with Millie merited honesty. "I was pretty bloody to him and he stormed off."

"What did you say?"

In a low voice, Suzy told her.

"My God!" Millie was stricken. "How could you? Don't you know what it must have cost him in pride to come and see you yesterday? He didn't know you'd been to see him earlier, and as far as he was concerned, he was making the running for the second time. Craig isn't the type to do that. I'd have thought he wouldn't even come back once. But twice! Oh, Suzy, he must really care for you."

In the face of such impassioned words it was hard to keep unemotional, but Suzy tried.

"It's a funny kind of running, when he keeps going back to Elaine."

"Can't you forget her? Just think of Craig."

"Can you think of bread without butter or bacon without eggs? They go together."

"You and Craig go together! Listen to me, will you? Go and see him and give him a chance to defend himself."

"I don't want a man who puts himself in a position where he has to be on the defensive."

"You don't want a man—period!" Millie snapped. "You're still searching for a paragon."

"Because I believe in old-fashioned virtues? I can't change my outlook and what's more, I don't want to, if you must know."

170

"What makes you so sure his outlook is any different from yours? Because he's played around with girls who want to play around? That doesn't mean he won't change once he falls in love. And that's all he wanted to find out: whether his love for you, and yours for him, would last. Meeting for the odd day or the sunny weekend is not the same thing as traveling on tour with a person. That's when you really get down to basics. I should know. And if the two of you could weather that, then you could weather anything. That was all he wanted to find out," Millie reiterated.

"And why he hared straight back to Elaine when I said no?"

"It was a pretty nasty no. You said so yourself. Anyway, you're making too much of it. Men don't regard sex the way women do."

"Tell me something I don't know!"

"To them, it's like sneezing when they've got an itchy nose!" Millie disregarded Suzy's sarcasm. "It's only when they fall in love that it turns into pneumonia for them, poor muts."

"Poor muts!" Suzy was incredulous. "You make it sound as if love's a death trap for them."

"Well, isn't it? Men are natural born hunters. Given the choice, don't you think they prefer to keep it that way, and roam wild?"

"Craig can roam wherever he likes. The farther from me, the better."

"Unfortunately for him, I'd say he was stuck on *you*. Which means his roaming days are over. But you've got to give him a chance to tell you."

"I gave him all the chance he needed."

"He has to make sure it's the real thing."

"Why are you so concerned about him?" Suzy asked suspiciously.

"I'm concerned about you, not him. I wasted seven years of my life, and I don't want to see someone I like, do the same."

"It won't take me seven years to get over him."

"Do you want to get over him? I thought you loved him."

Suzy sighed. "I do."

"Then listen to me, will you? I'm saying what I believe. He's serious about you, Suzy. If he weren't, he'd have made a pass at you."

"What do you think his travel offer was, if it wasn't a pass?"

"A choice."

Suzy did not answer.

"Don't spoil your life through jealousy," Millie said on a sigh. "After all, you aren't married to him. If you were, and he rushed around to someone else after you quarreled, you'd have reason to be hurt. But you're not even his girl friend. And what's more, you've given him more stick than anyone else. You can't blame him for turning to Elaine."

"It was cheap behavior."

"It was the behavior of a hurt man. A hurt *single* man. That's what you keep forgetting."

Suzy found she was being swayed by Millie's arguments. Maybe there *had* been more jealousy than morality in her reaction. And anyway, what gave her the right to moralize? Take people as they were, had always been her doctrine but, the first chance she had had of putting it to the test, she had failed dismally.

"What are you going to do?" Millie asked.

"Take your advice. I've been so concerned with my own feelings, I haven't given a thought to Craig's."

"Then tell him so. He's playing the finals this afternoon, and if he goes on court and loses, it will be your fault."

"Why?"

"Could you have written the best article of your career fifteen minutes ago?"

"No, but—"

"Then how do you think Craig feels?"

Suzy's defenses cracked completely. If she needed proof of her self-centeredness, she had it now. She glanced at her watch. It was twelve o'clock and play didn't begin on the center court until two. He might still be at the hotel.

"All right, Millie, I'll call him."

172

"Let me know what happens. And don't make me wait two days, huh? Remember it's *my* final tomorrow!"

Laughing, excited, and tentatively dabbling her emotions in the happiness pool, Suzy put down the receiver to clear the line and immediately dialed the Savoy.

Seconds later she was staring at the telephone in dismay. Craig had left for Wimbledon an hour ago. Should she call him there or should she try to see him?

Once again she dialed. This time she was met with polite officialese. Yes, Mr. Dickson was at the club, but he was not taking any calls. No, not even personal ones. No, it didn't matter *how* personal.

"Then can you put me through to Frank Ellman," she pleaded. "His manager."

But that wasn't possible either. Mr. Ellman was with Mr. Dickson and had left word not to be disturbed.

"If you leave your name I will see Mr. Dickson gets the message after his match," the voice at the other end said politely, and Suzy had no recourse but to do as she was told and then call Millie.

"You've got to see Craig before the match," Millie said emphatically. "Come over here and I'll drive you down. If you're with me, you can come to my dressing room, and we'll take it from there!"

"You're an angel!" Suzy slammed down the phone and raced out of the building.

Time was moving inexorably on and she knew it would be one-thirty before they reached Wimbledon. But that should still give her long enough to make her peace with Craig. It would mean confessing all her fears about him; her insecurity regarding their relationship and the future. But pride, which had kept her silent till now, was a very poor bedfellow. Unlike Craig, she already knew *how* poor.

Leaving her car in the parking lot, she flagged down a taxi and perched on the edge of the seat as they made the usual lunchtime crawl to the Savoy. Millie was waiting beside a limousine parked near the entrance, and Suzy flung a pound note at the taxi driver and dashed over to her.

"Put your foot on the gas, Charlie," Millie told the chauffeur. "If you get fined for speeding, I'll pay it."

"I could get my license endorsed," the man replied. "Or have it taken away. I'm sorry, Miss Queen, I'd like to oblige but . . ."

"Forget it. I understand."

At first they made excellent time and within fifteen minutes had Putney Bridge behind them and Wimbledon a short distance away. They should reach the tennis courts with plenty of time to spare.

But a mile from the grounds they hit a traffic snarl and, for the rest of the journey, moved at a snail's pace. It was a quarter to two when they reached the stadium and it was here that Suzy began to appreciate the value of Millie's help.

Recognizing the tennis champion, the usual security check was waived, and the limousine purred down the private road to the main grandstand. Crowds were already thronging the entrance but Millie dashed for the steps as if she were competing in the 100-meters Olympic. With Suzy breathlessly following, they raced along corridors and up and down concrete steps until they reached a narrow white door.

"You're on your own from here," the girl panted, and stepped to one side.

Suzy knocked on the door. There was no answer.

"He can't be here," she whispered.

"He must be." Millie's hand was raised to knock when a loud burst of clapping came from outside, proclaiming that the two men finalists had walked out onto the center court.

"We're too late." Suzy was almost in tears. "Oh, Millie, if Craig loses this match I'll never forgive myself."

"Let's go to the players' box." Millie grabbed her arm. "If we can attract Craig's attention during the warm-up, he'll guess you've come here to let him know you didn't mean what you said to him."

When they reached the players' box it was already packed, for it was the rare professional who tired of watch-

174

ing Craig play. But a space was immediately made for them, though it was some distance away from where Craig's manager was sitting.

"Even if Craig looks up, he won't see me," Suzy said distractedly. "He'll be looking at Frank."

"We'll make him see you," Millie said firmly. "The minute he lifts his head in this direction, stand up and wave."

Suzy nodded, not taking her eyes from the court where Craig and his opponent were steadily hitting tennis balls over the net. At least Craig's opponent was doing so, but Craig was consistently mis-hitting.

Look at me, Craig, she whispered silently. Lift your head and look at me.

But he went on hitting into the net, and as she watched, he tucked his racket under his arm and walked over to the umpire's chair. He rummaged beneath it and came back on court with another racket.

Look at me, Suzy willed, but her plea still went unheeded and the man below continued to serve into the net.

"One minute to play, gentlemen," the umpire said and the two players acknowledged his call. But neither of them looked in the direction of the players' box.

"He hasn't seen me," Suzy whispered. "If he loses . . ."

"Don't think that way," Millie said vehemently. "He'll win. He's the better player."

"Commence play, gentlemen." It was the umpire. The crowd quietened instantly and the match began.

Even afterward Suzy found it impossible to remember the game clearly. All she could bring to mind was the electric atmosphere of the court and the demonic power that Craig exuded. Not for nothing was he called the tennis robot, and watching him today, the nickname seemed an understatement. He commanded the court with a precision that was inhuman. She had thought she had seen him play brilliantly in the Italian Open, but it was nothing compared with the way he was playing now. This was power tennis at its most powerful; not a stroke was missed, not a point lost.

Craig's opponent, a young and versatile Dane, played

175

with the skill that had made him the number two seed, but he might as well have played with his feet for all the impact he was making against Craig. The almost unbelievable serves were returned with an ease that was almost derisory; while Craig gave spin to every one of his own and served so many aces that the crowd only murmured when he didn't.

Desperately the Dane changed his tactics, slowing down his game in the hope that a change of pace might spoil Craig's rhythm. But nothing made any difference. Craig took point after point. He was not only a robot but a computer: able to out-hit and out-think his opponent in every way: lobbing when he was expected to play down the line; making passing shots when drop shots were anticipated. There was nothing the Dane could do right, and nothing Craig could do wrong.

"No one can beat him today," Millie breathed. "I've never seen him play like this."

The words tolled the death of Suzy's hopes. Craig was not playing like a man with shattered confidence. Here was a man for whom the word "confidence" was as meaningless as it would be to a machine. For that's what he was: a machine. She had been a fool to think he was a flesh-and-blood person with the ability to care enough to be hurt.

A burst of clapping told her that Craig had won the first set six love. He walked over to his seat but did not sit down. Instead he swallowed some salt tablets and returned to his place by the net, ready to play the moment the umpire gave the call. It was an astonishing show of nerve. Look at me, he seemed to be saying. I'm as fresh as when I started and I'll be as fresh as this when the match is over. There was a murmur from the crowd; some of them considered his behavior arrogant, but all went quiet as the second set commenced.

If the first had been astonishing, this one was mesmeric. Craig smashed ball after ball across the court, his serve unanswerable. Valiantly his opponent fought back but he was helpless in the face of such an onslaught. Though he rallied to win two games, he lost the set in four straight games thereafter. By now the crowd knew they were watching a match that would go down in the tennis records, and there was hushed expectancy in the air. Every professional who was not engaged in playing their own game had crowded in to watch this one, and Suzy heard the whirring sound of cameras as newsmen prepared to film what they knew was going to be an historic final.

"No one has ever won three straights sets against Johannsen," Millie breathed. "If Craig does it, he'll set a record. Aren't you proud of him?"

"I don't feel I'm watching a man play," Suzy said helplessly. "It's almost as if he's been programmed to win."

Millie looked puzzled, but before she could question the remark, the third set was already under way. With quiet desperation Suzy watched Craig for a sign of hesitation, hoping that the comment she had made to Millie would prove to be unjustified. But it wasn't. This set was more merciless than the first two. Three nil in Craig's favor. Four nil. Then five and finally it was the last game.

No sound came from the crowd and only the drone of an airplane, high up in the blue sky, and the thwack of the tennis ball on grass broke the silence. Craig was due to serve and he did so with a speed that almost made the ball invisible. It fell dead at Johannsen's feet. The Dane looked at it and gave a philosophic shrug which Craig acknowledged by a slight lift of his racket. The second serve did the same and so did the third.

All at once it was match point and Suzy kept her eyes on the tall, lithe figure of the man she loved. She knew she was watching the birth of another victory and the death of her own hopes. A man who could play like this was not a man nursing a broken heart. Craig raised his arm. The ball rose high, the racket thwacked it and it was all over.

The crowd rose to its feet and cheered.

"Wasn't it sensational?" Millie exclaimed. "I've never seen a match like it."

Craig and Johannsen were moving to the side of the court where photographers' bulbs were already flashing. In the distance a carpet was being unrolled on the turf and the ball boys were assembling in a double line to await the arrival of the "Royal" who would present the champion and the runner-up with their trophies.

"Jeez, I bet you're feeling relieved," Millie said. "We'll go to Craig's dressing room as soon as the presentation's over."

"Not me," Suzy replied. "I don't want to see him."

"Of course you do. That's why you came here. Nothing's changed." The dark eyes roamed Suzy's set expression. "What's wrong with you? Aren't you pleased he's won?"

"Oh, sure. It proves that nothing is more important to him than tennis! If he can quarrel with me and then play like this . . ."

"He has great concentration." Millie looked bewildered. "We all know that. That's part of the reason for his success."

"It was more than concentration today," Suzy persisted. "It was total dedication. All he cares about is his career. Tennis is the real love of his life and no girl will ever match up to it."

"What's got into you, Suzy? Did you want him to lose?"

"You know I didn't. I only wish he hadn't won quite so convincingly. Be honest about it, Millie. Weren't you surprised by the way he played? You said yourself you were scared that my row with him would affect him on court. Yet he played the match of his life."

"That just shows he's got guts."

"It's more than guts. It's a blind obsession with winning. Me, Elaine, anyone else who comes into his life will only be secondary, and that's something I couldn't cope with. I'm just glad I found out before it was too late. When I marry, I don't want to come second to a tennis ball!"

Pushing her way through the crowd, Suzy headed for the exit. She heard Millie call her but she refused to turn, and it was only when the girl caught up with her halfway down the steps outside the players' box, that she was forced to stop.

"You don't mean what you've said," Millie pleaded. "You're overwrought."

178

"I meant every word. Craig doesn't need me—not the way I want to be needed. If Elaine's willing to take him on his own terms, she's welcome to him." Suzy held out her hand. "I'll say good-bye to you here, Millie. I won't come to the dance tomorrow night."

"You're wrong." Millie refused to take her hand. "At least give Craig a chance to talk to you again. His whole life's been committed to tennis. Once he's had time to adjust to you, he'll . . ."

"Change?" Suzy finished for her. "Don't try to make me believe that. If you marry someone on the premise that you'll be able to change them, you're heading for the divorce court."

"It isn't a question of changing someone. It's more like helping them to widen their horizons."

Suzy shook her head. It was impossible to make Millie understand how she felt. All she could do was to repeat what she had said.

"Please," Millie begged. "If you won't see him now, come to the dance tomorrow."

"No. It's over. I don't want to see him again." Suzy started to walk. The crowd had thinned, and progress was easier.

"You're so damned obstinate," Millie muttered, still keeping pace with her. "I wish I knew what else to say."

"How about good-bye? You'll be leaving England on Sunday and . . ."

"I've no intention of losing touch with you," Millie protested. "You're the only female I've ever been able to talk to. I won't let you walk out of my life, too. Unless you don't want to see me?"

There was unusual uncertainty in Millie's voice, and Suzy reacted to it.

"Of course I want to see you! But only if you promise not to mention Craig."

"By the end of the year I won't be talking tennis at all. I'm getting married, remember?"

"And starting to run a tennis ranch, remember? You'll

179

always think like a pro, Millie. You'll follow the game as if you were still playing. Tennis is in your blood, the way it is in Craig's."

"You mentioned him first." Millie was triumphant. "I didn't!"

Suzy nodded and continued walking.

"I still want you to be bridesmaid at my wedding," Millie said behind her.

"Australia's so far."

"I'll send you the ticket. You promised to come. I won't get married unless you're there."

"Don will have something to say about that." Suzy forced a smile. It was not very successful but it did something to lessen the gloom on Millie's face.

"If ever I can help you in any way," Millie said, "you only have to ask."

"I know." Suzy touched her hand. "And I won't forget."

"Yes you will," Millie said with unexpected insight. "You'll want to forget Craig and me and every damn person connected with the game. Oh Suzy, I wish . . ."

But Suzy did not wait to hear. With a murmur, she turned and ran.

XI

Work was Suzy's passport to forgetfulness throughout June and July.

She gave in her notice at the *Sunday Digest*. Bill received it with pleasure on behalf of his wife and displeasure on his own account, and Roger received it with annoyance.

"At least wait until you've found yourself a publisher," Roger said. "What will you do if you can't, come back with your tail between your legs?"

"When his Lordship is only too eager to have me work on his daily?"

"Even that would be better for you than to give up completely. Writers shouldn't just stay home and write. It's important to see people and to have contact with the outside world."

"I'm not going to a monastery in Tibet!" she joked. "I'll be right around the corner from you, pounding my typewriter in Bayswater."

Roger went on arguing but Suzy took no notice. No one's opinion mattered to her. Only the book was important. Somehow it had magnified itself into the most important part of her life; her *raison d'être,* and she settled down to complete it.

She was awash with words. Even when she was asleep she remained unrelaxed, her mind continually going over everything she had written and everything she still wanted to write. It was like being tied down in front of a recorder that could never be switched off.

In the past she had written best by remaining detached from her subject. But with the book it was the exact opposite. The more involved she became with her characters, the easier she found it to understand their motivations. They were no longer creatures of her own mind but independent people with their own thoughts; their own way of doing things, their own lives.

At the beginning of August she gave the finished manuscript to Anne, feeling herself to be the go-between rather than the author.

"If you don't like it, you must give me your word that you'll tell me," she pleaded. "I'm used to taking Bill's criticism, so I can promise you I won't burst into tears if you think this stinks."

"I'm delighted you are so full of confidence. It immediately makes an agent feel she's discovered a winner!"

"All I'm saying is that I want you to be honest with me."

"Honesty is my stock-in-trade! If I think you've been wasting your time, I'll tell you. I swear it. If only to make sure you go back to the *Digest* and stop Bill from blaming me because you left!" Anne glanced at the bulky manuscript and opened the first page. "*Tennis Ball Heart.* Hmm, I like that. If the story is no good, we can always sell the title!" She raised her eyes, saw Suzy's expression and grinned. "I knew that would get to you!"

"Am I so obvious?"

"Not more so than most new authors. They're either convinced they've written a masterpiece or positive they haven't. Either way it's always a cover-up for their fear."

"I'm not scared. If this one's turned down, I won't write another."

"I've heard that before, too. Leave it with me, Suzy

182

ove. I'll let you know when we get our first dozen rejection slips!"

Five days later Anne took her to lunch and told her that Hammond Ellison wished to publish her book.

"Ellison and Jay?" Suzy was not sure she had heard correctly. They were an ultra avant-garde house with an excellent reputation for discovering new talent.

"Better than that, my lovely," Anne replied. "The eminent one himself. With Hammond bullish for it, we're on to a winner."

"I can't believe it. I'd only thought in terms of a paperback."

"That'll come later. It will go as a hardback first. This won't be a quick potboiler, Suzy. This is going to be a prestige best-seller. And Hammond is the best seller I know."

"Are you sure?"

"Of course, I'm sure. He's—"

"I wasn't referring to Mr. Ellison. I meant the book. It's a readable story but I wouldn't put it in the best-seller league."

"You won't need to," Anne said dryly. "Others will do it for you."

Suzy looked at her hors d'oeuvres but found her appetite had been washed away by excitement. This couldn't be happening to her. Anne was exaggerating in order to make her feel good. How could anyone tell if a book was going to be a success? It did not make sense. And anyway, it hadn't been hard enough to write. There had been no sweat to it. Tears in plenty, of course, but they had been for Craig.

She picked up her fork. "I hope Mr. Ellison knows what he's doing."

"If you say that when you meet him, I'll throttle you!"

Suzy half smiled. "Perhaps I'll have gained a bit more confidence by then."

"I hope so." Anne peered down at her wristwatch. "You've got an hour and a half to work on it."

"You mean—"

183

"That's right. As soon as we've finished lunch, I've arranged to take you to his office. He's interested in meeting you."

"When do you think he'll publish the book?"

"As soon as he can. But we've got to agree to terms first. So curb your enthusiasm for his famous publishing house when you see him. If he doesn't give me the advance I want, we'll go somewhere else."

"Wouldn't it be better if I didn't meet him until you've come to some arrangement?"

"No. I want him to see you. If Hammond likes *you* as much as he liked your book, he'll supervise the publicity campaign himself. And if he does, we'll have it made. No one knows that side of the business better than he does. But like I said, he has to offer the right terms."

Anne named an advance that was double the salary Suzy had earned in a year.

"He'll never pay that," she protested. "Anyway, if I get a good royalty, I don't care about the advance."

"Heaven spare me from stupid authors!" Anne lifted her eyes skyward. "The bigger the advance you get, the more sure you can be that your publisher will put his back into selling the book. Not that we need worry about Hammond. If he likes it enough to publish it, I'm sure he will use his big guns to promote it."

"Then the advance won't matter." Suzy saw Anne's expression and said defensively: "You've just said so yourself. You said if Mr. Ellison . . ."

"I know what I said. But do me a favor, will you? When you meet him, just play the dumb blonde and leave all the discussion to me."

"You're the boss."

Suzy made a pretense of eating but the knowledge that she would be meeting the man who liked her book sufficiently to back it with hard cash, had put painful knots in her stomach.

"What's Hammond Ellison like?" she asked.

"Highly civilized, highly polished and highly intelligent."

184

Suzy's nervousness increased. "And he likes *Tennis Ball Heart?*"

"I said he was intelligent, didn't I? Which reminds me, he thinks the title's great, too." Anne beamed. "Nobody can recognize a blank, signed check better than our Hammond. And he's clever enough to fill in masses of noughts, too!"

"You're scaring me to death. If he's half as bright as you make him sound . . ."

"He's more so. Bright and *interesting*. He has a superb Nash house in Regent's Park, a gem of a place in Wiltshire and no wife. That's the interesting bit!"

"Or the brightest. He sounds the sort of man who can manage very well on his own."

Suzy's opinion was reinforced when she entered the marble-floored mansion off St. James's which housed the offices of Ellison and Jay.

A comely young woman led them up close-carpeted stairs to the first floor where another secretary, equally as comely, was waiting to take them into a large, book-lined room whose windows opened onto a wrought-iron balcony blooming with plants.

They also overflowed into the room, and where there were no books, there was greenery. Only the magnificent Sheraton writing table was devoid of either. This was graced instead by an antique silver inkstand, as spare and elegant as the man who rose from behind it to come forward to greet them.

"I can see I owe Anne an apology." He took hold of Suzy's hand and gave her a charming smile which included the older woman. "She said you were beautiful and I thought she was exaggerating."

He seated them both in front of his desk, in identical armchairs of velvet-and-gilt wood, and then resumed his own chair.

He was different from the way Suzy had pictured him. Younger—in his early forties and not fifties—with a smooth, pale face below smooth gray hair. His voice was smooth, too: saved from dullness by the wryly humorous

185

tone that edged it; as if he knew something amusing that he was not sure whether to share with you. Had she met him without knowing who he was, she would have guessed him to be a banker or a Harley Street specialist. Had she been told he was a publisher, she would have assumed it to be of expensive art books of the most esoteric kind.

Aware that she was staring at him, and that he knew it, she averted her eyes to his desk. Her manuscript lay there, almost hidden by the silver inkstand.

Following her gaze, he tapped it with his index finger.

"This book will be a best-seller, Miss Bedford. It is a word I do not use lightly, as Anne will tell you." His eyebrows, several shades darker than his hair, and seeming to be the most definite thing about him, met above his long, thin nose. "In fact, I am prepared to say that with the proper marketing, it could well be *the* best-seller of the year. My marketing," he added, without giving any extra weight to the words, so that for an instant Suzy found herself waiting for him to continue, before she realized he had finished.

"This is only an exploratory meeting, Hammond," Anne said before Suzy could make any comment. "I wanted the two of you to meet to make sure you liked each other. I'm a great believer in empathy, as you know."

"Indeed I do. And I'm sure Miss Bedford and I are most empathetic toward each other!"

Suzy laughed, then recollected Anne's injunction to emulate one of the three wise monkeys.

"I can come in tomorrow and talk to you about the contract," Anne went on, refusing to be sidetracked.

"That won't be necessary. We can settle it all now."

He stated a royalty percentage and an advance that took Suzy's breath away.

"That's not bad," Anne said dubiously, "but—"

"It's as high as I'm prepared to go," he intervened. "And far higher than you were going to ask for." He gave Anne the first genuine smile of the meeting. "Stop looking like one of the Valkyrie and go back to being your usual sweet self!" He allowed his amusement to encompass Suzy. "Anne
186

is the best agent in the country—if you didn't know that already—and I am the best publisher. So between us, you can see you will be in excellent hands."

"Certainly confident ones."

"That is a prerequisite of the publishing business!"

She smiled. "When do you hope to bring out my book?"

"In time for the Christmas market."

Anne gave a whistle. "That's cutting it fine. Will you have enough time?"

"No," he said. "But then we never do!" He spoke to Suzy again. "We will have to work fast, which is the way I like it. Then no one has a chance to get stale. If need be, we can print in Holland. We've just bought into a printing company there." He leaned further back in his chair and pressed the tips of his fingers together. It was a pontifical gesture but in no way made him look it. "We would obviously require an option on your next book."

"Of course."

"Not so fast, Hammond," Anne said. "You've bullied us quite enough for one afternoon. I'll talk to you about options another day, on our own. Suzy gets embarrassed to hear me talk money."

Hammond Ellison favored Suzy with another of his direct stares. "You don't look the easily embarrassed type. And far too intelligent ever to be that way over a subject as absorbing as money!"

"You're right," Suzy said, feeling Anne had made her look enough of an idiot. "If one has something to sell, it's one's moral obligation to get the best price for it."

"Moral?"

"The right thing to do. For oneself as well as for others. I'm a great believer in charity beginning at home!"

He chuckled, and still had a curve to his mouth as he escorted them to the door, coming down the stairs with them and standing at the entrance until they had walked several yards away from him.

"Aren't you thrilled, Suzy?" Anne practically danced over the pavement. "You must come and have dinner with us tonight. I'll get Bill to take us out somewhere."

"It would be more in order for *me* to take *you* out," Suzy giggled, drunk on expectation. "After all, I'm the one getting the advance! I nearly had a fit when he said how much."

"So did I. But Hammond likes to display largesse, and you obviously brought out the gentleman bountiful in him! He was very taken with you, Miss Bedford. I guarantee you'll be hearing from him."

"I should hope so." Suzy feigned innocence. "He'll be investing a lot of money in me."

"I didn't mean for that reason, violet eyes! Didn't you notice the way his nostrils flared when he saw you. Like a wolf scenting game!" Anne regarded her speculatively. "It will do you good to go out with a man like Hammond."

"But will it do *him* good?"

"Only you can answer that! But seriously, you haven't had any social life for months. You should start seeing people again."

"You can't socialize and write. It's one or the other."

"Compromise. All work and no play will turn you into a depressive."

"There's no danger of that. I just enjoy being on my own. It's a phase I'm going through."

They walked in silence for a few minutes.

"The book was written from the heart, wasn't it." Anne made it a statement rather than a question, but Suzy was not quite prepared to let it go at that.

"An author should always believe that—about her first book anyway."

"That's a cute answer, Suzy. Stick with it. You're going to be asked that same question a thousand times in the next year." Anne hesitated. "*Has* the book served its purpose or are you still in love with him?"

Suzy had too much respect for Anne's acumen to lie. "It's fading," she said carefully. "But it . . . Oh hell, yes. I'm afraid I still am."

"Then you should start to think about your next book. Work and play; that's the best therapy."

Intellectually Suzy knew Anne was right. But unhappily

188

facts had proved her wrong. She had almost worked herself into a frazzle writing *Tennis Ball Heart* and she was no nearer to forgetting Craig today than she had been three months ago. Each time she saw his name in a newspaper, her longing for him was as intense as it had always been.

He had been playing badly this past month and had lost several big matches, which had made her wonder if his private life could be catching up with his professional one. The thought had sharpened her jealousy and had given his image fresh life. So much so that she had felt he was watching her and that she had only to turn around sharply to encounter him beside her.

"Hammond was quite serious when he said he wants an option on your next book, Suzy." Anne was the agent now; no longer the friend. "And he'll want it within a year."

"No sweat about that," Suzy lied.

"Good." Anne did not sound convinced. "Second books are notoriously more tricky to do than first ones."

"You're a great help."

"I try to be. That's why I like facing facts. And fact number one is, do you have another plot lined up?"

"No."

"Then think of one. You've got to deliver the second book while the first one is still warm in people's minds." Anne walked on, then slowed. "Strike while the iron is hot, Suzy."

"I think that's such an original platitude!"

"You'll agree with me once you start seeing your royalty checks."

"I didn't write my book for the money regardless of what I said to Mr. Ellison." Suzy frowned. "How bloody pious I sound. I take that back. Of course I'm interested in the money I can earn as a writer, but I wasn't thinking of that when I wrote *Tennis Ball Heart*. I *had* to get that story out of my system, even if I'd thrown the book into the trash can once it was done."

"I know that, my dear. That's why I said you might have more of a problem with book number two. You can't wait

189

until you have another Craig Dickson to exorcise."

"Heaven forbid. I never want to go through that experience again."

They paused by some traffic lights and Suzy knew she had to face the fear from which she had been running for the past two weeks.

"Be honest with me, Anne. Do you think I have the ability to write a second novel? I didn't write this one, you know. It wrote *me*."

"Of course you've got the ability. You don't really think you wrote your book with hurt pride and a broken heart, do you? They only gave you the impetus. The determination and the effort came from within you."

"But saying I don't get another impetus?"

"That's where the royalty checks come in!"

Suzy smiled, though she was not convinced. Yet it would not help her to worry over the situation. She had brought her fear into the open and she must wait to see if it disappeared. The Muse could not be forced. Or could it?

She asked herself this question many times in the next few weeks and, no nearer to finding the answer, posed it to Roger when he took her to dinner in the middle of August; her first evening out with a man since the day of the Wimbledon Final.

"Writing is a habit," he assured her, without pausing to give it thought. "Think of it as a muscle that has to be used every day. The longer it lies dormant, the more slack it becomes. Sit at your desk every day and write write write. If rubbish comes out, tear it up and begin again the next day. Eventually a plot will come."

"What do I do if it doesn't?"

"Return to the *Sunday Digest*."

"Never."

He laughed. "There's your answer then. You'll write your magnum opus *secundus*, Suzy. I swear it!"

Cheered by Roger's words, Suzy heeded them. But they did not produce results, unless one counted an overflowing wastepaper basket. She toyed with the idea of returning to the *Digest*—even though she had told Roger she

190

wouldn't—but knew that were she to do so, she would not be able to throw herself wholeheartedly into her work. Like it or not, she was now an author, and must learn to regard the wasteland of her days as a gestation period that would end when labor pains began.

It was not the most apt simile she could have used, she decided ruefully one morning, more than a week later, as she surveyed yet another overflowing basket of rubbish. It seemed she was already having the labor—and lots of it— with nothing worthwhile emerging!

She was still pondering on this unhappy situation when Hammond Ellison asked her to have dinner with him.

For the first couple of weeks after meeting him, she had expected him to call, indoctrinated by Anne's belief that he would do so. When he didn't, she had been vaguely disappointed, but had soon forgotten him, more concerned to pick up the threads of her own social life with her contemporaries than to wonder about a man old enough to be her father.

But seeing him again, tall and distinguished outside her front door, she remembered her earlier expectancy, and felt unusually shy. She could imagine him with soigné women whose emotions were like froth on a soufflé: nice while it lasted but in no way sustaining.

Anxious to impress, she had dressed the part she felt he would like her to play. She knew she was not capable of sustaining it for long, but was well-pleased with the admiration in his eyes as they appraised her. A young claret but with a good body and a promise of more to come if allowed to mature properly, was what he must be thinking. She hid a smile. At this moment he was surprisingly easy to read. The knowledge that she could do so gave her confidence and made her smile more broadly still.

"May I share the joke?"

"I was thinking of myself as a wine and wondering how you would describe me."

"I think you have already decided that." His voice was dry.

"I'd still like to know if I was right."

191

She waited for him to speak, standing gracefully against the stairway. It was a good place to stand. The Wedgewood-green walls went well with the subtle tobacco brown of her dress, and acted as a foil for her guinea-gold hair, worn away from her face to make her look older.

"Champagne," he murmured, immediately proving her wrong. "You have too much depth to be a white wine and too much effervescence to be a red. So champagne, I think. Yes, definitely. Premier Cru—that goes without saying—and a Louis Roderer. They're inclined to be extra heady."

She laughed, as flattered as she knew he had meant her to be.

The evening progressed in the same way. He took her to an unpretentious restaurant on the outskirts of Dulwich, where the food was superb. He had ordered their dinner in advance and there was nothing for her to do except enjoy it, which she did, though she could not help asking him what he would have done if she had not liked this choice.

"Given you the menu," he smiled. "This is a restaurant, after all. But not many of my guests object to my selection."

"I suppose they'd have to be insentient before they did so! And who would admit to that!" She looked at the caviar blinis in front of her and thought of the baby duckling to follow. Hammond was right. No one would object to such a choice.

"Are you always a good judge of what people want?" she asked, then thought of his success in publishing and could have kicked herself hard.

"Only of what the people I like would want," he replied. "I am taking your question personally, and not as a business one. But on the question of food, I quite often entertain at home, and then my guests have a choice, the way they do here." One eyebrow lifted as he saw her unspoken question. "I would have taken you to my home tonight, Suzy, except that I did not want you to feel I was pressuring you."

"What makes you think I would have felt it?"

"If you don't know, then I'll plead the Fifth Amendment."

192

"You can't. You're not an American."

"My mother was."

"I'd never have guessed. You seem so English."

"I'm sure you mean that as a compliment!" He smiled. "But I lived in America, in Philadelphia actually, from the time I was five until I was fifteen. Then my mother died and I returned to live with my father."

"Was he a publisher too?"

"Yes. This was his firm. It was called Ellison's in those days."

"Is there a Mr. Jay?"

"No. It was my mother's maiden name. I incorporated it into the firm a month after my father died."

Suzy digested this piece of information along with her caviar. She sensed Hammond was waiting for her to make some comment but could not think of any that were flattering. Finally she settled for a diplomatic one.

"Was it because you felt your father had treated your mother badly? Adding her name to the firm, once it became yours, is the sort of symbolic gesture a young man would make."

"It had nothing to do with symbolism. My mother left my father for a man ten years her junior. He was completely justified to divorce her."

"Then why—"

"She used her own personal money to help the firm through a difficult patch. It was in the first year of their marriage. My father promised her he would add her name to the company as a thank-you gesture. She left him before he could do so." Hammond dabbed at his mouth with a napkin. "Once that happened, he felt it dissolved his promise. I didn't. It was as simple as that."

Suzy nodded. Simple it wasn't. Nor was Hammond. Now what sort of wine was *he* like? Neither red nor white nor even champagne. She thought about it, then knew. Vodka. Colorless, odorless, but with a kick like a mule.

"I always keep my word," he said, continuing the conversation. "And I like others to do the same."

193

"You must get frequently disillusioned."

He shook his head. "For that to happen, one must first have illusions."

She laughed. "*What* a clever dinner party conversation we're having!"

"Baked Alaska talk. It sounds more high-falutin' than it is!"

She laughed again. "So let's have rice pudding instead. That's very nutritious and sustaining."

"That sounds as if you're going to make some important statements."

"Not statements." She shook back her hair, forgetting it was not loose. "Questions though, if you don't object to answering them?"

"Not if you won't object to answering mine."

Given the freedom to unveil her curiosity, she was reluctant to do so. As if aware of this, he poured some more wine for her.

"Dutch courage, Suzy. I swear I won't bite you if you show yourself to be a curious little girl."

"I'm a curious big one. How is it that you are still unmarried?"

"What a dangerous question to ask these days!"

"Oh God!" Scarlet bloomed in her face. "I—I never . . ."

"Don't worry. I'm not." Having discomfited her, he looked pleased with himself. "I felt that marriage would curtail my ambitions."

"It's usually the other way around."

"That depends on the work one is doing. I travel a lot; I need to mix with many people and to keep long hours. A wife would feel unloved."

"Not if she had the mink and diamonds!"

"I wouldn't want that kind of wife. And the wife I would like . . . I think I am too selfish to make a good husband. I am single-minded and have always employed it in one channel—my publishing house. One has to work at success. If it comes by accident, you still have to work to retain it."

The conversation reminded her too much of what Craig

had once said, and she sought for a way to change it. Even as she did, she knew it was wrong to run away. She could not spend the rest of her life avoiding things because they brought back unhappy memories. It only encouraged them to keep pace with her. Bring out the memories and air them. That was the best thing to do. Like mites, they would die in the sunshine.

"You could always marry a woman publisher," she said aloud. "Then you could share your work."

"I hate competition."

"I'm sure you thrive on it."

"Not in a marriage. It wouldn't be conducive to contentment."

Suzy spread her hands. "I give in. I think you're probably very wise to stay single."

"I still see some doubt in those words."

"Only because I'm wondering if you will always feel the same." Head on one side she regarded him, unaware how beguiling was the curve of her slender throat. "Don't you ever get lonely?"

His laugh was too uninhibited not to be real.

"My dear Suzy. With all the friends I have? Anyway, loneliness is for the young and the unsuccessful old. If you enjoy your work, and it is also your pleasure, you are never lonely."

"I don't agree. Absolutely not. I enjoy *my* work. I love it, in fact, but it could never compensate me for a family."

"Then why are you still unmarried?"

"I'm only twenty-three. The word 'still' hardly applies."

"How right. I apologize. But you're so delectable—as we've just enjoyed such an excellent meal I hope you will forgive me for putting it in those terms—that I am astonished no man has succeeded in making you his."

"I intend to simmer a little longer, thanks."

"Is there no one special in your life?"

"No."

She saw the look he gave her and knew that her answer had been too quick. His next question proved her right.

195

"Has there been anyone special in the past?"

"Well, naturally." She was drawling and amused, the way she would have liked to be inside. "I'm not a baby, Hammond. I haven't lived in a vacuum. But there was no one who lasted. They all petered out to nothing. I suppose that one day it won't."

"I'm glad you still believe that. I would hate you to become a cynic."

"Like Jill in my book?" Suzy grasped the nettle. "Don't tell me you also think it was autobiographical? Really, Hammond, you should know better."

"I will, when I see book number two."

She pretended not to understand what he meant, and took the comment at face value.

"I haven't even started it yet."

"What's it about?"

"Nothing. I haven't an idea in my head. And if that sounds airy-fairy and as if I don't care, you couldn't be more wrong. I'm worried sick. I'd hate to be a one-book writer."

"Don't be silly, my dear. You're a born storyteller. And I'm not using that word the way my old nanny did! But if you're having trouble finding a plot, then let your mind lie fallow for a bit. You'll come up with something sooner or later."

"Saying it's later? It took me twenty-three years to find *Tennis Ball Heart*."

"Remember what Aspasia said to the acolyte: it's always difficult the first time!"

Suzy giggled. "I think I'll have it stitched into a sampler and hung over my desk."

"I meant it seriously, Suzy. Stop worrying about a plot. You're only having a problem with it because you're tired. You're an emotional writer as much as a cerebral one, and as soon as you are physically relaxed, you will find something you care about. That's when the old brain cells will start up again."

"I hope you are right. At this moment I feel as if they've all coagulated."

He paused while their plates were changed.

"I enjoyed your biography of Millie Queen. Anne sent me the cuttings from the paper."

"I enjoyed writing the articles. Bill wanted me to do it as a book, but I didn't feel I knew enough about her. In an article you say much less."

"I thought you said everything. You made her sound quite intelligent."

"She is. Fools don't become champions. You need more than strength and good eyes to play well. It's a tactical game."

"I stand corrected." He raised his glass to her. "I hope you won't need another newspaper assignment to give you your next plot."

She kept her face blank. Was this Hammond's way of telling her he still thought her novel was a testament to her personal life? He was such a devious man, it was difficult to know when he was being one.

"Maybe I'm the sort of writer who works best from a factual basis," she said.

"Then I'd better start scouring the papers for you."

She nodded, glad he had taken her at her word. Perhaps she should try to think of her encounter with Craig as a fact. An unhappy one, it was true, but a fact, and not an emotion. She must be grateful to him for supplying her with all the facts she had needed to write her first novel.

She tried to be grateful and failed. All she wanted to do was to cry.

"I'd like my next book to be humorous," she said.

"It's your choice. As I said earlier, plotless is a condition that will cure itself. Being witless would be far more of a problem for me to deal with!"

She laughed. "You have a marvelous knack of making me feel good."

"I can do better still. Think of your first hundred thousand."

"You're going to print so many?"

"Pounds, Suzy dear. I'm talking of money."

This was too much even for disbelief, and her face showed it.

"It's true," he said. "I may even be underestimating. You've written a best-seller. I told you that the first day we met."

"How can you be so sure?"

He tapped his nose. "This always tells me."

"Maybe I should retire and live on my laurels?"

"Over my dead body. You're a winner, Suzy. That's why you appealed to me. There are other reasons, too, but I don't think you are ready to hear them."

Before she had a chance to look curious, he started to talk about the last big book he had published. She was glad he did not pursue the topic in which he had clearly stated his interest. Me, Suzy thought, and wondered if Hammond always imagined himself in love with the young female authors he was currently promoting. If so, and bearing in mind how successful his company was, he must have a very strong libido.

But it would not do him any good where she was concerned. One day, hopefully, she would pick up the threads of her life and weave them into a pattern. But not yet.

Lie fallow, Hammond had suggested she do with her mind, and lie fallow she would; in every way.

XII

Despite Suzy's determination to keep herself emotionally aloof from Hammond, she found that association alone brought them closer.

In a strange way their age gap made it easier for her to relate to him. She saw him as an old friend—a surrogate father even—yet one who had the advantage of understanding everything she was trying to say. And how skillfully he encouraged her to say it. Her evenings with him became long monologues of self-discovery; each one uncovering another layer of her mind, until she wondered what would happen when there were no more layers to peel away.

He laughed when she said as much. "The human psyche is a self-perpetuating onion. The layers can never be peeled away. As one is uncovered, another one forms."

She was charmed by the description. It made her seem a constant source of interest. She almost told him so, until she realized her reaction was exactly the one he wanted. Damn him, Hammond Clever Pants Ellison. She was responding to him like putty in the hands of a glazier.

The knowledge did not displease her. After all, the best

way to forget one man was with another. And there were now whole days when she did not think of Craig; when she was convinced she had forgotten him. But then there were other days. Black ones in which vivid images of him played themselves out in front of her eyes: his mischievous pleasure when he had dropped her in the pool and his agonized remorse soon after; the childlike way he had fallen asleep on the hammock, and the not so childlike kisses they had shared soon after; the determined manner in which he had beaten Martelli at the stadium and the ice-cold precision with which he had pounded his way to his fourth Wimbledon Championship.

Wimbledon. Her Armageddon.

With relief she allowed Hammond to take over every aspect of her life. She knew the situation could not last—that one day he would want their relationship to change—but for the moment she clutched at it like a greedy child with a bag of sweets. Sugar was addictive, like smoking or drinking coffee, and if she were with Hammond often enough, she might become addicted, too.

He displayed a solicitude toward her that no man of her own generation would have done. She liked it; and that she could accept it without feeling any qualms of feminism, surprised her. But then Hammond had a way of making all causes, whatever they espoused, seem crude and unnecessary.

"When the time is right," he was fond of saying, "the problem will go; one doesn't need to wave a flag or drive a tank. All you need do is wait."

"Political prisoners want their freedom now!"

"The young are so impatient."

"And you aren't?"

"Of course not."

He would immediately disprove this by a burst of activity that would result in TV or press coverage for the book he was quietly and personally promoting. Yes, Hammond was a complex man to understand. All his logic was on the surface.

200

On the last Sunday in October there was a long interview with Craig in one of the newspapers. It detailed a great deal of his early life and asked what the four-time Wimbledon Champion and three-time World Champion was planning to do in the future. "At the top for a few more years," one of the paragraphs stated, "and a great player for the next ten. But after that—what?"

Suzy flung the paper to the floor. It lay there mocking her and she picked it up and read the rest of the article. It said nothing she did not already know, and she realized that this interview, like all the others she had read, gave no clue to the inner man.

The inner man. What a joke that was. There was no inner man. She had found that out for herself. There was only a tennis machine.

Hammond, on the telephone, was a welcome diversion.

"Would you like to see a copy of your book?" he asked blandly.

"You don't mean it?" Her voice rose with excitement. "When did you get it? There was no post today."

"The printer was coming up to town and he dropped it in. I'll bring it over."

"Oh, please, and stay to lunch if you don't mind potluck."

"Just to be with you is luck enough."

It was all very well to offer someone potluck, but what went into the pot was another matter. Thanking heaven for frozen foods, she took out packages and cartons, then went to the window boxes that lined the windows of the living room and cut some tarragon and chives. Within the hour a succulent smell was wafting through the small rooms, and she lowered the heat of the oven, put the lid firmly on the pot and went to bathe and change.

At one-thirty Hammond arrived with an enormous bunch of chrysanthemums.

"Now I know Christmas is a-coming," she said, looking down at the brilliantly shaggy heads.

"It was all I could get," he apologized. "Hothouse blooms aren't easily come by on Sunday."

201

"I'm not complaining!" She reached up and kissed him on the cheek. "These are beautiful, but they do remind me of winter."

"That's all to the good. This winter is going to be an exciting one for you. Full of fame, fortune and lots of hard work."

"Anne told me about the publicity tour you've planned for me."

"I arranged it only because she said you'd like to do it."

"I would. It will give me a chance to get away from the typewriter."

"Like that, is it? I was hoping to see part of your second story pretty soon."

"You can see it now."

She made her voice as casual as his, knowing they were both posing. Hammond was as anxious to see her manuscript as she was to show it to him. If it was no good, the sooner she discovered it, the better. She opened the drawer of her desk and extracted a pile of papers.

"Read it while I finish the lunch. And help yourself to a drink."

Twenty minutes later she peeped through the door and saw him immersed in the pages. With a sense of excitement she saw he had no drink at his side. Surely that was a good sign? Deciding to give him more time, she made a fresh fruit salad, and when she went into the room to get some Cointreau, he did not even look up to acknowledge her presence. She let another ten minutes go by, then wheeled in the trolley.

"Is this all you've done?" he asked, setting down the pages and coming to the table.

"There's cheese and biscuits." She determinedly misunderstood him.

"The story, damn you!" He put his hands on her shoulder. "It's far better than *Tennis Ball Heart*. You amaze me. Behind those cornflower eyes of yours there's a mind like a razor." He released her and took his chair. "When an author's successful with a first book, the critics start sharpening their knives to massacre the second one. But you're

202

going to blunt every instrument. Not only will they have to put their knives back in their sheaths, they'll have to bring out their bouquets!"

"Honestly? You're not just saying it?"

"Have I ever?"

"No, but—"

"Then don't doubt me now. And don't doubt yourself either."

She set the dishes on the table and pointed to the serving spoons for him to help himself. "You're marvelous for my ego, Hammond."

"Your literary ego only. You have no other. For a beautiful girl, you're singularly unconceited."

"You're doing your best to change that." She glanced briefly at the flowers that overfilled three vases.

"I'd like to give you more than flowers," he said, making no attempt to pick up his fork and eat. "You are a source of constant delight to me and I love you." He looked at the meat gently bubbling on his plate and half smiled. "This isn't quite the way I had planned to propose to you, but maybe it's rather fitting. In a way you are like food to me— appetizing, nourishing, sustaining, ambrosial!" He pushed back his chair and came around the side of the table to stand close to her. "You are everything to me, Suzy. You know that."

Wildly she sought for a way to temporize, afraid that if she did anything else she would lose his friendship. Why hadn't she worked out ahead of time what she wanted to say? She had seen it coming for weeks but had pushed it to the back of her mind.

"Think about it," Hammond said. "I have obviously taken you by surprise."

"You haven't." Her honesty won the day, though she knew it might cost her Hammond. "I've known what was in your mind for a long while. I'd have been a fool if I hadn't. But it's no use. I don't love you."

There was a moment's silence.

"Straight from the shoulder and not a cliché in sight," he said whimsically. "One more reason why I won't take

203

no for your final answer. Is it because you think I'm too old for you?"

"That's a cliché, if ever I heard one!"

"Then I *must* be in love!"

She smiled. "I've never given your age a thought. Except to think how much nicer it is to go out with an older man."

"But you don't love me. Are you in love with someone else?"

"You asked me that the first night you took me out to dinner, and I said no."

"I didn't believe you then, darling girl, and I don't believe you now." He returned to this chair and picked up his fork. "Is it anyone I know?"

"No." She realized she had to say more in order to satisfy his curiosity. "He—he doesn't live in England."

"How did you meet him?"

"When I was on an assignment."

"And he doesn't love you? I find that hard to believe."

She forced a mouthful of food down her throat. "You're too flattering, Hammond. Not every man I meet falls flat on his face!"

"Then they must be propped up by iron bars! You are beautiful, intelligent and kind. It's a rare combination." He held out his hand and slowly she put hers into it. "I do love you, Suzy, and I want to marry you. I won't change my mind. If you should change yours, I expect you to let me know."

"I will," she promised. "But, please Hammond, don't bank on it."

He released her hand and resumed eating. "By the end of the week I should have finalized the most important interviews in your tour. I'll tell my secretary to send you a copy of the itinerary. Perhaps you'll let me have your thoughts on it."

Suzy forced herself to concentrate. How tactful Hammond was, and how clever not to press her in areas that he knew were still tender. She wished she could make him see she was not going to change her mind. Yet to say so sounded rigid rather than positive. How could one be so

204

sure of not changing when everything in Nature changed? Oh Lord, she thought. I'm thinking like a chat show introduction instead of being myself. But I don't know what myself is. Not anymore.

But what better way was there of finding out than with a man like Hammond?

"Relax, Suzy," he ordered in his quietest tone. "Your mind's working overtime and it isn't necessary. Forget my proposal and think about your book."

"I can't close off my feelings. I'm not as clever as you are." She was waspish, to her surprise, but he laughed, and she knew it was because he had achieved his objective of stirring her out of her introspection.

"You're too clever by half, Hammond Ellison. One day you'll meet your master."

"I have, but she isn't yet my mistress."

Silently Suzy headed for the kitchen. She was watching the percolator when the telephone rang. She heard Hammond answer it, then he came to the door.

"A call for you from Australia."

Craig's name sounded like a clap of thunder in Suzy's head and she was unable to speak. It was a good thing, too, for Hammond's next words dashed her hopes.

"It's Millie Queen. Take the call, and I'll bring in the coffee."

Shakily Suzy complied. Millie's voice was as clear as if she were in the room and not on the other side of the world.

"Don and I are getting married six weeks from today," she announced gaily, "and I'm reminding you that you promised to be my bridesmaid."

"I didn't promise."

"I'll send you the ticket."

"It has nothing to do with the ticket." Suzy thought of her super-rich future, poor for lack of Craig. "I'm promoting my new book, Millie, and I can't get away. I wrote and told you about the book, didn't I?"

"Yes, you did, but I won't let you use it as an excuse. If I were getting married in Tibet, you'd come over like a shot, but because it's Australia and you're scared of meeting Craig, you won't come."

"Do you blame me?"

"That's the wrong word to use. I'm disappointed. I didn't think you were a coward."

"I'm not."

"Then come over for the wedding and face him."

"No. You've made a good try, Millie, but it won't work."

"Then I'll try again. If you don't come over for the wedding, Craig will know that he's the reason."

"That's ludicrous."

"Why? He knows we're friends and I told Elaine I was expecting you."

"You had no right to say that." Suzy was angry and did not hide the fact. "I never definitely said I would come."

"I know. And you're quite right to be annoyed with me." Millie did not sound in the least contrite. Happy with her Don, it would take more than a girl friend's anger to disturb her. "But I just couldn't stand the way Elaine was carrying on. She's been a real pain in the you-know-where these past few months, and I just felt like sticking a pin in her!"

"You didn't have to use *me* as the pin!" From the corner of her eye Suzy saw Hammond come in with the coffee. "I'm afraid you will have to get married without me. I have a phobia about being a bridesmaid."

"So be an honored guest. I won't take no for an answer. And I'm still going to tell Elaine you're definitely coming over."

"No!"

"Even if you don't, it will still give her a few sleepless nights. Wouldn't you like that?"

Suzy managed a laugh. It was more to fool Hammond than Millie. She had to make him think this was an innocuous girl-to-girl conversation.

"I'm staggered that she's still his current girl friend," she said.

"A very switched-on current. She scorches anyone who tries to get near him."

"If he didn't want it that way, he'd cut the wires."

"I don't think he cares or notices how she behaves. He's wilder than ever, Suzy. Elaine went to some family wedding in Texas and he was out with someone else before her plane even took off."

"Is that supposed to make me feel glad or sorry for her?"

"I don't give a damn about her. It's *your* feelings I'm bothered about."

"Then don't be. *I'm* not bothered anymore."

"Then why won't you come over for my wedding?"

It was a good question and Suzy did not know how to answer it without giving herself away all over again. Anyway, she couldn't be honest; not with Hammond listening.

"This call must be frightfully expensive for you," she said lamely.

"Frightfully," Millie mimicked. "So answer my question quickly."

"I already have."

"You know Craig's lost his form?"

"Are you talking about tennis?"

"What else. I was just hoping you might feel a bit responsible for it."

"Me?" Suzy was indignant. "It has nothing whatever to do with me."

"I think it has. If you were back in his life again, he'd settle down."

"Oh, do stop it, Millie." Suzy's temper was only held in check by Hammond's presence. "I'm sorry, I can't come to Australia, but I'll see you the next time you're in England. Good-bye and lots of luck."

Before Millie could answer, Suzy put down the receiver.

"There wouldn't be any problem in arranging for you to go to Australia," Hammond said behind her. "Your book comes out there three weeks after it appears here, and we could get some good publicity from your trip."

She bent over the coffee cups. "It's kind of you to suggest it, but it isn't necessary. There's nothing so important about Millie's wedding. She's making an unnecessary fuss about my being there."

"You're making an unnecessary fuss in refusing to go."

207

His words were softly spoken, but as she handed him his coffee and met his eyes, she knew she had to be careful what she said. In the normal course of events she would enjoy a trip to Australia—which Hammond probably knew—and to refuse one when it was offered to her, had made him suspect her reasons.

"If you want me to go to Australia," she said laconically, "then I will. But I hadn't thought it was so important."

Humor quirked his mouth and she knew he had seen through her quick acquiescence.

"Every book that's sold is important," he said in a businesslike voice. "Especially a first book. Besides, it's years since I was in Australia. Would you mind if I came along with you?"

The answer needed no thought. What better way to show Craig he meant nothing to her than to arrive in Australia with such an eligible bachelor in tow? Especially one who would make it clear he was in love with her.

"If you had said that in the first place, I'd have accepted Millie's invitation without an argument."

"You mean you will use me as a cover?"

Her cup rattled in its saucer. "A cover against what?"

"Against the man you are running away from."

"I'm not running away from anyone."

Dark eyebrows arched disbelievingly. "You are in love with a man who is not in love with you. I guessed that long ago. I wasn't deliberately listening to your conversation, my dear, but I could not help overhearing it, and it didn't require much deduction to know what it was about."

Suzy tried to remember exactly what she had said to Millie, and what Hammond could have gleaned from it. She was not sure if he was casting a fly or if she had really given herself away. It was impossible to recall every word. She stared at Hammond, but as always could not even begin to guess what he was thinking.

"I'm sorry you misconstrued what I was saying to Millie," she said. "I was only talking about Craig Dickson and his antics off the court. I met him when I was writing her biography and we had a mild fling. Unfortunately Millie's

208

got the bride's disease of matchmaking, and nothing will convince her that Craig and I were through months ago."

"Were you both through, or was it only Craig Dickson?"

Suzy resisted the impulse to tell Hammond to mind his own business, but knew that such a reply would undo everything she was trying to establish.

Wandering over to her desk, she leaned against it casually and sipped her coffee. He watched her, waiting for her to speak.

"My parting from Craig was mutual and amicable." Suzy was delighted that she sounded so firm. "I can't understand why you should think otherwise. I'm sure the same thing must have happened to you many times. You meet someone and get bowled over by them for a few weeks, and then the whole thing peters out."

"The way yours did."

"That's what I'm trying to tell you. It was over ages ago." Her lips moved upward in a smile, the muscles at the sides of them feeling as if they were being manipulated by a lever. "You should be glad it happened this way. If it hadn't, you would never have had *Tennis Ball Heart!*"

Hammond eyed her thoughtfully. "So that's why your Carlton is such a swine. When I first read the book I felt you could have softened him without losing any of your venom. But you couldn't, could you? You had to show him in the way you saw Craig Dickson. They're the same man."

"Not quite. There are some similarities."

"The end is similar, too."

"How can you say that!" She was amazed. "Jill marries Carlton."

"And you'd like to marry Craig. That's why you gave the book a happy ending. At least your heroine got some satisfaction even if you didn't!"

"That's a—a foul thing to say."

"Vicarious pleasure is what a great many people have to settle for. You, too, if you can't get him out of your system."

"He *is* out! How many times must I say the same thing? What I feel for Craig has nothing to do with love. It's anger and hurt pride. Mainly pride, as a matter of fact, which you

209

have done an enormous amount to restore."

"We try," he said with irony, and she half moved toward him in apology.

"I'm sorry, Hammond, I should have told you all this before."

"I don't see why. I'm not your keeper, my dear. Your publisher and your friend, yes. Your husband, too, if you will have me. But that doesn't mean I want to be your father confessor! Far from it. Your past—what little there is of it"—his smile robbed the words of cruelty—"has helped you to grow up and has also given us a first novel of distinction. Let us leave it at that."

Relief made her feel so heady that she was almost drunk with it. She should have known she could rely on Hammond. Meeting him was the best act that Fate had done for her. Sexual excitement stirred, making her aware of her breasts and stomach. Her eyes showed it and she did not care. She kept them fixed on him, waiting for him to make the next move.

"I still think we will go to Australia, Suzy. As I said before, it's a worthwhile market. An excellent one on a percentage basis. They have a far higher ratio of book buyers than over here."

Suzy only half heard him. Shock robbed her of desire. She had shown Hammond she would accept him and he had rejected her. How clever he was. There would be no Pyrrhic victory for him. When he laid physical claim to her, it would be in his own time and on his own terms.

"Very well," she said in her coolest tone. "I'll drop Millie a note and let her know she can expect us."

"Do that." He paused. "Don't hate me for it, Suzy. One cannot run away indefinitely—and writers never should! You must see Craig Dickson again and exorcise him properly—or improperly—if that's the best way for you to do it."

"We . . . I . . . we never did."

"I wasn't asking you."

"I know that. But I wanted you to know."

Hammond continued to look at her and she ran a tongue

over dry lips. "You're right to make me go to Australia. I know it. But at this moment in time, I'm damned if I can be grateful to you."

"Thank the Lord for that. The last thing I want from you is your gratitude!" He touched her fingers lightly, stretching out his hand to do so. "Finish your coffee while it's still hot. Cold coffee tastes bitter."

XIII

Three days after arriving in Australia—days filled with press and TV interviews that were almost like inquisitions—Suzy met Craig at the farewell party which Larry gave for his most famous of all protégées.

She had thought about their meeting for so long that when it eventually took place it was an anticlimax.

Believing that reality could never equal love-fevered memories, she was unprepared for the way Craig exactly mirrored her image of him. He was the male *supremo* of the tennis world; exuding sexual vigor and charm in equal doses. His golden skin was darkened to bronze by the Australian sun, and his eyes glowed as brightly as if they had lamps behind them. Not the hard brightness of electricity, but the warm, luminous glow of oil: sensuous and glistening. Like yellow-green beacons they regarded her, reminding her of the tiger she had once felt him to be. His brown hair was bleached almost silver in the front, and the inevitable strand fell across his forehead. Did it grow that way or had he cultivated it because he knew that every girl who saw it longed to have the right to push it back, as she herself could have done if it hadn't been for Elaine.

"So we meet again, Sweet Sue. I never expected you would fly over just for Millie's wedding."

His American accent was the same but his drawl was more pronounced; legacy of his life with Elaine, she decided bitterly. The knowledge seared her, firming her weakness into strength.

"I didn't only come for the wedding, Craig, but also to publicize my new book."

"How could I have forgotten that! I've been hearing nothing but *Tennis Ball Heart* for the last three days. I think you should share some of your royalties with me, Suzy. After all, I was the model for your hero."

"Not a very model hero," she said lightly. "And you can't expect me to agree with what you've said. The story was a figment of my imagination."

"If you say so." A mocking smile curved his mouth. "Where will your imagination take you for your next book?" His eyes moved beyond her. "To the guy with the gray hair?"

"You'll have to wait for my next book to find out."

"A bit old for you, isn't he?"

"What a very young-man thing to say!" She knew a sense of triumph as she saw the surprise on his face. "The guy with the gray hair, as you so succinctly described him, is my publisher, Hammond Ellison."

"How clever of you. Did he take your book before he saw you, or afterward?"

Color flooded into her cheeks. She felt the wave of heat but could do nothing to stop it. Craig saw it too and looked slightly ashamed.

"That was a foul thing to say, Suzy. I apolozie. Whatever else you are, you're a good writer. I'm sure your book was taken on its merit."

She moved her head slightly to show acceptance of his apology, but found it impossible to speak. Craig's accusation had hurt too deeply to respond to instant healing.

"You're obviously going to go from success to success," he went on, making handsome amends, and then spoiled it by saying: "But I still consider myself partly responsible for it."

"Always the egoist, aren't you?"

"Even more so since I read your book. But tell me something. If I'm Carlton, did you model Jill on yourself?"

"Hardly," she replied, remembering the happy ending.

"I thought not." His voice was more drawling than ever. "After all, she loved the guy, warts and all, which is something you could never do. You're only interested in perfection. In the myth rather than the man."

"I am not looking for perfection."

"You could have fooled me."

"Almost any girl can!" she flashed.

"Still the old saber-tongued Sue," he mocked. "But I hope you meant what you said just now. If you don't lower your standards, you could end up an old maid."

"I doubt it."

Her eyes turned automatically to Hammond who chose that moment to look across the room and raise his glass to her. She smiled back and then, glancing at Craig, saw he was watching her.

"So I was right after all," he said. "Sweet Sue has finally come home to roost."

"Most women do."

"And your career won't interfere with your marriage, either. Lucky Mr. Publisher."

"I think I'm lucky too."

"Do you?" The color of his eyes darkened, as if the light behind them had dimmed. "Are you in love with him, Suzy?"

She bent her head to her glass of champagne. The bubbles fizzed and burst, reminding her of the way her own hopes had gone.

"Why this interest in my private life? Or do you always keep tabs on your ex-girl friends?"

"You were never my girl friend."

"It wasn't for want of your trying."

"Do you blame me? You're a gorgeous-looking bird and I'm highly susceptible to them. Chase anything in skirts—that's me. And a pushover for shapely legs, even if they're on a piano!"

214

"Oh, stop it! If you're trying to annoy me—"

"Never! I was merely trying to show you how wise you were to see me in my true colors."

"Then it's a good thing for you that Elaine is colorblind." The smile vanished from Craig's face.

"You know, I'm beginning to feel sorry for Hammond Ellison. Marrying you will be like binding yourself in a hair shirt that's been washed in citric acid."

"I must remember to tell that to Hammond the day I marry him."

"When's it to be?"

The yellow in Craig's eyes was more pronounced and seemed to tinge his skin. Either that or he had changed color. She pushed aside the hope that she might have hurt him. It was both dangerous and foolish to indulge in wishful thinking.

"We haven't set the date yet," she replied.

"Don't wait too long, Suzy. Lover boy isn't getting any younger."

"Is that the only way your mind works?"

"It's the normal way. Have you thought what your life will be like with him fifteen years from now? Or will you sublimate your desire in your books?"

The glass shook in her hand and he reached out and took it from her. "I'm sorry, Suzy. I don't know why I'm talking to you like this. I must be a dog in the manger after all."

"It's understandable." She was smooth as syrup. "I'm the one that got away."

"Yes." He stared fully into her eyes. "I'm just one big ego, as you've always said, and I always remember my failures. They're so rare."

"Craig!" A small, raven-haired girl rushed over and caught him by the arm. "They're dancing out on the lawn and you promised me the first samba."

With a nod to Suzy, he moved away. She gulped down the rest of her champagne and wondered how soon she could reasonably leave the party. For the moment it had to be endured, and stoically she went in search of Millie. Maybe happiness could rub off.

As always Millie was surrounded by a crowd of people, and Suzy was content to stand among them and let the conversation wash over her, soaking away the hurt that Craig's words had caused.

"I'm so pleased you decided to come over after all." Millie was beside her, edging her away from the crowd and not stopping until they were almost alone in a corner. "I told you it was the best thing to do, didn't I? Have you seen Craig yet?"

"A few minutes ago. He hasn't changed."

"Have you? That's more to the point."

Before Suzy could say anything to this, Don saw them and bounded over.

"So my old lady bullied you into coming here! I was afraid at one stage that she'd insist we fly to London and be married from there."

"Whatever for?"

"Because Millie says you're her mascot. Without you, she assures me we wouldn't be getting married."

"What absolute rot!"

"No, it isn't," Millie protested. "You got me to talk about myself in a way I would never have done before. It made me see myself, too, and that was scary. I suddenly realized that you can't keep winning the rat race without becoming a rat!"

"Millie's right," Don agreed. "Maybe she was ripe for a change when you came into her life. But if you hadn't, or if you had been a different kind of girl, it might have taken her longer to discover what she was doing to herself."

Millie linked her arm through Don's and grinned at them both. "You can't begin to imagine what a penance it's been for me to play in these Australian tournaments. I can't wait to say good-bye to competitive tennis and the whole mish-mash that goes with it."

"And you were the one who's been encouraging *me* to make it my life."

"The background to your life," Millie corrected.

"And a background for Craig," Don said.

Suzy felt naked. Did everyone know of her love for Craig? Millie was a talkative character but surely she hadn't gone blabbing to everyone about it?

"Millie only told me about you two the day she called you and suggested you come out for our wedding. I gave her hell for bullying you the way she did, and she then told me why."

"You haven't mentioned it to—"

"Nobody else knows," he assured her. "And my little lady will keep her mouth shut, too."

"I'd no idea you were coming out here with a good-looking guy like Hammond," Millie said.

"Without Hammond, I wouldn't have come."

"So you do still love Craig?"

"How do you work that out?" Don asked, bewildered.

"With female logic."

Millie gave him a good-natured push and told him to circulate for a while. Only when he had obligingly done so, did she speak again.

"Is there really something going between you and Hammond or are you using him as a cover?"

"Yes to the last part of the question and I'm not sure to the first."

"You could do a lot worse if you've definitely ruled out Craig."

"He ruled *me* out," Suzy said. Then because she could not bear to talk about him, she said: "What will Larry do after you're married? Has he found someone else to manage?"

"No. He's going to join us at the ranch. He's tired of traveling too. It's wonderful the way things have worked out for me, isn't it? This time last year I figured I'd be playing tennis till I dropped. Now it's a whole new ball game." Millie tugged her hair, portent of a question to come. "You've changed your life, too, haven't you? I never imagined I had a literary lion following me around in Rome!"

"Only a cub as yet."

"With sharp teeth and claws, though. I'm in the middle of reading your book and it's had me in stitches—when I'm not licking my wounds."

"*You* aren't in it," Suzy said quickly.

"You can't deny that Craig is."

"You mean Carlton?"

"I mean that two-timing, womanizing, tennis-playing hero of yours! Did Craig mention it by any chance?"

"No. And do you mind if we change the subject. I came here for your wedding, not to dissect my unimportant romance with an unimportant man."

"Fair do," Millie said, unabashed. "From now on I'll mind my own business."

"I wish I could believe that."

Suzy smiled at the American girl. It was hard to remain cross with her for long. Her sunny disposition disarmed one and it was easy to see why she had been such a successful player, commanding not only respect but affection. Unlike Craig, who commanded adulation.

Damn Craig for infiltrating all her thoughts. In desperation she sought for Hammond, and found him talking to Larry.

He caught hold of her hand as she came to stand beside him, though he did not speak to her. But his clasp told her that he knew the evening had been traumatic for her, and she gained comfort from it.

Within a few moments he had managed to extricate them both from Larry's company, and looked at her with his usual ironic expression.

"Did I detect a smoke signal earlier, or was I imagining it?"

"It wasn't a smoke signal; it was practically a bush fire! I'm so tired I could pass out."

"Then we'll go. You've done what you set out to do."

She gave him the compliment of not asking what he meant, and followed him as he edged a way for her through the crowd. The party was becoming noisier and drunker, and already some of the older people were making their departure.

218

"Would you like to go somewhere else for a drink?" he asked. "Or do you wish to go straight back to the hotel?"

"The hotel, please." Remembering she had told him she was tired, she intended to carry on with the pretense, even if he did not believe her.

He did not speak again, except for trivial conversation, until he unlocked the door of her suite and preceded her in to switch on the lamps.

She went directly to the window and stared at the view of Sydney Harbor. Its magnificence diminished the depth of her pain and brought it into perspective. Was this what Hammond had meant when he had said that going to the moon had given man another perception of himself?"

"You have a busy day ahead of you," he spoke directly behind her. His breath fanned her cheek but he made no attempt to touch her. "You must get a good night's sleep, Suzy. If you'd like a couple of sleeping pills . . ."

"What for?"

She swung around as she spoke, in time to see the slight dilation of his eyes. She waited for him to make a reference to Craig but, as always, she misjudged him, and he merely bent forward and kissed her on the brow.

"Then have a good rest sans pills. I'll call you at nine."

Alone, she went back to staring through the window. Of course, Hammond would not refer to Craig. He was far too wise. Unlike Craig, who had made it quite clear how he felt. Still, she had been plain-spoken with him. Neither of them had come out of their encounter well, though Craig had had more justification for being angry. Her book alone had seen to that.

Wishing she had accepted Hammond's offer of a sleeping pill—merely thinking of Craig had made her on edge—she climbed into bed. She was booked to remain in Australia another week, but after Millie's wedding on Saturday she would have no need to meet the tennis crowd, which thankfully meant she need never see Craig.

Promptly at nine the next morning Hammond telephoned and arranged to collect her in an hour.

"What's on the agenda today?" she asked. "I think you

219

should give me a proper schedule, then I could plan what I want to wear."

"I'll do that," he promised. "It was remiss of me not to have done it earlier. Your first appointment today is a press conference in my suite with some out-of-town weekly papers. You won't find that much of a problem. Then this afternoon you'll be awarding the Sylvester Trophy."

A tingle ran through Suzy's body. The Sylvester Trophy was one of the most important tennis tournaments. Not only did it offer a large cash prize to the winner, but entry to it was eligible only to the ten top seeded players in the world. And today, Craig was competing in the finals against a fellow American. Hammond had not been remiss in omitting to give her a schedule of her engagements; he had been deliberate.

"Suzy?" he asked. "Are you still there?"

"Where else?" she said lightly. "My mind was just rummaging through my wardrobe."

He chuckled. "You always look beautiful."

"I'm bright, too," she said, and knew from his indrawn breath, not quite disguised, that he had been expecting some attack. Well, she would not disappoint him.

"Why *me* to present the award? I'm not much of a celebrity."

"You're a new one, my dear, and that means something, too. Apart from which, everyone's saying you used Craig as the hero for your book, and it will be excellent publicity for you to give him the prize."

"If he wins. He's been off form the last few months."

"If he loses, we might get even more mileage out of the publicity. Someone's bound to say he got rattled because you were there."

"That's a good reason for me not to go. If Craig loses, I don't want it to be because of me."

"You can't cry off now. It's all arranged." Hammond paused. "You could always phone him and wish him well. That should appease your conscience."

"I don't have any conscience where he's concerned," she snapped, and banged down the phone.

She was immediately sorry, knowing it had given her away to Hammond. But he had wanted to make her angry. He obviously believed that the best way to get rid of the past was to burn it out with a blowtorch.

By ten o'clock, when he came to collect her, she was in control of herself, and gave such good value to the visiting press that Hammond was delighted. The fact that she herself had been a journalist always softened the most abrasive reporter, and though no Australian could ever be described as easy, they gave her a smoother ride than they would otherwise have done.

It was noon before she and Hammond were alone, and she kicked off her shoes and lay back on the settee.

"Think what a lovely afternoon we could have had on the beach," she said, pointing to the blue sky beyond the window. "Just you and me."

"And a thousand other bodies! Hold the seduction over until tomorrow, my dear. This afternoon you're fully booked."

"You did it deliberately," she reproached. "Why?"

"You know why. I'm a believer in the kill or cure method."

"I saw Craig at the party, didn't I?"

"One dose of medicine isn't enough."

"I don't need more. Writing my book was all the cure I needed."

"You looked about to have a relapse at Millie's party," Hammond said bluntly. "You were so bright and bubbly with Craig Dickson, I thought you were going to explode."

"All right, so I overreacted. But that's what most people would have done in my position. We can't all be as calm and controlled as you."

"I'll beat you if you say that again."

"I'm sorry." She meant it. "But you make me angry when you don't believe me."

"You make *me* angry when you lie. Don't do it, Suzy. It's a waste of your time. I know you too well."

His crisp command was like cold air on a soufflé, and instantly her bravado collapsed.

221

Aware of it, he relented and went over to the tray of drinks, almost depleted by the reporters. He found an unopened half bottle of champagne and poured out two glasses.

"How did you manage to hide this?" she asked, accepting it with pleasure.

"By hiding it!" He glanced at his wristwatch, a Philippe Patek, as elegant as its wearer. "I suggest we have lunch up here. Then you can still relax."

"I'd like that."

There was a knock at the door and he rose to let in a waiter wheeling a trolley. Suzy looked at the cold lobster and assorted salads, the large bowl of fresh fruit and the silver bucket that held a German hock.

"You'd already arranged it." She was half amused, half irritated. "No wonder you say you know me!"

"But not completely." He leaned forward and drew her up. "That is a pleasure still to come."

At two-thirty they were being greeted by the officials at the stadium. They were a different breed from the faintly supercilious ones she had seen at Wimbledon, and tended to be hard-nosed types who acted as if professional sport was a way of taking exercise with pay. As a layman she found it a refreshing attitude, though listening to one official having an argument with a player, she could appreciate why the tennis stars preferred the British ones.

She had hoped to be seated with the directors and organizers of the competition, but found herself being led to the section reserved for managers, family and close friends of the players.

"Hello, Suzy." Craig's manager, Frank Ellman, greeted her like a long lost friend, and she introduced him to Hammond before squeezing along the row to seat herself beside Millie and Don.

"I shouldn't really be here," Millie confided. "It meant skipping an appointment with the dressmaker and she was furious. But I had to see the match."

"What are Craig's chances?" Suzy asked in exactly the right uncaring tone.

222

"It's hard to say. He's been so erratic lately that even the bookies don't know what odds to give! It's like that old nursery rhyme. When he's good he's very very good and when he isn't, he's a disaster!"

"One of the Sydney papers said the Tennis Robot needed some new parts," Don chipped in. "Not that Craig gives a damn. He still draws bigger crowds than anyone else."

"Because he's a great player," Millie said staunchly. "And he'll be great again. Frank told me he's trying to persuade him to take a few months' rest. He's sure he's only stale."

There was a burst of clapping as Craig and his opponent walked out on court. Immediately Suzy's mind went back to Wimbledon, and she quickly turned to smile at Hammond, disconcerted to find that it was Frank, with Hammond now on the far side of him.

Oh God, Suzy thought in despair, it'll be bad enough coping with my own nerves while Craig plays, let alone with Frank's. He was perspiring slightly and dabbed at his neck with a colored handkerchief.

Below her the two players divested themselves of their sweaters, tested their rackets and greeted the umpire. Craig glanced up at the box, his eyes moving along the seated rows of people. His eyes met Suzy's and a shuttered look came down on his face as he turned away.

Beside her, she heard Frank mutter.

"What did you say?" she asked.

"Just talking to myself."

He leaned forward, his full attnetion given to the scene below.

Craig had taken his place on the base line. There was an isolation about him that was almost tangible, and his opponent seemed to sense it, too, for he glanced at Craig and half raised his hand, as if to ascertain he was all right. Craig acknowledged the movement by half lifting his arm, though the rest of his body remained motionless. Once more Frank muttered beneath his breath, but Suzy knew better than to ask him if anything was wrong; even if there were, he would not tell her.

The warm-up began and balls went backward and forward over the net. Craig stared straight ahead, smashing ball after ball far out of the court, as if unable to control his strength. The umpire signaled for play to commence and both men took up their positions. Johnny Jackson was due to serve and Craig waited at the base line. His racket was loose in his hand and he gave no visible sign of expectation. He could have been a statue.

The serve that came at him was low and fast, skimming the net to land several yards short of his feet. With uncanny swiftness he lunged for it, making a passing shot that had the crowd gasping. The point was Craig's, and his opponent served again. This one went to twelve rallies, with both men making brilliant saves. But again Craig won the point with a seemingly impossible return. There was no need to ask if he was on form today. The crowd settled back to watch what they knew was going to be a great match, and which Suzy knew was going to be another Wimbledon.

Craig played every point as if it was the match one. He raced across the clay for seemingly impossible returns which he made possible time and time again; out-pacing, out-thinking, out-playing his opponent on every occasion.

He won the first set without losing a game and, as at Wimbledon, paused only to take some salt tablets and wipe the sweat from his face before returning to the court. He seemed like a man possessed, his concentration so intense that the outside world had ceased to exist for him.

"I can see why he's called the Tennis Robot," Hammond commented to Frank, leaning forward to do so. "He looks totally devoid of feeling."

"He's got too much feeling," Frank replied. "But he's learned how to control it."

"I suppose that's one of the reasons for his success. Control. He's lucky to have such a gift."

"It wasn't a gift." Frank did not take his eyes from Craig. "He worked at it. By Christ, he did."

"Quiet, please," the umpire called and the second set began.

It was almost a repetition of the first. Craig still played like a machine, but now he was in top gear. He served aces for each one of his own serves and returned Jackson's with such Machiavellian cunning that he again took the set six-nought. By now everyone realized they were watching a man at his peak. Even the usual ooh's and aah's of excitement had become muted. Tension was too tightly strung to be voiced.

Suzy longed to run away. Looking at Craig was like looking at a machine. How did Frank have the nerve to say Craig had emotions? Anyone could see he was programmed like a computer. Tennis Ball Heart. What a joke that was. He didn't have a heart.

"I never thought I'd see him play like this again so soon," Frank mumbled as, the second set over, his attention momentarily relaxed. "It's the second time in six months."

"You mean he only plays like this at certain times?" Hammond asked with interest.

"The last one was at Wimbledon. But the time before that was ten years ago."

"Then why is he called the Tennis Robot? I assumed it meant this type of play." Hammond indicated the court with an inclination of his well-sculptured head.

"This isn't playing like a robot," Frank said. "This is tennis from the gut. Don't be fooled because he looks like a robot out there. You can take it from me that he's aware of everything that's going on, and he's using all his strength to make himself forget it."

"You mean he's split himself in two?" Hammond questioned.

"Right. One part of him is up here—with us, with the crowd, with anything and anyone else he's thinking about—and the other part, the one that's dominant, is forcing him to block out the world and concentrate only on the game. But the effort of doing so is taking all his strength. If he relaxes his guard for a single instant, he'll be knocked out."

"No one can knock him out today. He's invincible."

"He'll knock himself out." Frank leaned farther across Suzy, so that no one around them could hear him. "Once this match is over, he'll collapse. It's happened twice before, so I recognize the symptoms."

"What brings it on?" Suzy spoke for the first time, her curiosity stronger than her desire to remain uninvolved.

"Shock of some kind. The first time was when his mother died. She'd been a good player in her day, but not great, like Craig. But she knew he could go to the top and she sacrificed her whole life to that ambition."

"His ambition, or hers?" Hammond asked, and the way he did not look at Suzy, told her the question was as much for her as for him.

"Hers to begin with," Frank said. "Then she fired Craig with it. He was fourteen when I first saw him play and even then you could tell he was going places. He wasn't just a tennis freak either. He was good at sports and academically bright. His mother hocked everything she had to give him the right start and education. At college, when he wanted to take a job to pay for his studies, she wouldn't let him. Nearly went berserk to stop him, in fact. They were really close, those two. I never saw anything like it. Not maudlin, you understand—she was too tough to let that happen—but real, bone-deep love and respect." The weathered face, with its open countenance, looked strangely reflective. "Respect. That outlives a great many other emotions, I guess." He sighed. "Anyway, the day before he played his first American title match, she died. I expected him to scratch the game but he wouldn't; said he owed it to his mother to go out and win. I didn't think he could make it. I pleaded with him to change his mind. I felt it would harm him psychologically to go out and play badly. But he wouldn't listen to me; I don't think he even heard me."

"And he played and won," Hammond stated matter-of-factly.

"Right. The way he's playing today. He demolished his opponent in straight sets and then came off the court and collapsed. He told me a long time later that he couldn't remember playing a single point." Frank watched as Johnny Jackson took his position on the base line. "It's my belief that when Craig can't take any more emotion he blanks out his mind. Shuts up shop, as it were. He did the same at

Wimbledon in June." Frank glanced at Suzy. "You remember the way he played there?"

"Everyone remembers it," Hammond said before Suzy could speak. "It caused a great deal of comment."

"He collapsed after that match, too," Frank went on. "Out like a light for twenty hours, and still doesn't remember a single stroke of that game. Remarkable, isn't it?"

"It sometimes happens to people under stress," Hammond said. "The mind is like an electric current and when it becomes overloaded, it cuts out."

"A good thing for Craig that it does," Frank said with a dryness rare to him. "Generally, he never knows when to stop."

"He obviously does know," Hammond smiled, "so I wouldn't worry about him."

"I can't help it. I've practically lived with him since he was fourteen. Even when he was at college I moved close to help him continue with his training. He's like a son to me." The lined face puckered into a smile. "I see him more than my own son."

The third set began and Frank straightened and turned to watch. Suzy tried to watch, too, but half her attention was given over to what Frank had said. If Craig only behaved like this when he received a severe emotional shock, what shock had he suffered prior to his match at Wimbledon? She could not believe it was her quarrel with him. If he blanked out each time he quarreled with a girl, he would have played half his matches like a zombie.

She forced her mind back to the present one. Jackson was putting up a tremendous fight to stay in the game. He was running all over the court and getting back incredible shots, only to have more incredible shots returned to him. Yet he managed to win the first game, which drew enormous applause, and even picked up two points in the second game, by brilliantly lobbing when Craig had expected a return to the backhand. But that was the last time the umpire spoke Jackson's name. From then on it was all downhill, with Craig battering him remorselessly to win the third set and the trophy at six games to one.

Jackson vaulted the net and pumped Craig's hand with admiration, knowing there was no shame in losing to such a player. Craig acknowledged the handclasp by the merest flicker of his head, and though he raised his eyes to the crowd who were roaring their acclamation, there was no smile on his face.

"I must get down to the court," Frank said hurriedly, and grabbed Suzy by the arm. "You're going to be photographed with him, aren't you?"

She looked at Hammond, who nodded and rose.

"I'm coming, too," he said, speaking to Frank. "If Craig's gone into the same state he was in at Wimbledon, he won't know what's happening to him. You may need me there."

"There'll be plenty of officials," Suzy protested, unwilling to have Hammond with her when she saw Craig.

"Officials have big mouths," Frank grunted. "Can you see what a story it would make in a newspaper? 'Tennis Robot' is a title we can live with, even 'The Man with a Tennis Ball Heart.'" A brief smile punctured his face. "But 'Champion with Amnesia' is something we can do without!"

"Then let's get down," she said hurriedly, and pushed forward.

When they reached the court, it was thronging with people, Craig and Johnny Jackson in the middle of them and Frank elbowed his way close to stand by Craig. Suzy, trying to stay near Hammond, was pushed to one side, and watched helplessly as the crowd closed over her again.

She was on the verge of panic when several burly officials linked arms and cleared a path for her. A small, dapper-looking man appeared by her side and she guessed him to be Thomas Sylvester, chairman of the company which had sponsored the match.

Forcing a smile to her lips, she advanced to the table set up at the end of the court, where Craig and his vanquished opponent were waiting for her. Craig looked at her without returning her smile, his eyes blank as opaque glass. A couple of people made short speeches, then she was handed the large silver trophy to present to the winner.

"Congratulations, Craig. You played a fantastic match."

228

She was aware of Frank and Hammond directly behind him. But Craig seemed unaware of anybody. In silence he took the silver dish from her, but made no move to go. She had the feeling he was nailed to the ground.

"Aren't you going to kiss her?" someone asked, and cameras were held aloft.

Craig bent his head and did so. His lips were firm and unyielding, cold as ice, and she shivered and stepped back.

"How does it feel to win the Sylvester Trophy for the second year running?" another man asked.

Craig did not answer and Frank closed in and put his hand on the muscular brown one.

"The boy's exhausted. Can't you see that? Let him rest for a while and he'll give you all the interviews and pictures you want later."

None of the photographers or reporters took any notice, and bulbs and questions flashed out as Frank steered Craig across the court to the narrow passageway that led to the dressing rooms.

"Keep to the other side of him," Frank muttered to Hammond. "All I'm short of is for him to collapse on me."

Hammond linked his arm with Craig and Suzy ran alongside. Craig had still not said a word and she could not take her eyes away from his face. His color was normal, apart from the flush caused by the exercise of the past hour, and he looked as handsome as he had done last night. But there was something missing from him. It was like looking at a copy of him, perfect in every detail, except for the vital one of life.

They reached the inside of the main stand but instead of turning to the dressing rooms, Frank headed in the opposite direction.

"The rear exit," he explained. "I'm taking him straight back to the hotel. If he stays here, I'll never be able to keep the papers away from him."

They reached the rear exit and came out into the sunshine. A small crowd of fans were clustered there, and more came running forward as Craig was recognized. But the main crowds were by the front gates, and it was comparatively easy to dash toward the big chauffeur-driven car that awaited them.

Frank pushed Craig into the back, then stepped aside for Suzy to follow. She hesitated, and Hammond took command in his usual debonair way.

"We have our own car, thanks. If Suzy comes with you, she might attract more attention."

Frank nodded and jumped into the back seat. Craig was sitting bolt upright, staring ahead at nothing.

"Move," Frank ordered the chauffeur, and the car glided away.

"It's frightening to look at him," Suzy said and could not suppress a shudder. "I once saw someone hypnotized; they were told they were a statue and they acted exactly the way Craig's acting now."

"He'll come out of it," Hammond soothed. "Don't dramatize it, my dear. By tomorrow he'll be his normal self."

His normal self and back with Elaine. Suzy frowned. Where was the Texan girl now? Probably in Craig's empty dressing room, wondering where he was.

"Do you want to go to the hotel or would you like to do some sightseeing?" Hammond asked.

"The hotel, please."

She was in no mood to enjoy scenic splendors, and sat tensely in their car during the short drive to the hotel. Craig's behavior was not something she could dismiss, for it opened up a train of thought that she needed to explore. She had tried to reason it out during the match but had gotten nowhere conclusive. Nor could she do so now. If Craig only behaved like this when he received a severe shock, she had to find out what shock he had received today. Today and at Wimbledon last June. It was all so muddled. Yet through the muddle one common factor stood out. She had quarreled with him prior to his match in London and again here. But could a quarrel with her have such a devastating effect on him that he had to block it out in such an anesthetizing manner?

Only if he loved her.

She closed her eyes. She wanted so desperately to be-

230

lieve this that she was afraid to trust her own judgment. She couldn't knowingly leave herself open to hurt again. She was beginning to get over him; could almost believe that six months from now she would be able to think of him without regret. So wasn't it better to leave things the way they were?

"Feeling tired?" Hammond inquired, and she shook her head.

"Just a bit disturbed," she confessed. "I've always thought of Craig as so vital, that it was awful to see him acting like a zombie."

"Maybe *I* should go into a trance state, too," Hammond said. "It seems to be an excellent way of gaining your concern. Underneath your cool-gold exterior, you're a warm-brown girl!"

"You don't need to do anything drastic to get my attention." She moved closer and relaxed against him. "Knowing how steady and unflappable you are, is part of your charm for me."

"I don't want to be charming with you." His voice was light. "I want to be violent and demanding and passionate."

She straightened swiftly, disturbed by what he had said, and annoyed that she should be.

"I—I still don't know how I feel," she stammered.

"That's why we came out here, remember? For you to think and evaluate."

Think and evaluate. How typical these words were of Hammond. How could she explain to him that thinking and evaluating were impossible while she was still overwhelmed by feeling? By hers for Craig and Craig's for . . .

For whom? If she knew the answer to that, she would be wise indeeed.

XIV

To Suzy's dismay, Hammond spent the rest of the afternoon talking about Craig's behavior.

Even at dinner he stayed on the same subject, seemingly unaware of her own reluctance to do so. This was so unlike Hammond, who was always closely—sometimes too closely—in tune with her mood, that she was certain he was doing it for a purpose.

He's baiting me like a fish, she thought angrily, but I'm damned if I'll swallow the hook. She spooned the last of her vichyssoise and kept her face a mask of indifference. They were dining in the main restaurant of their hotel, and though the surroundings were plush, the diners were tacky and boisterous.

"I wonder if the Australians would be so free and easy in their manner if they lived in a cold climate?" she asked, cutting across Hammond's dissertation on trance states.

He looked briefly taken aback, then he smiled. "Rough and ready would be a better description. Under all their bluntness they're a rigid people. Narrow too, compared with the British."

"If by narrow, you mean they have old-fashioned virtues—"

"What's virtuous in being old-fashioned? Would you go to an old-fashioned dentist or doctor?"

"No, but—"

"Then I've made my point. Every age has its own values. If changes occur, it's because people want those changes. New ideas bring new pressures to bear."

"Like birth control?"

"And going to the moon; that gave us a whole new perception. Once you realize how small you are in the universal scheme, all your values alter."

"The car and the airplane affected attitudes, too," she said, glad they were on a safe subject and firmly hanging onto it. "And television, too. That's opened up the world to everyone."

"Of course. Without television, where would professional sports be today? Take people like Millie and Craig, for instance. If—"

"You take them," Suzy said, annoyed at the way he had manipulated her back to the one subject she did not wish to discuss. "I'm not a sports fan and I find it a boring subject."

"Then let's forget sports and concentrate on the people who make it. Craig, for instance."

Suzy set her fork on her plate. "You are being surprisingly unsubtle, Hammond, and so, it seems, must I. I don't want to talk about Craig. Is that clear?"

"I'm afraid not. If he no longer means anything to you, I fail to see why you should object to talking about him."

"Dissecting is the word you should use," she retorted. "What's the purpose of it?"

"Do you need me to remind you again why you came here?"

"I've already told you that I've got my answer. What do I have to do to convince you—write it in blood?"

Hammond looked as if he found her comment crude. But *he* should complain, when he'd been bulldozing away at her feelings for the past six hours.

"I do not love Craig," she said, "and I don't want to talk about him."

"I think you do love him, Suzy."

"You can't love someone who doesn't exist."

"I am afraid one can. That's what love is often about!"

She acknowledged the truth of this cynical comment but could not think of an answer to it.

"Whether or not Craig is the sort of man you *want* him to be, is beside the point," Hammond continued. "What's more to the point is that feeling the way you do about him, you couldn't marry anyone else." ·

"Hammond, I—"

"Don't deny it, darling. Please respect my intelligence more than that."

"I feel so awful," she said miserably.

"Because you love Craig or because you don't love me?"

"Both."

He managed a smile. "A typical woman! She always wants to eat her cake and have it, too!" He raised an eyebrow at her. "Well, my dear, you should look on me as a Christmas cake, not a sponge. I won't go stale on you! If you and Craig don't manage to work things out, I'll still—"

"No, Hammond, that wouldn't be fair to you. The one thing I've learned from coming here, is that second best—no matter how close it is to being first—can never be enough for me."

"You'll change your mind about that, too, when you're older. Though come to think of it, by that time *I'll* be too old to take advantage of it!"

She did not smile, for she knew that for him it was no joke.

"The young hate to compromise," he went on. "Whereas the older one gets, the more virtue one sees in it. One can even find virtue in defeat."

"I never did."

"Because you are still too young. But take me as an example. I want to marry you but you have turned me down. So I review my life and decide that it may be for the best, after all. I have been a contented bachelor for so long,
234

that I might have found marriage—even to someone as lovely and intelligent as yourself—too restricting."

"You probably would have," she agreed, knowing he did not believe a word of what he was saying. But if this was the way he wanted to play it, then so would she.

"What do you intend to do about Craig?" he asked.

"I don't know. I would like to talk to Frank before I make any decision."

"Why not do it now? It's only nine-thirty. I'm sure you'll find him in their suite."

She pushed back her chair, then saw Hammond's smile and stopped in confusion.

"I'll talk to him later." She sat down.

"Please don't, my dear. I can't bear you sitting here restless for the remainder of the evening. Your nervousness is already affecting my enjoyment of this excellent steak."

Gratefully accepting the way out, Suzy left him.

Within minutes she was at the door of the suite Craig shared with Frank. She knocked tentatively, and almost at once it was flung open. Frank's expression told her he had been expecting someone else.

"My supper," he informed her as he saw her glance over her shoulder. "I ordered it twenty minutes ago and, ah, here it comes."

She stepped aside as a waiter wheeled in a trolley, placed it by the window and left. There was no sign of Craig and Suzy glanced at the doors on either side of her.

Interpreting her look, Frank pointed to his left.

"You can't talk to him, I'm afraid. He's dead to the world. As soon as I got him onto his bed, he flaked out. He's been sleeping ever since."

"Aren't you worried?"

"No. The first time, I was scared plenty, and even at Wimbledon I didn't like it. It had been ten years since the last occasion, so it gave me quite a shock. That's why I made him see one of your doctors in Harley Street. What he said to us made enough sense for me to stop worrying." Frank strode across the carpet and opened the door of Craig's room. "Have a look for yourself," he said, without

235

lowering his voice. "You can switch on the radio or wail like a banshee and he won't hear a thing."

Hesitantly, Suzy stepped forward and looked at Craig. She was reminded of the other two occasions when she had seen him asleep; in Rome and at Marvin's house in Sussex just before Wimbledon had begun. At both times she had been struck by his vulnerability, but tonight there was something more in his unconsciousness: an inertness that spoke of a deeper exhaustion; almost as if he were in a coma. Because there was something poignant in watching a man made so defenseless by sleep, she stepped back into the sitting room.

"You see," Frank said prosaically, following her and closing the door. "He looks quite normal."

She marveled at the manager's insensitivity, and to her discomfiture he chuckled and said:

"I don't see him with your eyes, Suzy. You love him differently from the way I do."

"I don't—" She stopped, unable to lie. "Is it so obvious?" she asked finally.

"Most girls who meet him fall in love with him," Frank said with brutal honesty. "You're no different from the rest."

"Thanks. You're making me feel great."

"What's true is true. Craig's a handsome son of a bitch and he's a celebrity. Put the two together and you get a package that women can't resist."

"You make us sound like dolts."

"Who's arguing!"

Ruefully she acknowledge the truth of this, which somehow made it more difficult for her to begin what she wanted to say. Perhaps it might be better if she said nothing. Yet she had come here to find out why Craig had reacted the way he did, and it would be cowardice to run away.

"I suppose you're wondering why I'm here?" she murmured.

"I gave up wondering about Craig's girl friends years ago!"

Her uneasiness increased, adding to her belief that she was only one of many in Craig's life. Yet that still did not

236

stop her from wanting to know the reason behind his collapse at Wimbledon, and again here, today.

"You said Craig only goes into this peculiar state when he wants to blank out something painful," she said, "and . . . well, what I'd like to know is what was he trying to blank out at Wimbledon?"

"You're going back some." Frank seemed surprised. "I haven't a clue. He never gave me any reason for it."

"He must have said something."

"Nope. Not even a hint. I swear it. Like I said to you earlier today, he was out for twenty-four hours and when he recovered he acted as if nothing had happened."

"Didn't he do anything different? Please think carefully, Frank, it's awfully important to me. Did he mention me at all?"

Frank shook his head. "All he said was that he'd changed his mind about the coming weekend. Elaine had gone off to some chateau in the Loire and he'd turned down the invitation to go with her. After the match, when he'd recovered, he asked me to book a flight for him to Tours."

"Did he say why he had changed his mind?"

"Nope."

"Or why he had refused to go with Elaine in the first place?" Suzy knew she was pushing but she could not help herself.

"Craig never said a word—about anything. He can be pretty close-mouthed when he wants. He's nowhere near the extrovert he pretends."

Disconsolately she was forced to agree. His nightly calls to her from the States had been long on time but short on intimacy. She was no nearer to knowing the real Craig, if one existed, than when she had first met him.

"Do you think he'll marry Elaine?" she asked.

"Could be. But she's not the only girl he . . ." Frank went to the trolley. "Do you mind if I have my supper now, Suzy? I could eat a horse."

She nodded and perched on a chair as he gustily drank some soup.

"I get so wound up when Craig's playing a big match

237

that I never eat until it's over. Craig's the same. He just has a light breakfast."

"But that was hours ago."

"I know. But short of feeding him intravenously, what can I do!" The manager's look was humorous. "He's fit as a flea, honey. Fasting for a day and night won't kill him."

Frank pushed aside his soup bowl, burped and then lifted the lid of a silver entrée dish and heaped some chops and potatoes onto his plate.

"Have you finished with the questions?" he asked, his mouth full, his expression happy. "You're sitting there as if you're on the wrong end of a pin!"

"That's what Hammond said."

"Your publisher. He seems a nice guy. Craig thought so, too."

Suzy was instantly alert. "Did he? Was that all he said?"

Frank nodded, busily chewing. "He muttered something about him being the right type for you, but a bit—well, you know . . ."

"A bit too old," Suzy finished. "Craig told me that himself."

"Then you know as much as I do. Look, Suzy, why don't you wait until you can talk to him yourself when he wakes up? If you want to know why he reacted the way he did at Wimbledon, he's the best one to tell you."

"If he didn't tell *you*, then he's hardly likely to tell me."

"That doesn't follow. We both mean something different to him."

"You are more special than I was." Suzy went to the door. "There's only one Frank in Craig's life, but there are dozens of girls."

"That's true." Frank was, as ever, depressingly living up to his name. "Care for some coffee? I'm going to order some more."

"No thanks."

"Would you like me to call when he wakes up?"

"No. I'm on a TV show early in the morning, and I want to get a good night's sleep."

"Can you?"

His expression showed awareness of her mental state. He was a kind man, she decided. Being with Craig for so long had taught him not to pry into people's minds. But he was letting her know that he understood the misery in hers.

"I'll probably take a sleeping pill," she said, then tried to be funny. "Or read my own book!"

He smiled. "I'll see you at the wedding, then."

She looked blank for an instant. "Good Lord, I'd forgotten it was tomorrow."

"Craig's an usher, so you'll see him there."

"With Elaine."

"I guess so."

Frank bent to examine the last contents of the entrée dish in front of him and Suzy went out.

She was by the elevator when Elaine came out of a room nearby.

"Jesus!" she exclaimed, her blue eyes sharp. "Still running after Craig?"

Suzy stared fixedly at the door of the elevator.

"You still don't know when you're wasting your time," Elaine continued. "You aren't stupid, so you must have the hide of an elephant!"

The sliding doors parted and Suzy thankfully slipped past them. They closed and she let out a strangled sigh. Elaine's words, more than anything Frank had said, made her suddenly realize how distastful she was acting. How could she have questioned him so shamelessly and given away the last vestige of her pride? When Craig found out, it would make his day.

Wildly she reached for the stop button. She must go back and tell Frank not to say anything about her visit. The lift shuddered to a halt and she stared at the control panel. If she went back now, she was more than likely to meet Elaine in the suite. The thought of this was so unpleasant that she could not face it.

She pressed the button for her own floor. She would speak to Frank on the telephone instead. It would serve the same purpose.

The moment she was in her own room, she dialed his

number. He answered at once and she kept her voice low in case Elaine was within earshot.

"Don't tell Craig that I came along to talk to you," she said.

"Are you sure?"

"Yes. Promise me, Frank."

"You've nothing to worry about, George." Frank's voice was hearty, his response so quick that she wondered bleakly how many times he had been faced with a similar situation: one girl phoning about Craig while another one was with him.

Anger and mortification kept her awake despite a sleeping pill, and by eight-thirty next morning she had been dressed and waiting for Hammond for three hours.

He did not ask her what had happened the previous night, and kept up a flow of trivia during the drive to the studio.

At first she was grateful for his diplomacy, but by the time they reached the TV station she was fuming with rage. Did he have to act as if nothing had happened? To treat her like a child who could be cajoled from one mood to another? Didn't he know she wanted to wallow in her misery; to scream and shout and rant; above all, to confide?

"Don't you want to know what I found out about Craig?" she burst out in the middle of the studio foyer. "Or are you going to wait to read it in my next book?"

"I didn't think it necessary for me to tell you I was interested," he said quietly. "I thought you took that for granted.

"You're not the sort of man one can take for granted."

"That's the nicest compliment you've paid me."

"Don't be so clever," she snapped, and then recovered her sense of humor and, with it, her proportion. "My going to the suite was a waste of time," she informed him. "Craig was asleep, in a stupor almost, and Frank didn't have a clue as to his behavior. He said a few things about Elaine but nothing that I didn't already know. Craig doesn't confide in him, so there was nothing he could tell me beyond the fact that he blanks out when he's under too much stress."

240

"So you're back to the starting point."

"Not quite. One can never go back. And I wouldn't want to, even if I could. Craig's behavior, blackout or trance, call it what you will, doesn't affect the situation. What I said about him still stands."

"So does the way you feel."

"I'm changing," she said quickly.

"Miss Bedford?" A twanging female voice brought Suzy around to face an attractive-looking brunette. "I'm Jean, Mr. Melville's assistant. He's asked me to welcome you to his show and to tell you that he will meet you in the studio when you come back from makeup. If you'd care to follow me . . ." She looked at Hammond. "You too, Mr. Ellison."

"I'm not appearing on the show."

"Mr. Melville would like you to do so."

Raising an eyebrow at Suzy, Hammond accompanied them to the makeup room where a brisk young lady dabbed and powdered them.

"I'm beginning to wish I hadn't agreed to come on this show," Suzy murmured to Hammond as they followed Jean down a seemingly endless corridor. "I was watching one of the chat shows this morning while I was getting dressed, and someone on it referred to our host as Melville the Mouth!"

Hammond chuckled. "I'm sure you will be able to handle him. And even if you can't, it will still give you enormous publicity." He eyed her as they reached the door of the studio. "I'm sure you will do fine, Suzy. Most men cave in when they see a natural blonde with long legs!"

She sniffed. "Well, stand by to rescue me in case he's immune."

They entered the studio proper and Ronnie Melville came forward to greet them. Unlike his reputation, he was soft-spoken and gentle mannered. Beware the gentle disarmer, Suzy thought, and was immediately put on her guard.

"I'm glad you could come on my show," he smiled. "I adored your book, Miss Bedford. I found it . . . But we won't talk about it now. I don't want to spoil the impact."

241

He led her toward a small brocade settee that stood on a carpeted dais. A couple of easy chairs were beside it, as well as a table and a copy of *Tennis Ball Heart*. Arc lights were focused on the dais and it was blisteringly hot. It was only as she sat down that she saw the huge blown-up photograph of Craig behind the settee. She tightened her lips, then made an effort to relax them. At least she was being forewarned.

It was the only warning she was to receive. Barely had the introductions been made on camera, when Ronnie Melville bluntly told her that he knew she had modeled the character of Carlton—the "hero" of her book—on Craig Dickson.

"You could just as easily say I modeled him on all the other sportsmen who put their professional success before anything else," she said. "After all, to be a champion, no matter at what, you need to have total dedication to what you are doing."

"But wouldn't you agree that your hero—if one dares call him that—bears more resemblance to Craig Dickson than to anyone else? After all, you *have* written about a tennis star."

"Because I lived for a while with Millie Queen and I got the idea for the story while I was with her."

"Is *she* in your book?"

"Not consciously."

Ronnie Melville pounced. "If you could have written Millie Queen into it *unconsciously*, couldn't you have done the same with Craig?"

"Could any girl be unconscious when Craig Dickson's around?" Suzy asked, wide-eyed.

Her TV host chuckled. "Although you deny he's in your book, do you also deny that at one time he was in your life?" Small eyes twinkled at her without any humor. "And to jog your memory, Suzy, if it needs a jogging, that is, here's a picture of the two of you kissing at Rome Airport only six months ago."

Suzy stared at the TV monitor a few yards out of camera

range and saw a newspaper picture of Craig kissing her on the mouth.

"Oh, *that*," she cooed. "Craig's always kissing girls good-bye. It's when he starts kissing them without saying good-bye . . ."

There was a general laugh and Hammond gave her an appreciative wink.

"Can I take it you haven't yet met Mr. Right?" Ronnie Melville persisted.

"That's a leading question."

"Which leads me to Hammond Ellison, your publisher and good friend." The Australian turned to the man beside him. "I'm almost tempted to call you Suzy's Svengali."

"I'm delighted that you haven't," Hammond rejoined, as relaxed as if he were conducting the interview himself. "Because no one created Suzy as a writer. She has a natural talent and I was lucky enough to be at hand when it blossomed."

"Then how do you see yourself?" the Australian persisted, falling into the quagmire of Hammond's simile. "As the nourisher of the blossom? The gardener, perhaps?"

Thank God he didn't say as the manure, Suzy thought, and catching Hammond's eye, knew he had thought the same.

"I see myself as Suzy's publisher," he said blandly, "which is what I am."

"Then, as her publisher, can you tell me what you see in store for this lovely little lady?"

"A great future as a writer. Her first book is a best-seller, as you know, and her second one, which I have already been privileged to see, will be even more successful."

"Does that take the lid off a sporting profession, too, or is it set in a different milieu?"

"It's about people," Hammond hedged, and showed by his tone and expression that he wanted everyone to know this was what he was doing. "The choice of career may affect one's lifestyle and earning capacity, but human emotions are the same whether one's a dustman or a doctor.

243

A politician or— But I'd better not say anymore in case I get into trouble."

"I can't imagine you being indiscreet, Mr. Ellison," Ronnie Melville said. "Except deliberately. So are we right to assume that the next book is about a politician and a prostitute?"

"I'll answer that question nearer to the time of publication. Meanwhile, your viewers can absorb themselves with Suzy Bedford's great first novel!"

"Spoken like her publisher!" the Australian applauded. "Or would I be wrong in assuming you are more than that? Rumor has it that you may be her real-life hero!"

Suzy's body stiffened and she was glad that the question had been put to Hammond and not to herself. She was counting on him to keep her pride intact without committing either of them to an outright lie, and knew that no one could do it better.

"Rumors are good for selling books," Hammond smiled.

"But is this particular one true? Are you in love with Suzy Bedford?"

"Everyone who knows Suzy loves her. But for the moment Suzy's too busy enjoying her well-earned success to think of marriage."

"So she turned you down, eh?" the Australian said triumphantly, and rounded on Suzy. "You must be extremely confident of your talent, Suzy Bedford, to reject a proposal from your publisher! Not many first-book authors would have the courage to do that."

Suzy gave him a sweet smile. "I also have sufficient confidence in my talent to turn down another interview with you, Mr. Melville!"

For an instant he looked startled, then he roared his approval. "I do believe the little lady is mad at me. But my shoulders are broad and my back is strong. What's more important is that I've asked the questions most of my viewers would have asked if *they* had the chance. And I've got the answers, too!"

He went on talking, winding up the show with a refer-

244

ence to the book itself and the success it was achieving around the world.

The lights on the camers went out and Hammond gave Suzy the signal to rise, which she did with speed, anxious to leave while she still had her temper under control.

"What a ghastly man!" she said as they returned to the hotel for her to change before going on to Millie's wedding. "Why can't they be satisfied to interview me as an author and not as a sex object?"

"Because you *are* a sex object," Hammond smiled. "Enjoy your beauty, my dear, don't resist it."

"I still hate being asked personal questions."

"I'm the one who came off worst," he said equably. "I didn't mind admitting you'd turned me down."

"You needn't have said it. You could easily have parried the question."

"The truth is better. The papers will pick up the story and for a while we'll get some peace."

Their car stopped at the hotel entrance and Hammond stepped out with her but remained where he was.

"I haven't a thing to wear." He smiled. "So I'll wait here for you. Try not to be long."

"Twenty minutes," she said, "but give me five minutes' leeway because of the damned elevators."

With two minutes to spare, she was back, a symphony in blue that made Hammond's eyes light up. How much simpler her life would be if she could love him, she thought wistfully as they re-settled themselves in the car.

"It wouldn't work," he said, reading her thoughts.

"Don't be so clever."

"I'm cursed with brains," he was gently mocking, "and they tell me not to dream impossible dreams."

"You never would," she agreed. "You aren't the type to wander by lone sea breakers and sit by desolate streams."

"I'd prefer to say that I don't see myself as King Canute. I'm clever enough to know when the impossible's impossible!"

She laughed, as she knew he wanted her to do, and was

245

relieved when they reached the large, splendidly modern church where Millie was to marry her Don.

There were large crowds outside it, but police were holding them in check, and she followed Hammond through the narrow path kept forcibly clear. So would the crowds congregate for Craig if and when he married Elaine. Suzy pushed the thought aside and caught Hammond's arm as they entered the church.

They had barely settled in their seats when the organ boomed out Mendelssohn's "Wedding March" and Millie came down the aisle on her father's arm. She was no storybook bride trembling in tulle, but a confidently radiant young woman fully in charge of herself. Only as Don— defying convention—turned to look at her, did she momentarily falter before giving him a smile of such tenderness that Suzy had no fear for the girl's happiness.

The ceremony droned on, elaborate and seemingly endless, and Suzy tried not to look for Craig but inevitably found his tall, wide-shouldered back. He needed a hair cut, she thought, looking at the brown hair that almost reached his shirt collar, and felt such an aching need to touch it, that tears filled her eyes. The minister's voice changed pitch and the organ burst into song. Craig moved his head and Suzy saw he was looking at Elaine, who was beside him. It seemed a prophetic thing for him to do and she lowered her head to her hymn book, keeping her eyes wide open and unblinking, in case the tears fell and Hammond should notice them.

There was a final crescendo of sound and the service came to an end. Everyone started to push their way out except Hammond, who pulled Suzy in the opposite direction.

"We can't go into the registry," she exclaimed.

"We aren't. But there's a side exit."

"How do you know?"

"I spent my time profitably while you were changing," he smiled, and led her out to a side street where their limousine was parked. "God, it's hot." He eased his collar. "I hope the reception's being held out of doors."

246

"It is. Don's aunt lives in Sydney and she offered them the use of her garden."

"I suppose we should be thankful it wasn't held somewhere in the bush! At least Sydney's civilized."

Walking on the velvety lawn a quarter of an hour later, Suzy saw quite how civilized. Transplanted, the setting could have been in America or England were it not for the magnificent view of Sydney Harbor.

"I didn't see you crying at Millie's wedding," Hammond said as a waiter appeared before them and they helped themselves to champagne.

"It's silly to cry at weddings."

"I'll cry at yours," Hammond said softly.

"Now you *will* make me cry." She gulped at her drink. The bubbles tickled her nose and she coughed, almost choking as she saw Craig coming toward her.

In his morning suit he looked unfamiliar. The dark jacket gave him a maturity he did not have in the familiar white of tennis, and it made her realize that despite his boyish, bronze vitality, he was nearly thirty. His expression was as sober as his appearance.

"Hello, Suzy." He nodded briefly to Hammond, then turned back to her. "I'd like to talk to you."

"Talk away," she said gaily.

"Alone. I'm sorry, Mr. Ellison."

"There's no need to be," Hammond said quietly. "I was expecting you."

He moved away and Suzy went to follow, but found Craig in front of her.

"You're not going yet, Suzy. I intend talking to you whether you like it or not."

His voice was no longer drawling and his words slurred one into the other, so that for an instant she wondered if he were drunk. But his eyes were steady, and though there was color in his face, it came from tension, not alcohol.

Unwilling to make a scene, or to have him make one—which from the way his hands were clenching and unclenching seemed more than possible—she allowed him to lead her down the sloping lawn to a more secluded part of

247

the garden. This did not satisfy him either, and after a quick glance around, he skirted several more clumps of bushes until he reached an artificial pond. A rustic bench stood beside it, and unceremoniously he pushed her down on it, then sat beside her, his knees touching hers.

She tried to ignore his closeness, but though she could control her expression she could not control her breathing. Her breasts rose and fell and he saw the movement. His eyes rested on the soft material that swathed them and the color in his face intensified.

"I—I saw you—on television," he said jerkily. "I was in bed an—and Frank switched it on."

"It was a farce," she said coolly. "I've told Hammond I won't do anymore of those kind of shows."

"That one served its purpose."

"Really?"

"You know damn well it did! If you'd been as honest as your publisher, you could have saved me a day of hell."

She swallowed nervously, refusing to let herself think, in case her thoughts were the wrong ones; as they always seemed to be where Craig was concerned.

"Look at me," he said thickly, "and tell me if it's true."

"If what's true?"

"That you aren't going to marry Hammond Ellison. That you turned him down."

"Oh, *that*," Suzy said with praiseworthy casualness. "That was just talk."

"Was it?" He leaned closer, his breath warm on her temple. "Don't lie to me, Suzy. I've got to know the truth. Are you going to marry him?"

She kept her head lowered. Craig's nearness was overpowering. His hands rested on his knees; the fingers were long and supple, the nails spatulate. The knuckles showed clearly, each one standing out and stretching the skin, so that it looked paler than the rest. It told her how tightly he was pressing them down.

"Answer me, Suzy," he said again. "Are you going to marry Hammond Ellison?"

"No. At least, not in the foreseeable future." She jumped up and went to stand close to the pond. "But don't let's talk about me anymore. Tell me how *you* are. Are you feeling better?"

"I haven't been ill." He rose to join her. "What made you think I was?"

"I—I—"

Too late she saw she had given herself away. Yet not quite.

"I spoke to Frank last night. I rang up to see how you were."

"What for?" His puzzlement was genuine. "There was nothing wrong with me."

"Not physically, perhaps. But . . ." She stopped, then said abruptly: "Do you remember me giving you the silver trophy?"

He half turned away from her and was silent for what seemed a long time, but could only have been seconds. "No, I don't, as it so happens. It was clever of you to guess. Or did Frank open his big mouth and tell you?"

"You mustn't blame Frank. He didn't say a word until we—until I made it clear I knew something was wrong with you. But no one else guessed," she added quickly, and remembered what Frank had said last night when he had seen her watching Craig asleep: "You look at him with eyes of love." If only she had seen Craig with those eyes when he had played at Wimbledon six months ago. If she had, they might both have saved themselves from heartache. But on that long ago day in June she had seen his behavior as heartless; had not guessed it to be the exact opposite. Because he felt too much, he had to cut out all feeling. All she needed to know now was what that feeling had been; at Wimbledon, and again here, yesterday.

"It's only happened a couple of times," Craig said. "It's nothing."

"You mean it was nothing when your mother died?"

His indrawn breath was audible. "Frank does have a big mouth."

249

"And again at Wimbledon," she persisted. "And also yesterday." Craig had forced her to come here and talk to him, and talk she would, even if he did not like the subject.

"It's my way of coping with stress," he said slowly. "I talked it over with a psychiatrist once, and he assured me there was nothing to worry about." He gave a husky laugh. "You're enough to make any man go into a *permanent* state of trance!"

She said nothing and went on looking at him. She could only see a part of his profile: a hazy fringe of eyelash and the curve of his cheek, the color of honey and the texture of downy silk. He was still silent and she knew he was not going to say any more.

"Are you trying to tell me *I* was the reason for the way you behaved at Wimbledon and on court yesterday?"

"Yes." He moved, and now she could not see any part of his face. "I love you, Suzy. I have for a long while. At first I thought it was like all the others, but then I knew it wasn't. I was happy just to talk to you; to be with you; to hold you without wanting more. Of course, I did want more," he said, "but I was prepared to wait. That's why I wanted you to come around the tennis circuit with me. I thought it would give you a chance to see the way I lived and the stresses you'd have to cope with. It would have given you time to decide if you loved me enough to make it your life too."

"What would you have done if I had told you I didn't need time to decide—that I already knew how I felt about you and would have gone with you anywhere?"

He swung around to face her.

"I would have married you so fast, it would have made your head spin."

"Married me? Last June? I didn't know you were thinking in terms of marriage."

"Why else do you think I wanted you with me? No," he said swiftly. "Don't answer that. There's no need. You assumed I only wanted an affair—another girl to join the fan club."

250

"You can't blame me. It's the way you've always lived. Even now," she could not help adding.

He took the point, and looked angrier still. "You're right. I won't deny it. I've been sleeping with Elaine for the past six months, and with other girls, too. You made it clear you didn't want me and I wasn't going to live the rest of my life pining for you. The only problem was that other girls didn't help to forget you. They made me feel worse. I would try to pretend they were you and . . . and when they weren't, I'd end up hating them!"

"You didn't; and you still don't give the impression that you hate Elaine. I saw the way you were looking at her in church today."

"It was a look of pity," he said quietly. "I had already made up my mind to talk things out with you, and even if I couldn't . . . even if we didn't . . ." He rubbed the back of his neck in a gesture half irritable, half embarrassed. "I couldn't go on seeing Elaine. It isn't fair to her. I know you don't like her and I can appreciate why, but she loves me and—I—I've just been using her. Once I saw you and Ellison on that chat show this morning, I knew I had to see you and put things straight between us."

Suzy tried not to let herself be carried away by what Craig was saying. She would hear him out completely. Only then would she form a judgment. She waited and he went on looking at her. There was indecision on his face, and it was so unusual to see it there that she longed to make the first move.

"I love you, Suzy." He spoke thickly. "I wanted to ask you to marry me that Sunday we went to see Marvin and Lydia. The day I flew in from Holland."

"Why didn't you?"

"I was scared. I had to be sure you loved me, the man, not the tennis star. I know you said you didn't like all the glamour and the publicity that surrounded my life, but it can still create a dazzle that blinds you. That's why I wanted you to be with me before you committed yourself. I was scared that once I retired, you'd find me too limited."

"Limited?" She almost choked on the word. "You've got to be joking. What about those hour-long telephone calls we had? Do you think I found you too limited then?"

"I think—I thought you saw me as someone you enjoyed cutting down to size. You were always doing it, you know. And today you would be even more justified. You're a celebrity in your own right, Suzy. You have the kind of talent that won't deteriorate with age. You won't be over the hill at thirty-five, the way I will. When I'll be long forgotten by my fans, your readers will be multiplying."

"That's great," she said. "There's nothing like a reader for keeping your bed warm and holding your hand when you're ill. Honestly, Craig, you must be crazy."

"Am I?" he asked huskily, reaching out for her. "Oh, Suzy, if you knew the hell I've put myself through these last six months."

"What about me? You weren't the only one to suffer." Contrition made her hands tremble as she pressed them to the side of his face. "When I think of the terrible things I said to you, I could cut out my tongue."

"You do pack a hefty verbal punch," he admitted. "I guess it's why I blacked out at Wimbledon. I came to your house all set to propose and you practically kicked me in the teeth."

She twined her arms around his neck and pressed her body close to his. Unlike the other times when she had done so, his response was not immediately physical, and she was pleased.

"You should have been tougher with me," she whispered. "But you were always so reasonable. A nice straight hook to the chin might have brought me to my senses!"

His chuckle was thin, as if the torment was too near to be ridiculed. She remembered his match yesterday, and pulled back slightly so that she could look into his face.

"Why did you black out on court when you played Dick? We hadn't quarreled."

"I might have been able to cope with a quarrel." He looked into her eyes, not hiding the feeling that burned in his own. "You said you were going to marry Hammond and
252

it was so obviously the right thing for you to do, that I couldn't see any way of fighting it. When I saw you with him at the match, it was more than I could take. The rest is history."

There was triumph in knowing her power over him, but also compassion. His strength was no longer something she had to fight against, but something she had to protect. Craig the superstar, was also Craig the child.

She moved back against him and his arms wound themselves around her.

"I tried to see you before your match at Wimbledon," she said. "I'd like you to know that. But when you won, it seemed to be a sign that you didn't care. I even came to your suite last night, but you were dead to the world."

He looked astonished. "Frank never said a word."

"I told him not to. I saw Elaine as I was leaving and . . ." Suzy faced and voiced her jealousy. "I was so mad, I could have killed her!"

"She wasn't as much of a fixture in my life as she made out," Craig informed her bluntly. "If I couldn't have you, I was going to have a lot of others."

"And now?"

"Now there's only you."

"That could be for a long while."

"For the rest of my life, Suzy." His hands moved up to rest against the sides of her breasts. "I'm willing to quit tennis anytime you want. I know this isn't the life you like and—"

"My life is with you," she interrupted. "Wherever you are. When you're out practicing, I'll be working on my next book. It's an ideal arrangement."

"Until we start a family." His lips rested against her mouth. "But by that time I'll have quit anyway, and we can live in my house in California—it'll be built by then—or anywhere else you like."

An answer seemed unnecessary and she put her hands behind his head to keep his mouth on hers. Passion rose swiftly, the fiercer for having been so long denied. His body stiffened and he jerked her closer and put his own

253

hands low on her hips, holding her tightly against him.

"I hope you don't want a long engagement?" he murmured against her lips. "Otherwise, I'll have to go into another trance state to keep myself under control!"

"I wouldn't be too sure about my own control either," she confessed. "But I'd like us to be married in front of my parents."

"Next week?"

"Yes, please." She savored the touch of his mouth and was disappointed when his lips left hers.

"Not here, Suzy," he said in answer to the question in her eyes. "The way I feel right now, I daren't start kissing you. But thank the Lord it's only an afternoon reception. With any luck, we can sneak away by four."

"I can't imagine what you've got in mind."

"It's not in my mind!" Hungrily, he stared into her face. "The times I've dreamed of holding you like this . . . There's so much I want to say that I don't know where to begin. But first, I'll scratch my matches for the next month. By the time we return to England and I make an honest woman of you—"

"I *am* an honest woman!"

"Count the minutes, Sweet Sue!" His mouth hovered over hers but he resisted the temptation. "As I was saying, by the time we're married, we'll be left with three clear weeks. Just long enough for a honeymoon. Any ideas where you'd like to spend them?"

"In bed with you!"

"Funny you should say that. You must have read my thoughts."

She grinned. "Let that be a lesson to you, Craig Dickson."

"You won't scare me that way. Since you're going to be my only woman from now on, I'll have nothing to hide."

Their shared laughter enveloped them, binding them closer. But to Suzy it did more than that. It showed her what the future could be; and she liked it.

She liked it very much indeed.